As he followed her inside his penthouse for what he was sure was about to be mind-blowing sex, Jonathan realized that he didn't know her name.

"Don't you think it's time we finally exchanged names?" he asked, kicking the door shut.

"Why?" she replied, raising a brow. "Isn't it better this way? You know, less complicated."

"I suppose."

"C'mon, don't tell me you're going to chicken out now that I'm here," Ciara teased.

Jonathan thought about it for a minute. She was challenging him to live dangerously. Do the unexpected. The problem was, he was so used to being predictable that he didn't know how to proceed. Maybe she was right. It would be less complicated this way. Clearly she had no idea who he was.

"If that's the way you want it," he said finally.

"Yes, it is," Ciara stated emphatically. "Can you handle that?"

"If you can, then I'm game," Jonathan said, and moved closer.

Books by Yahrah St. John

Kimani Romance

Never Say Never
Risky Business of Love

Kimani Arabesque

One Magic Moment
Dare to Love

YAHRAH ST. JOHN

first began writing at the age of twelve, and wrote more than twenty short stories. When she finally sat down to complete her first full-length novel, she was offered a two-book contract. Both novels received four-star ratings from *Romantic Times BOOKreviews*. In 2005, Yahrah was nominated for an Emma award for Favorite New Author of the Year at the Romance Slam Jam.

A member of Romance Writers of America, Yahrah is an avid reader of all fiction genres and enjoys the arts, cooking, travel and adventure sports, but her true passion remains writing. She currently lives in Orlando, but was born in the Windy City—Chicago. A graduate of Hyde Park Career Academy, she earned a Bachelor of Arts in English from Northwestern University. Presently, she works as an assistant property manager for a commercial real estate company.

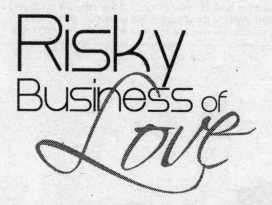

Risky Business of Love

YAHRAH ST. JOHN

KIMANI
ROMANCE

 KIMANI PRESS™

ISBN-13: 978-0-373-86029-6
ISBN-10:   0-373-86029-3

RISKY BUSINESS OF LOVE

Copyright © 2007 by Yahrah St. John

www.kimanipress.com

Printed in U.S.A.

Dear Reader,

Thank you for sharing Jonathan and Ciara's journey of love. I am grateful for the opportunity to write their exciting tale of passion, politics, broadcast news and, of course, scandal.

Despite the many obstacles in their path, Jonathan and Ciara risk it all for love, which makes the old saying true: anything worth having is worth fighting for.

Please feel free to contact me and share your thoughts on their love story at yahrah@yahrahstjohn.com or P.O. Box 772443, Orlando, FL 32877-2443. Also, please be sure to check out my Web site at www.yahrahstjohn.com for the latest contests and book signings in your area.

Until we meet again, peace be with you.

Yahrah St. John

Acknowledgement

I am blessed to have many family members and friends who support me and my writing career. They understand my need for space or my lack of free time when it comes to my writing. I wish I could thank them all, but there wouldn't be enough space. So, let me thank my family first—the Mitchells, the Smiths and the Bishops.

My father Austin Mitchell for his enthusiasm, support and faith in my abilities. Gita Bishop for not just being my cousin, but a big sister, as well. You're always looking out for me. To my second moms, Aislee Mitchell and Beatrice Astwood, for their love and dedication.

My friends until the end, Tiffany Harris, Therolyn Rodgers, Dimitra Astwood and Tonya Mitchell, and my sister Cassandra Mitchell for listening to my story ideas, reading drafts and offering advice and suggestions.

Finally, I'd like to thank my readers for their continued support of a new writer such as myself. You make me want to be a better writer!

All of you are a source of great strength, and contribute to my success.

Chapter 1

"You're on in five." Cameraman Lance Johnson pointed the lens on Ciara Miller, general assignment reporter for Philadelphia's WTCF-FOX Channel Twenty-Nine News.

"Wait a sec," Ciara replied, smoothing down her shoulder-length hair with one hand while holding the microphone in the other. She was about to speak when the roar of ambulance sirens screamed in the background. Once they were no longer within earshot, she turned away from the devastating murder-suicide scene in front of her on a balmy afternoon in early July.

Lance smiled as he looked through the lens. Ciara was breathtaking. He was captivated by her smooth bronze skin, brilliant hazel eyes, full lips and defiant chin. Ciara had a way of seducing the camera with her delicately carved features and exotically high cheekbones. The honey-blond hair surrounding her oval-shaped face only added to her allure. The new hair color was daring but not too bold as to offend viewers. She'd said she wanted to make a statement, and that she had. Ciara was always the epitome of fashion and today was no exception. She was wearing killer-red Prada pumps, a slim black skirt and a vibrant red silk blouse.

He'd known Ciara for the last five years since they'd both begun working at WTCF fresh out of college. Barely making minimum wage, they'd been paired together and had instantly developed a rapport. Their long hours and grunt work had paid off as they'd steadily moved their way up the newsroom ladder. Ciara was now a staff reporter and Lance an assistant photographer, but Ciara had bigger dreams and he knew she would achieve them; the girl had tenacity.

Lance gave her a thumbs-up signal, lifted the camera on his shoulder and directed it her way. Poised and ready for battle, Ciara gave the on-screen intro to her package for the second block of the five o'clock news.

"The scene here today turned deadly for a young wife and mother," Ciara said as the camera focused in on the Spanish-style home that now served as a crime scene. "Hector Rodriguez accused his wife of infidelity and then turned the gun on her and then himself late yesterday evening. Witnesses say that Mrs. Rodriguez came home yesterday to discover her husband enraged after she was late coming home from work. Neighbors say they heard loud voices before hearing gunshots.

Authorities indicate that Hector Rodriguez trashed the home in a jealous rage before shooting himself and his wife. Detectives indicate that a full investigation will take place. This is Ciara Miller reporting for WTCF-FOX News." Ciara smiled into the camera.

"How was I?" she asked, batting her long curly eyelashes at her best friend and coworker. She absolutely adored Lance. He knew her inside and out. She could always be real with him. It was a shame he was so darn smart and good-looking, and with that athletic physique she could eat him up with a spoon. "Unh, unh, unh, unh," Ciara murmured, shaking her head. But she couldn't go there, they'd decided a long time ago that they'd rather have a platonic relationship than ruin a great friendship.

"Beautiful as always," Lance replied, turning off the camera and closing the lens cover. "And you know that." He set the camera inside the open OB truck that he used to send live feeds back to the newsroom.

"Yeah, I do," Ciara said grinning, "but a little praise never hurt." She watched the medical examiner's van drive away as the police secured the perimeter of the crime scene.

Lance wrapped the cord around his arm and walked it back to the truck. "Since when do you need to be told you're fabulous? You know you've got what it takes."

"Have you told that to Shannon recently?" Ciara asked. "Because she won't give me a break. She keeps sending me out for lightweight entertainment stories. Today was the first time I've gotten to report breaking news."

Ciara had tried for months to convince WTCF's new television director, Shannon Wright, that she was more than a pretty face, to no avail. Had Shannon even looked at her résumé?

She'd been at the top of her class at Johns Hopkins and had obtained a master's degree in journalism at Columbia University. She'd worked at Columbia's television station, the *Columbia Daily Spectator* and the yearbook. She was a member of the National Association of Black Journalists and had worked at the station for over five years. She'd started out as a production assistant before moving on to become a general assignment reporter.

Ciara excelled at pushing herself. So what if that interfered with her cultivating lasting personal relationships; she was willing to make the sacrifice to get to the top of the heap. Her looks wouldn't last forever. Talent was the key.

"You'll have your day," Lance said. "You just have to be patient."

"As you well know, patience is not one of my virtues," Ciara replied.

"Ain't that the truth," Lance laughed, opening the passenger side. "You'd better get in. I've got to get back and edit the footage."

Ciara hopped up in the van and buckled her seat belt while he closed the door. Lance may have thought that was the end of it, but Ciara had other ideas.

"Now is not the right time for me to announce my candidacy," Jonathan Butler said to his father, Congressman Charles Butler, and Reid Hamilton, his father's chief of staff and personal adviser. They were in his father's office strategizing on Jonathan's campaign while his father paced the floor reciting the speech he was going to give to the press the following day. "I should let you step down first. I don't want to appear overly zealous."

Charles smiled as he watched his son. Admiration shone through in his oval-shaped brown eyes at his son's stately presence. Six foot three with massive shoulders, his son towered over other men, including him. He carried himself with the same dignity and grace that Charles had conveyed during his twenty-five-year tenure serving the good people of Philadelphia. He had a bright future ahead of him and had done the right thing starting off in law before becoming an alderman. Charles was sure that Jonathan would be as capable a leader as he was. It was just a shame that he had to step down because of a heart condition.

"Why not announce it at your father's retirement press conference tomorrow? It would be a prime opportunity with maximum coverage," Reid replied.

"I agree with Reid," his father said. "Capitol Hill has been rumoring for months that you'll take over my seat. Why not end all the speculation?" Charles was sure the press would be eager to meet his handsome, dark-haired son.

"How would it appear to the public if I announced my candidacy directly after your speech? It would show a complete lack of respect for what a wonderful congressman you've been. The public would see me as a capitalist."

"There will never be a right time," Charles Butler returned.

"That may be true, Dad, but now is definitely not it. I haven't even hired a campaign manager or a media consultant." He'd done some preliminary legwork by getting an office, but there was still more to be done.

Jonathan saw the shocked expression on Reid's face. Reid must have assumed that because he served as his father's campaign manager that he was the logical choice for Jonathan. Jonathan, however, had other ideas. He appreciated Reid's input thus far, but he wanted someone he knew and trusted leading his campaign, and his best friend, Zach Powers, was just that man.

Jonathan intended to speak with Zach over lunch. Zach had just finished a successful campaign with Governor Green and Jonathan was sure Zach could do the same for him.

"I'm sorry, Reid." Jonathan folded his arms across his chest. "I meant to speak with you. I hope there are no hard feelings?" Jonathan extended his right hand.

"No, not at all." Reid returned the handshake and faked a smile.

His father spoke up on Reid's behalf. "Jonathan…"

"It's okay, Charles," Reid interrupted him. "If Jonathan wants to hire his own right hand, leave him be."

"No, it's not fair," Charles Butler huffed. "You're practically a member of this family. Jonathan, why would you even think of going with a stranger?"

"Dad, I've made my choice and I don't intend on arguing about this. Now, if you'll excuse me, I have a few items to attend to." Jonathan grabbed his overcoat and leather briefcase sitting on the floor and headed out the door.

Once the door closed, Charles faced his best friend and closest adviser. "Don't worry, Reid. I'll talk to him."

"Don't bother," Reid said. "If your son feels he can find a better man to lead his team then by all means let him."

"Thank you for understanding." Charles patted Reid's back and walked back to his desk.

"No problem," Reid said and grabbed the folder of notes he'd previously prepared on Jonathan's campaign and walked to the door. "I'll leave you to your speech." Reid closed the door behind himself.

Livid, he stalked back to his office and shut the door. He slammed the file on his maple desk and plopped down in his swivel chair.

How dare that two-bit snot disrespect him in such a manner? After everything he had done for the Butler family, after all the hours he'd spent, the personal sacrifices he'd made and Jonathan dared hire another manager? Who did he think had helped Charles get elected? Reid was responsible for Charles Butler's successful twenty-five-year run in Congress every bit as much as the man himself.

Reid knew the ins and outs of politics more than most. He'd had over thirty years in the business. He'd run all of Charles Butler's campaigns and won every

single one of them. Jonathan had no idea what it took
to win an election. What he needed was to be taught a
lesson—he couldn't mess with a real man. Reid would
show him that he would not be tossed away like the
gum on the bottom of his preppy-boy shoe.

Oh yes, Reid mused, rubbing his chin thoughtfully.
Jonathan Butler was in for a rude awakening.

Ciara and Lance returned to the station with a few
hours to spare to put the entire piece together for the
five o'clock news.

They rushed down the hall, parting ways at the
studio control complex and newsroom. The studio was
bustling as the stage crew prepared for the evening's
newscast. WTCF-FOX Channel Twenty-Nine was one
of the smaller television stations in Philadelphia and
that was fine with Ciara. Opportunities were always
more plentiful at a local station.

Ciara walked over to her desk and turned on her
computer while listening to the police and fire department scanners for breaking stories. She was organiz-
ing her notes when her boss, WTCF's television news
director Shannon Wright, stopped by her desk.

Tall and frail with dull, lifeless red hair and brown
eyes, Shannon wasn't much to look at and could use a
serious makeover, but when it came to the station,
Shannon was the top dog and Ciara was stuck with her.

"So, how'd it go? Did you have any trouble?"

Ciara turned around and stared at Shannon. What
did Shannon think—that she was a newbie? She was
capable of putting a package together.

"Yes, Shannon, I have it all together," Ciara replied, placing her notes back in the folder.

"Were you able to get an interview with a member of the family?"

"No, I'm sorry. They weren't giving any interviews."

An annoyed look crossed Shannon's pale face. "Did you try, Ciara?"

"Of course I did, Shannon," Ciara said exasperatedly. "No one else got interviews either. The grandparents arrived and spirited the children away before the press could ask any questions."

Shannon nodded. "What's your angle then?" Shannon sat beside Ciara's desk.

"How abuse can happen in a small neighborhood and no one knows anything about it. Thought maybe I could explore further and do a piece about women's shelters."

Shannon smiled. "Sounds preachy, Miller." She stood and folded her arms across her chest. "As reporters, we're supposed to report the news, not make broad assumptions."

"I know that, Shannon, I just thought we could make this story more human and not focus solely on the victims."

"You're too soft, Miller," Shannon lectured. "You've got to toughen up or you won't last long in this business."

Shannon swiftly walked away, leaving Ciara feeling completely defeated. Why did she insist on riding her so hard? From day one she'd taken an instant disliking to Ciara and she couldn't figure out why.

Ciara took a deep breath and calmed herself. It would not be to her advantage to get on Shannon's bad side. Without her approval, a reporter's packages might never see the light of day. Somehow she had to convince Shannon that she was a valuable part of the WTCF family. She had to believe that one day soon Shannon would realize what a gem she had.

After Shannon had left, Ciara walked down the hall to the studio control complex, hoping to review Lance's footage for the day, when she received a call on her cell.

Opening her flip phone, Ciara answered, "Hello?"

"Baby girl, is that you?" Diamond Miller asked from the other end.

Ciara rolled her eyes heavenward. "Who else would be answering my phone?" she replied sharply.

"No need to get snippy, Ciara," Diamond replied.

"Sorry," Ciara apologized halfheartedly. "What can I do for you, Diamond?" She called her mother by her first name because Diamond refused to be thought of as the mother of a twenty-eight-year-old daughter.

"Well, uh…" Diamond paused as she flipped open her baguette purse and pulled out a box of slim cigarettes. "I was hoping you might be able to spare a little cash." She smiled at the bartender as he pushed a free cocktail in front of her. Diamond gave him her best head toss and wink. He beamed. Works every time, she thought. She returned her attention to her only daughter. "I'm a little short on cash. C'mon, help your mama out."

Ciara sighed. "I just lent you money last month, Diamond. Really, this borrowing has got to stop. I'm not made of money, you know."

"Of course, sweetie." Diamond laid it on thick. "It's just that I had a bad night at poker with the girls."

Ciara doubted that was the real reason. Since she'd been a child, Diamond had been terrible with money. Ciara supposed that it was because even at forty-five her mother still looked like a goddess. Nary a wrinkle could be found on her smooth brown skin, and dancing had kept her fit. But what could Ciara expect from a former Las Vegas showgirl?

"Diamond, I don't know if I can swing it. I'll have to check my finances and get back with you."

"Promise me it'll be soon."

"I promise," Ciara said, closing the phone. What had she ever done to deserve a mother like Diamond?

Jonathan was in the middle of reviewing a case he was consulting on with a colleague when his father walked into his office at City Hall later that afternoon.

"Jonathan," Charles Butler began. "We need to talk." He closed the door behind him and came toward Jonathan's large cherrywood desk.

"I suppose you've come to plead Reid's case," Jonathan stated, putting the confidential file in his desk drawer.

"Of course," his father replied. "Reid has been a big part of this family for years. He deserves your respect."

"He's been part of *your* life, Dad," Jonathan replied. "Not mine."

"Because of Reid, I never lost an election. I am retiring undefeated."

"Bully for you," Jonathan returned, "but that doesn't

change my feelings on the subject. I have never cared
for Reid and I most certainly don't want him running
my campaign."

"I understand," Charles sighed. "To each his own,
but you understand I had to try."

"And your opinion is duly noted." Jonathan stood.
"But I'm my own man, Dad. And I decide who I want
to run my campaign."

"Fine, but at least throw him a bone." His father
would not let up. "Let Reid be your adviser. You know,
make suggestions on the campaign."

"That's what I have Zach for," Jonathan replied.

"I know. But do this for me."

"All right, Dad," Jonathan conceded. "Just as long
as Reid and you understand that I run the show." The
days of Charles Butler running the show were over.

And to prove it, he met up with his best friend, Zach
Powers, for dinner later that evening at the Prime Rib
in Center City.

Jonathan had known Zach since boarding school,
where they'd been roommates and had played lacrosse
together. Even when they'd gone their separate ways
in college, they'd still remained friends. Jonathan
trusted Zach to have his back.

Jonathan smiled as Zach approached the table. Ele-
gantly dressed in a tailored Gucci suit and Italian
leather loafers, Zach was a major player and he knew
it.

"It's good to see you, Zach," Jonathan said as his
best friend joined him.

"Not that I'm not happy to see you, but why are we

here? Why all the secrecy?" Zach asked, taking a seat opposite Jonathan.

"C'mon. You know the press as well as I do. If they smelled a story, it would be front-page news," Jonathan replied. He paused when the waiter came over and filled the water glasses.

"I wanted to ask you in person to be my campaign manager."

"Pardon?"

"You heard correctly. I want the best and brightest on my team. And that's you."

Jonathan had seen what Zach had done for Governor Green and Mayor Floyd. Both had been new to the political arena and had been facing tough competition from the incumbents, but Zach had adeptly convinced the public to vote for them. Zach was a skilled campaign manager and Jonathan intended to capitalize on his success, and it just so happened that he was finally available.

"You don't have to lay it on so thick, Johnny boy. I'm your friend, so you know I'll be there to support you. Whatever you need, I'm your man."

"Thank you." Jonathan shook Zach's hand. "I knew I could depend on you." He turned around to give the waiter his dinner selection of rack of lamb.

"What I don't understand though, is why not Reid Hamilton?" Zach inquired. "He's been your father's right-hand man for years." He stopped and gave the waiter his menu. "I'll have the roast prime rib."

"Reid may be the right man for my father, but he most certainly is not the right man for me," Jonathan stated.

"Is there some sort of bad blood between the two of you?" Zach inquired, sipping on his mineral water.

Jonathan shook his head. On the surface, Reid was slick and smooth. Jonathan didn't know if it was his smugness or the way he always seemed to know it all, but something about Reid rubbed him the wrong way. Call it intuition if you will, but he'd never liked the man.

"No, I simply don't trust him."

"Well don't be afraid to speak your mind," Zach replied. "Though I'm flattered by your faith in me, but are you sure you're ready to go out into the minefield that is the political arena? You know there's nothing but lions and bobcats."

"I'm well aware of all the players," Jonathan said confidently, "and I'm ready to play the game."

"Are you sure?" Zach asked. "I thought you were having fun in the city council."

"I was," Jonathan replied, "but I'm ready for something new. Something bigger."

"And are you ready for all the ladies that are about to fall into your lap? As a single congressman, every socialite on Capitol Hill is going to want to snag you."

"The socialites you speak of are all interchangeable. I haven't found a unique one out of the bunch." He'd spent his life enjoying the fairer sex. It was no secret that he loved women, but none had ever sustained his attention for long.

"Maybe you're expecting too much," Zach offered.

"I want the total package. Attractive. Intelligent. Articulate. A sophisticated woman with a body made for sex."

"You sure don't want a lot," Zach chuckled.

"I know, I know. It's a tall order. Do you think such a woman exists?"

"Ah, you never know," Zach said. "Mrs. Right could be right around the corner."

Chapter 2

After a working dinner, all Jonathan wanted to do was kick back and relax. He found himself at a local bar in Center City. Ordering a Corona, he took a seat on a stool and soaked in the scenery around him. The bar didn't consist of much: a small dance floor, a pool table and a dartboard in the corner.

He was discussing the pool game with the bartender when she walked in. She was stunning in a red silk blouse with a deep V neckline and a short black skirt that revealed a killer set of legs. She oozed sex and it made Jonathan immediately want the siren in his bed. He'd never picked up a woman before with the sole intention of sleeping with her, but then again there was a first time for everything.

Straight honey-blond hair hung generously down her shoulders, making him want to reach out and run his fingers through it and make it unruly. He tightened the grip around his bottle and groaned.

"Ummm, now there's a hot one," the bartender commented, filling up several bowls with beer nuts.

"Have you seen her in here before?" Jonathan inquired.

"Not that I can remember."

"Hmmm." That meant like him, she'd come for a break from reality as well.

Sultry and sexy, she strutted past him and went straight to the pool table. She struck up a conversation with several of the bar patrons already engaged in a game. They were as mesmerized as he was and easily allowed her access.

He watched her sashay over to the wall and grab a cue stick. One of the men, more bold than the others, came over as if to show her how to hold a stick, but she shook her head. Clearly, she was self-confident about her pool game. With all eyes in the room on her, she leaned down and swiftly hit a ball into the left corner pocket. Two more followed suit amid whistles and catcalls.

Walking around the pool table, she handled the cue stick with ease, landing several more shots. And just as easily as she'd insinuated herself into their game, she exited and came toward the bar.

Ciara sighed wearily. She hated coming to places like this. They reminded her too much of her mother's dancing days, but oddly enough it was bars like this that made her feel the most comfortable after a long, hard day.

"Can I get a whiskey sour?" she demanded, leaning back against the bar and surveying the room.

"Mighty strong drink for a lady," Jonathan stated.

Ciara squared her shoulders. "And how would you know what I need?" she asked defensively. She'd had a hard day at work with Shannon riding her tail and she was in no mood for a do-gooder. All she wanted was to drink in peace.

Jonathan grinned. Apparently, the lady had a hell of an attitude. "I don't, but if you want to drive home this evening then you had better not have too many of those."

"And how do you know I intend to drive home?" she asked, glaring at him.

Jonathan noticed that anger had caused her hazel eyes to turn slightly green. He felt his manhood swell immediately. It had been too long since a woman had turned him on this quickly.

The bartender slid the drink her way and she wasted no time in emptying the contents of the glass and pushing it back his way.

"Another, please," she said with authority. Perhaps she had something to prove.

"Slow down," Jonathan said. "Those things can creep up on you." He took another swig of his beer.

"Thanks for the advice, but I know how to take care of myself," Ciara replied, finally turning in his direction. When she did, she was blown away.

She didn't think they even made 'em as delicious as

him anymore. Tall. Broad shoulders. Skin the color of buttermilk. And that square jaw and those chiseled cheekbones. Ciara felt herself warm instantly. Back in her college days, a tall, fair-skinned, attractive brother would not have remained single for long.

"I'm sure you can," he replied, raising his bottle and clicking it against her glass. "Cheers."

"Cheers." Ciara attempted a smile. "Listen, I'm sorry, okay? I had a bad day at work and I just came here to get a drink and decompress."

"I understand." His face split into a wide grin. "Mine wasn't the best either." Outside of Zach agreeing to be his campaign manager, he hated being bullied into letting Reid be his adviser, but he didn't want to be at odds with his father. "Why don't you tell me about it?"

Her eyes rolled upward and Jonathan took that to mean she didn't want to talk. And that was fine with him. He'd be content just sitting beside her and looking at her. She was a beautiful woman and it had been a while since he'd felt an instant attraction to someone. It surprised him because he was usually cautious by nature. Hell, in his profession he had to be. He always thought first before acting, but this time was different. This time he wanted to act on his desires.

Ciara caught the passionate stare from the stranger at her side. It was pretty hard not to. He made no effort to hide his obvious interest in her.

Ciara lifted the glass to her lips and gulped some of the fiery liquid. Warmth immediately flooded through her veins. Maybe a little fun with a mysterious stranger might do her some good. Get her mind off her lack of upward mobility in her career.

"What do you say we get out of here?" Ciara suggested, brushing her arm against his. The sheer magnitude of his presence both overwhelmed and excited Ciara, causing her to feel a vibration deep within the pit of her stomach and that was from only a touch. Imagine what the full-court press would feel like?

Jonathan raised a brow. If he understood her intent, then she wanted him as much as he wanted her.

"Are you sure about that?" Jonathan asked because once they got started he wasn't sure he'd be able to stop.

A spark of fire flashed in Ciara's hazel eyes.

"Then let's get out of here," Jonathan replied, tipping back his head and draining the contents of his bottle. He grabbed his suit jacket off the back of the bar stool, grasped her by the hand and quickly led her out of the bar.

They were both quiet on the short drive to his penthouse. Jonathan secretly wondered if she wanted to back out. He sure hoped not; they had come this far and there was no turning back now. He'd been on edge the moment he'd seen her walk into the club. He'd known from the way she'd seductively stuck out her fanny while playing pool that this moment was a foregone conclusion.

With the late hour, traffic was light and they were at his building within minutes. When the car came to a complete stop, excitement surged through every fiber of Ciara's being. She hadn't been this naughty in quite a while, but boy did it feel good! Making love with this stranger would not only be scandalous, but totally sinful. He looked like a man familiar with a woman's body and how to please it. Ciara easily imagined those big strong hands roaming over every inch of her body and she was ready to get it on.

She didn't wait for Jonathan to come around and open the passenger door. Instead, she hopped out and followed him. He punched the up elevator button and impatiently they waited for it to arrive.

On the ride up, they were both silent for several minutes, each electrified by the other's nearness. Jonathan was the first to give in and pull Ciara into his arms. Dipping his head, he did exactly what he had wanted to do since first spotting her and that was kiss her senseless. Ciara responded with equal enthusiasm to his hard and searching kiss. She blocked out where she was and focused on the exciting stimuli of Jonathan's soft lips and warm tongue as it dove inside her mouth. Her breasts grew heavy and the place between her thighs became slick with moisture. When the elevator finally came to a jolting halt, they separated slightly dazed.

"This way," Jonathan said, exiting the elevator and pulling Ciara toward his penthouse apartment. Reaching inside his breast pocket, he pulled out his key, but fumbled inserting it into the cylinder, so Ciara took it from him, inserted it herself and entered the foyer.

As he followed her inside, Jonathan realized that he didn't know her name. "Don't you think it's time we finally exchanged names?" he asked, kicking the door shut.

"Why? Isn't it better this way?" she replied. "You know, less complicated."

"I suppose."

"C'mon, don't tell me you're going to chicken out now that I'm here?" Ciara teased.

Jonathan thought about it for a minute. She was challenging him to live dangerously. Do the unexpected. The problem was he was so used to being predictable that he didn't know how to proceed. Maybe she was right. It would be less complicated this way. Clearly she had no idea who he was and that he was running for office. If she had known, she could decide to use it against him down the road. Maybe it would be better not to exchange names. "If that's the way you want it," he said finally.

"Yes, it is," Ciara stated emphatically. She wanted one passionate night in this stranger's embrace and afterward they would go their separate ways. Just how she liked it. "Can you handle that?"

"If you can, then I'm game," Jonathan said, hungrily staring at her.

Ciara's anticipation heightened at his intense gaze and the thought of him tantalizing her entire body for the rest of the night. "I hope you know that I didn't come out tonight with the intention of getting laid."

"Neither did I," Jonathan admitted. "But I'm sure glad we met." Whether it was due to her come-hither look or her amazingly curvy body, all Jonathan knew was that any resolve he'd had vanished. Bracing one hand against the wall over her head, he leaned in and pressed her body against the wall. He moved his groin against her hot flesh and swiftly, he covered her mouth with his.

The gentle caress of his lips was a delicious sensation that Ciara wanted to savor over and over again. She parted her mouth and allowed him to deepen the kiss and stroke his tongue intimately with hers. "Has anyone ever told you you're a fabulous kisser?" Ciara said, pulling away from him and tossing her purse on the hall counter. She was completely aroused.

Jonathan smiled. "A time or two." He wanted her so bad he wasted no time tossing his overcoat on the floor. He hastily started undressing as he made his way to the living room.

A sense of urgency rose in Ciara, too, as she followed him. "Let me help you with that." She reached down and helped him unbuckle his pants. Once his belt was unlooped, she threw it across the room and his pants fell in an instant. "A briefs man. Oh, I like," she growled, kicking off her pumps.

Jonathan's libido was in overdrive. He quickly unbuttoned her silk blouse, which revealed a lacy bra underneath. Earlier he'd wondered how her breasts would look and now he would find out. Quickly, he unhooked her bra and tossed it aside. He was immensely pleased by the sight before him; her full C-cup breasts were ample and he hungered to taste them, but first he wanted to rid her of all clothing.

Lowering the zipper, he helped her wiggle out of her skirt with trembling fingers until it fell in a puddle on the floor. Ciara watched Jonathan's gaze travel down to the scrap of material covering her feminine mound and heard him utter a low groan beneath his breath. It didn't take long for Ciara's damp bikini panties to soon follow the same path as her skirt, until she stood naked in front of him.

Jonathan's eyes raked boldly over her and mere seconds passed before they both reached for each other at the same time. He curled his arm around her waist and pulled her firmly against his full arousal. He wanted her to know how turned on he was. Ciara understood his meaning and, instead of backing away, she grabbed both sides of his face and brought his mouth firmly down on hers and they fell to the couch.

Jonathan was completely in charge, using one hand to bring both her arms above her head. Then he nuzzled and nibbled at her earlobes and neck. He continued his ministrations by planting tantalizing kisses along the hollow of her neck, causing Ciara to throw her head back in abandon and moan aloud.

His tongue's path continued downward, stopping only when he came to the swell of her breasts. That was when Jonathan lowered his head and latched on to her right breast, sucking generously as if he were a newborn baby getting milk from its mother. While his tongue teased and pleased her upper body, Jonathan used his hand to slide down her taut stomach until he reached her core. When he did, he lightly stroked her womanly nub as if he were gently stoking a growing fire until she became slick and wet.

Ciara moaned her pleasure when Jonathan turned his attention to the other breast, laving the nipple with his tongue until it turned into a rocky pebble. "Yes, oh yes," Ciara said.

"That feels good," she whispered, encouraging him.

But she wanted more. She wanted to feel his hot, enlarged shaft pulsating inside her.

"I want you now," Ciara ordered.

"I want you, too," he said, but he wanted to do it the right way and take her in his bedroom and make love to her slowly. His body couldn't wait, though; his manhood was throbbing for release.

"Then take me," Ciara said, boldly meeting his molten stare. She wanted him right then. Wherever and however.

Jonathan bent down, grabbed his pants and pulled a condom out of his wallet. He quickly sheathed his enlarged penis, protecting them both. Lifting Ciara's leg, he plunged deep inside her moist haven. He pulled back slowly, allowing Ciara's body to register his thick, hard member inside of her before filling her completely. Then he began a steady pumping motion, bringing them to the edge of a precipice before slowing the pace again.

"Wrap your legs around me," he said, bodily lifting her off the couch. When he ground his hips intimately against her and squeezed her buttocks, exquisite pleasure took hold of Ciara, causing her to clench her thighs tighter and tighter. Her fingers dug into his shoulders and she kissed his ears, neck and chest, inhaling his musky masculine scent.

Jonathan uttered a low growl in the back of his throat when he felt her muscles contract around him. As their bodies rocked with that age-old rhythm, Ciara's breathing became more shallow and she gasped for breath. And when Jonathan gave one final thrust, a burst of bright light surrounded Ciara as she spiraled out of control and into the abyss. Seconds later, a shudder racked Jonathan's body and he fell on top of her. After a moment, he rolled over onto his side.

"Wow!" Jonathan whispered in her ear, smoothing down her hair with one hand.

"That was pretty amazing!" Ciara exhaled as she finally caught her breath and laid her head down against his chest.

"You're telling me," Jonathan said. He wiped his brow and swallowed hard, hoping to force more air into his lungs.

"Ready for the next round?" Ciara inquired.

Jonathan smiled. The woman was insatiable! "Slow down, we've got all night."

The next morning Jonathan awoke feeling alive and exuberant, but when he turned to gather the mystery woman in his arms, he found the bed empty. The only reminder of the night before was an indentation of where her body had lain.

Disappointed, he rubbed the sleep from his eyes. He'd hoped to share breakfast with the woman who'd sated his every desire last night and this morning. But instead of sleeping over, she'd skulked off. He guessed she didn't want to be reminded of her scandalous behavior in the morning light. But oh how great it had been! Whoever she was, she'd known exactly how to please him.

Twenty minutes later, Ciara inserted her key into the lock and rushed inside the apartment she shared with her sister.

It was nearly seven o'clock and if she didn't hurry, she was going to be late for work and Shannon would probably have a cow. She was heading toward her bedroom door when the bathroom door opened and Rachel appeared through a cloud of mist.

"And look who shows up the next morning," Rachel commented, cinching her robe tighter around herself. "Do you know how many calls I made when you didn't come home?"

Ciara hung her head low. "I'm sorry, sis," she replied, rushing to her room. Rachel followed behind her and watched Ciara sort through her closet for something to wear.

"It would be nice if you'd called. I was worried," Rachel said, sitting down on Ciara's four-poster bed. "It was so unlike you to stay out all night. You always come home."

Ciara smiled when she looked at Rachel because it was like looking at a younger version of herself, except Rachel was several inches taller and had darker hair. She had similar facial features as Ciara and the same almond-shaped eyes.

"I know, I know," Ciara said as she undressed. "It's just that the mystery man last night was so different from all the other men I've been with. I can't explain it, really." Once she was in her undies, she grabbed her robe from the bedpost and tied it around her middle.

"It was that good, huh?" Rachel asked.

"Better."

"Just be careful," Rachel advised. "You know nothing about this man. He was a complete stranger."

An image of his naked form flashed before Ciara's eyes, causing her to smile naughtily. "I know enough." Who could forget those big strong hands and that big powerful member as it thrust into her aroused flesh over and over. Ciara had to blink several times to control her racing hormones.

"Besides that," Rachel sighed.

"C'mon, Rach, you've got to know what an adrenaline rush it is when you're with a man." Ciara's hazel eyes lit up as she spoke. "It's like when you're on a really great roller coaster and it's so thrilling that you have to get back on again and again. Just to feel that rush of excitement. Well that's what this feels like." Ciara left her bedroom and grabbed a fresh towel out of the hall closet.

"Well, then I'm glad you enjoyed yourself," Rachel said.

Ciara wondered if her comment was genuine because Rachel was much more cautious than she was. She rarely dated while Ciara was known for leaping before she looked.

"So are you going to see him again?"

"No!"

"Why not?"

"Because it was a one-time thing never to be repeated," Ciara replied. "Although I must admit he totally relaxed me last night. You should try it sometime, little sis." Ciara smacked her on the butt with the towel and rushed off to the bathroom, leaving Rachel to stare openmouthedly after her retreating form.

* * *

"Are you ready?" Charles Butler asked as he rose from behind his desk and stood in front of his son, Jonathan. They were in his office and on their way to his resignation speech at Independence Hall later that morning.

"Give me a minute, okay?" Jonathan said, pushing past his father and adjusting his tie in front of the mirror. With all the people surrounding him of late, Jonathan couldn't breathe.

"Here, let me do that, honey." Dominique Butler jumped up from the couch and helped her son with his tie. As she stared into his piercing brown eyes, Dominique couldn't be more proud of her handsome, articulate and charismatic son. She had little doubt that all of her husband's constituents would be lining up to vote for her son.

"Is all this hoopla really necessary?" Jonathan wondered aloud to whoever was listening. "I'm not even announcing my candidacy." You'd think he was, considering how his parents were wound so tight. But he guessed he shouldn't be surprised; he'd been working toward this moment his entire life.

For years, he'd worked on his father's campaigns, had stood by his father's side countless times when he'd run for Congress. Not to mention the fact that he'd run his own successful campaign for city council. Now that his father was stepping down from his congressional seat, Jonathan was more than ready for this next challenge in his career. He'd dreamed of this moment.

"You have no idea," Charles Butler said, grabbing

his son's shoulders. "You may not be announcing today, but rest assured the press is scrutinizing your every move. They didn't just fall off the turnip truck. They know an announcement is forthcoming so you've got to be on top of your game."

"The press are like vultures," Reid Hamilton chimed in. "They are always looking for a crack in your façade."

Of course he would agree, Jonathan thought. Reid knew how to suck up to his father. Jonathan had never much cared for the man. Thought he was too smooth and slick, but his father had always thought the sun and moon shone on Reid.

"All done," Dominique said, patting her son's chest. He peeked over her shoulder. His mom sure made a damn good tie. Then again, she'd had years of practice.

"Thanks, Mom." He softly kissed her cheek. "And I appreciate all the advice, guys, but I'm prepared for the challenges ahead."

"Don't let your arrogance stand in your way," his father criticized.

"I'm not arrogant, Father," Jonathan returned, picking up his speech notes and glancing over them. "I'm just confident in my abilities. How much longer?"

Just look at him, thought Reid, inwardly seething. So smug and so sure of himself. Who did he think he was? Reid glanced down at his watch. "The press conference will convene in about fifteen minutes."

"Reid, could you give us a minute?" Charles asked his soon-to-be ex-chief of staff.

Once the door was closed, Charles laid into his son.

"All right, son. Before we go out there, is there anything you want to ask me?"

"Just one thing," Jonathan asked. "How did you manage to do this job for so long?

Charles Butler chuckled. "A stiff stomach."

Ciara was on her way to check the assignments board when Shannon stopped her later that morning. Ciara suspected it was because she'd missed the daily meeting. "Ciara, I've been looking everywhere for you," Shannon said.

"Why? What's going on?" Ciara asked excitedly. Maybe Shannon was finally giving her a story she could sink her teeth into.

"Becky started having some abdominal pains, so I sent her off to the hospital."

"Oh no, what about the baby?" Ciara asked. Her colleague Becky was only six months pregnant. It would be much too soon for a delivery.

"We can only hope that she's okay," Shannon replied.

"Well, Becky will be in my prayers." Ciara started down the hall, but Shannon stopped her.

"That's good to know, but that isn't why I was looking for you. Becky's absence has left a hole on the political beat and I need someone to replace her quick."

Ciara shook her head. Please not her. Ciara hated politics. It was as boring as a pile of rocks. Ciara had seen poor Becky going to the endless benefits, fundraisers and rallies, and she wanted no part.

"Shannon, please."

"Sorry, kid. No can do," Shannon replied. "I need a reporter and you're it. Congressman Butler is announcing he's stepping down today and I need someone there like yesterday."

"And that's news?" Ciara asked.

Shannon rolled her eyes upward. The kid still had a lot to learn—news wasn't all about homicides or weather disasters.

"I'm just joking," Ciara replied. "When and where?"

"At Independence Hall at 11:00 a.m."

Ciara glanced down at her watch. It read ten o'clock. "Thanks a lot, Shannon. That sure doesn't give me any time."

Shannon shrugged her shoulders. "Then I guess you had better get a move on it, hadn't you?"

When Shannon turned and walked away, Ciara rolled her eyes upward. She would show that witch what she was capable of and then Shannon would be begging her to take the top anchor's spot. Grabbing her notepad and tape recorder, Ciara went in search of Lance.

An hour later, she pushed her way through the crowd of reporters to get a prime location for Congressman Butler's resignation speech at Independence Hall. "Excuse me. Excuse me." Lance was right behind her, serving as a shield when some reporters gave her dirty looks.

"Okay, this is perfect," said Ciara once they'd finally made their way to the front of the pack. "I want you to get a good shot of Congressman Butler." They'd discussed what she was looking for and her expectations for the story on the drive over.

"Will do," Lance said, focusing his camera on the podium. "Have you heard that his son may be running for office?"

Ciara turned around to face him. "Yes, I'd heard that rumor, but nothing's official yet. Though I'm sure he's a shoo-in. He comes from a political family with a spotless reputation."

"Have you seen him before? I heard he's quite attractive," Lance teased. He knew how Ciara enjoyed pretty boys.

"Hmmm, I doubt he's all that," Ciara commented. "Those political types are always stiff fuddy-duddies."

"Is that right?" Lance asked as the Butlers took the opportunity to appear at just that moment. Ciara would sure be surprised though because Jonathan Butler was a far cry from one of those political types. Matter of fact, he looked exactly like Ciara's cup of tea.

"Well, of course." Ciara whirled around, but when she did she nearly lost her balance because the drop-dead gorgeous Jonathan Butler was not a stiff fuddy-duddy at all, but the sexy mystery man from last night.

Ciara was completely thrown as the Butlers stepped onto the podium. Charles was first, standing center stage, while his wife, Dominique; son, Jonathan; and campaign manager, Reid Hamilton, flagged either side of him. Several female reporters nearly pushed her aside as all eyes focused on the handsome specimen of a man standing in front of them.

Charles Butler approached the mike and gave a brief

speech that summarized what the press already knew—
that he'd enjoyed his tenure in office, but after twenty-
five years he was stepping down due to angina.

Ciara heard none of it though because her heart was
thumping so loudly in her chest, she could hardly think.

How could her one-night stand be Jonathan Butler?
It hardly seemed possible. Maybe she should make a
fast exit before he noticed her.

Lance looked down at his counterpart, saw how
fixated she was on the dazzling politico and asked,
"What was it you said about political types?"

Ciara blushed. "Ummm, I don't remember," she
lied. She knew exactly what she'd said, but that statement didn't apply to a man like Jonathan Butler. He was
an enigma, to say the least.

If she ran away, she'd appear like a coward, kind of
the way she had earlier that morning. No, she had to
face Jonathan Butler head-on, and her job gave her the
opportunity to catch his attention. Ciara pushed her
way back up to the front of the pack. Thankfully, her
mother had taught her how to stop a man in his tracks.
Charles Butler surveyed the crowd and Ciara raised her
arm, hoping he would call on her, and after several
questions about his health, she got her wish.

"The lady in the front, you have a question?"

"Congressman Butler, some might consider the announcement that you're stepping down as a prime opportunity to introduce your son, Jonathan Butler, as
your successor. Would that be a valid statement?"

Charles Butler was temporarily flabbergasted.
"Well, uh…" Charles Butler stammered. Jonathan

couldn't remember a time when his father had gotten flustered by a pretty face, so he stepped to the podium to cover for his smitten father.

And that was when he saw her.

Chapter 3

She was stunning. Jonathan would never forget how that honey-blond hair had luxuriously lain across his pillow. From where he was standing, she was as delicious a sexpot in the morning light as she'd been in the moonlight. A hint of cleavage peaked out of her buttercup suit jacket, making any man curious to find out what other pleasures she hid underneath.

"I'm here in an unofficial capacity. I'm here as a son, supporting his father," Jonathan replied, smiling down at Ciara. She returned it with a knowing smile of her own. So, she recognized him from last night? Let the games begin, he thought.

"Well, that doesn't exactly answer my question, now does it, Mr. Butler?" Ciara replied silkily, looking up at him beneath heavy eyelashes.

Jonathan raised an eyebrow at her unwillingness to take no for an answer. And was she giving him that same come-hither look? Because if so, he would and could most certainly oblige.

"Do you intend to run at some point in the future, Mr. Butler?" Ciara flashed Jonathan a sexy grin, eager to be the first to get the scoop.

Lance looked down at Ciara. He couldn't believe Ciara's boldness. Here she was flirting with Jonathan on-screen. He hoped Shannon didn't see this.

"I may run for public office at some point in the future," Jonathan answered evasively.

More like the immediate future, Ciara thought but she let it rest. She'd hit her mark! Jonathan Butler was flustered.

"One final question for Congressman Butler. What's next on the agenda for you?" Ciara asked, batting her eyelashes at the senior Butler.

"Mostly a whole lot of golf," Charles Butler replied.

"And with that last statement, the press conference is concluded," Reid said, coming forward to the microphone. "We thank all the members of the press for their attendance." Then he turned and glowered at Jonathan. He couldn't believe that young snot was flirting with a reporter in the middle of a conference. Didn't he know how unprofessional his behavior was? Jonathan Butler had no place in the public arena and Reid was determined to ensure he did not succeed in his election quest.

"Son, I think you…" Charles Butler began, but Jonathan shooed him away.

"Not now, Dad," he said, his eyes never leaving

Ciara's. He longed to have her tiger eyes gaze at him again, and no one was getting in his way.

"Excuse me for a moment." He patted his father on the shoulder and stepped down from the podium.

When he reached his destination, he found her speaking with her cameraman. Jonathan tapped him on the shoulder. "Excuse me, do you mind if I interrupt?" he asked Lance, eager to talk to the woman who'd garnered his attention the moment he'd laid eyes on her at the bar.

His eyes traveled slowly down her curvy frame, taking in her buttercup pantsuit and low-cut jacket with one of those lacy things underneath. He loved the vibrant, sun-kissed hair, pert breasts and long, shapely legs that the formfitting fabric clung to. Her beautifully clear café au lait skin was perfect with the exception of a sexy mole near her mouth.

He seized her beautifully manicured hand and lightly brushed his lips across it. A tingle of excitement rushed through Ciara at the feel of Jonathan's lips on her skin. She remembered what it felt like to have his lips on other parts of her body, which caused her skin to color a bright red.

Another reporter bumped into Ciara. Jonathan's reflexes were impeccable and he placed his hand on the side of her back to steady her, sending an electric current right through Ciara's spine.

"My, my, my, Mr. Butler, you certainly are gallant." Ciara fanned herself.

"My pleasure," Jonathan said, honoring her with a breathtaking smile, all the while inching closer. Ciara stepped backward to escape the heat being generated by his nearness.

"You know that's quite a bold move you made earlier, calling me out on my announcement."

"Really?" Ciara touched her chest, drawing Jonathan's attention to her sumptuous endowments. "C'mon, you're the news story here. Not your father. Everyone wanted to know if you were running for office. All I did was let the cat out of the bag."

"So your cornering me on live television was strictly for the public?" Jonathan asked, captivated by the honey-coated tone of her voice.

"No, not completely." Ciara smiled. "It was personal as well as professional."

"So you were trying to be provocative?" Jonathan queried.

"The public loves it and my news director will eat it up."

"Well, your plan worked. You most certainly know how to titillate and not just the public," Jonathan replied, remembering how he'd felt planted inside the tight warmth of her cocoon.

Ciara flushed. "Now, now, Mr. Butler, remember we are in public."

"I know exactly where we are," Jonathan replied smoothly. "And since I have you cornered," he whispered in her ear, "perhaps you can tell me why you snuck out of my bed last night."

Ciara boldly looked up at him. "I didn't sneak out of your bed. I walked. And furthermore, our evening together was over."

"And I take it that's how you would like to keep it?" Jonathan inquired.

"Wouldn't you?" Ciara asked. "I doubt your father would approve of your one-night stand with a member of the press."

"I do not need my father's approval. I see whom I choose."

"Very well stated but hardly true, Mr. Butler. In case you haven't noticed, you're smack-dab in the public eye," she said, whirling around so Jonathan could view several curious sets of eyes watching their every move.

"I think it would be prudent to leave our one night together as just that, one night. No matter how enjoyable." She smiled seductively at him, revealing a set of pearl-white teeth. "It would not be wise for us to continue our association."

Jonathan leaned down so that only she could hear him. "Don't tell me, you're afraid of a little challenge?"

Ciara breathed in his musky masculine scent. It was very intoxicating and she instantly stepped back. "No, not at all," she replied.

"Then join me for dinner tonight."

As much as she might want to join Jonathan Butler for dinner, her mind cautioned her against it. He oozed charm and was dangerous to her peace of mind. Last night had been about more than just buck-wild sex; he'd gotten to her and that would never do.

At this point in her career, she couldn't afford to get tied up in all that messy love stuff. She needed to focus her energies on becoming an anchor. Of course, a high-profile relationship with a would-be congressman just might do that. Perhaps she should reconsider. She could enjoy him as well as boost her career.

"Are you asking me out on a proper date this time?"

Jonathan grinned. "As I recall, that wasn't what you were looking for last night."

"Touché."

"How about dinner?"

"Perhaps," Ciara answered. "Only if it includes dessert." She winked at him.

Jonathan couldn't resist smiling at her audacity and rose to the occasion. "That could be arranged." He grinned. "How about seven-thirty?"

"Sounds perfect."

"Great, I'll pick you up at the studio."

Ciara thought about that and shook her head. She in no way wanted their relationship to leak out to the rest of the press.

"No can do. Why don't I meet you?"

"Capital Grille on Chestnut Street at seventy-thirty."

"I look forward to it," Ciara tossed over her shoulder and started toward the door, but Jonathan halted her.

"Wait, I still don't know your name," Jonathan commented.

"It's Ciara. Ciara Miller," she replied, sauntering over to Lance.

Ah, now there was an unusual name, Jonathan thought as he rejoined his father's contingent, but one that fit her extremely well.

Lance joined up with Ciara at the door and asked, "So, what happened?"

Ciara turned around and noticed Jonathan watching her backside from across the room, but he quickly looked away when she caught him.

"I have a date with Jonathan Butler tonight," Ciara said once they were outside.

Lance opened the van door and began hauling his equipment into the back of the truck before joining her inside. "I'm not surprised you snagged a date, especially after the way you out-and-out flirted with him at the press conference."

"Who me?" Ciara asked, feigning ignorance.

"Yeah, you," Lance said, nudging her in the middle. "You better hope Shannon doesn't pick up on the vibe."

"Oh please," Ciara said. "Shannon wouldn't know flirtation if it hit her with a ten-foot stick."

"Son, what are you thinking?" Charles berated his overly eager son after the reporter had left. "Fraternizing with a member of the press. Do you even realize how every aspect of your life is scrutinized?"

"The press is just waiting for you to screw up. So they can be there like a pack of wild dogs to pick up the scraps," his mother added.

Jonathan patted his father on the back. "Trust me, Dad. I know what I'm doing. It's just dinner after all."

Reid laughed inwardly at Jonathan's public display. Here he was on the eve of an election that was practically guaranteed and he was hooking up with a pretty television reporter, of all people. Reid couldn't ask for better luck for Jonathan to get his comeuppance.

"Do you even realize how lucky you are, Jonathan?

To be in the position you are?" his father queried. "People are waiting for you to fail."

"Of course I do, Dad." Jonathan's voice rose slightly and several reporters looked over at them. "Because you never let me forget it," he snapped underneath his breath. All he'd heard all his life was that he was next in line. He had to do everything perfectly or be prepared for the consequences, and when his father was Congressman Butler, those were always stiff.

When he'd been in boarding school, he and a couple of other ninth graders had played a prank on the dean by toilet papering his house. Jonathan had hoped he'd be kicked out and allowed to be normal like other kids instead of going to social functions playing the dutiful son, but it was not meant to be. He'd thought he could get away without his father ever finding out, but not so. Charles Butler had shown up to the Phelps School in all his glory and had caused quite a commotion. Pretty soon, Jonathan had been back in school and under strict supervision in detention.

Reid jumped in. "Can we have this conversation in the car, please?" he implored as he directed the Butlers toward the exit.

Jonathan looked down at Reid's hand on his arm and glowered at him. Reid quickly removed it.

Jonathan sucked in a deep breath once they were outside. He allowed his parents and Reid to precede him before entering the limousine Reid had waiting. He was so tired of his father ruling his life. He was a grown man capable of making his own decisions.

After several long moments, he got inside the vehicle. Jonathan seethed while en route back to his father's office because his father kept hounding him.

"Who is this woman, really?" his father asked aloud. "You know absolutely nothing about her."

"Your father's right," Reid agreed. "All of a sudden she shows up just when you're about to announce your candidacy. It could be a setup. What's her name?"

"Oh, c'mon," Jonathan said, ignoring Reid's question. He had no intention of giving him her name so he could treat her like a common criminal. "You guys are making too much of one date." All of this cloak-and-dagger stuff truly wasn't necessary. Why? Because his father may know about politics, but Jonathan knew women. He would know if he was being played.

"And you are taking this too lightly," Reid countered.

"Maybe, Reid, you've forgotten what it's like to date," Jonathan said, taking a dig at his father's right-hand man. "But for the rest of us, when you meet someone you like and they like you, you go out on what's called a date. It's as simple as that."

"Well, I guess we'll have to wait and see if she has an ulterior motive," Reid replied, putting on his sunglasses and looking out the window. He couldn't believe how arrogant Jonathan Butler was.

"Yes, we shall," Jonathan said.

When she returned to the studio to prepare for the twelve o'clock newscast, Ciara ran right into her co-worker, Chelsea Allen.

It didn't bother her one bit that one of her closest

friends at the station was Caucasian, though it may have bothered some. Ciara was color-blind. Furthermore, there was none of the backstabbing that came with competing for the same positions. Chelsea was the antithesis of Ciara. A brunette with pale skin, Chelsea wore baggy clothes to hide her size-fourteen figure. But she sure was the best makeup artist Ciara had ever come across.

"Ciara, where have you been? Shannon's been looking everywhere for you."

"Oh, Lord." Ciara rolled her eyes. "Is she breathing fire?"

Chelsea appeared stumped. "Isn't she always?"

Ciara laughed. "I suppose you're right. So what does the dragon lady want now?"

"Something about a story she wants you to cover."

"Am I the only reporter around?" Ciara wailed, grabbing Chelsea by the arm and pushing her into the ladies' room nearby.

"Is it me?" Ciara pulled a brush out of her purse and proceeded to smooth her golden locks until they shone. "But doesn't it seem like she enjoys giving me a hard time?" Ciara asked, surveying herself in the mirror. All in all, she was pleased with her appearance and turned to face Chelsea.

"You're her whipping boy—I mean, *girl*—right now," Chelsea said, touching up her lipstick with a fresh coat.

"I wish she'd find someone new to pick on. I mean, it's not like I'm not a seasoned reporter. I've been at the station for five years." Ciara folded her arms and pouted.

"Cheer up." Chelsea patted her shoulder. "Pretty soon, Shannon will find something or someone new to focus her energies on."

"Maybe she should get herself a man, release some of that pent-up energy, then she wouldn't be so focused on the rest of us."

"It sure couldn't hurt," Chelsea chuckled. "Wait a sec." She stared into Ciara's eyes. "Does this mean that you've found yourself such a man to relieve stress?" she teased.

"Who me?" Ciara played coy but couldn't resist grinning from ear to ear.

"Yeah you," Chelsea replied. "Don't you hold out on me. You know I'm living through you vicariously."

"Well." Ciara paused for effect. "If you must know. I've met a truly amazing man. He's absolutely gorgeous, tall and has the most well-defined body I've ever laid eyes on."

Chelsea's eyes grew wide at every adjective Ciara used to describe her fine mystery man. "And? Who is he?"

"You wouldn't believe it if I told you," Ciara said, glancing around the restroom to make sure they were the only two people there. She bent down and peeked under the stalls, but didn't see anyone.

"Well? Spill the beans," Chelsea said, frustrated.

"It's Jonathan Butler," Ciara said. "We met last night at a bar and the sparks flew."

"You mean that gorgeous fox that's supposed to run for his father's congressional seat?"

"Nothing's official yet," Ciara said.

"Yeah, but we all know it's going to happen," Chelsea responded. "So when are you going to see him again?"

"I'm not going to say anything more. You know the walls around here have ears." Ciara glanced around the restroom. "And I don't want this to leak until I'm ready to use it to my advantage." She had probably said too much, but she was so giddy with excitement, she couldn't contain herself.

"Okay," Chelsea replied. "We'll talk more over lunch."

"As long as I'm not stationed in Timbuktu, I'm all yours," Ciara said, shutting the door behind her. Neither of them heard the toilet flush several moments later or saw Shannon exit from the restroom with a broad smile on her face. The station manager wanted ratings; well, Shannon had just hit the jackpot.

Lunch with Chelsea was all girl talk as always. Ciara enjoyed filling her best pal in on all the details of her date with Jonathan and watching her eyes bulge out with envy, but unfortunately she had an unenjoyable task ahead of her and her name started with a *D*.

Her mother, Diamond Miller, telephoned her three times at work, asking Ciara when she would come by with the money. Why couldn't she get the money from her boyfriend? thought Ciara as she drove up South Street. Although known for its ten blocks of party bars, some areas were somewhat sleazy with homeless people, hookers and drug dealers. It was the slums and, although it may have been her roots, she hated being reminded of her humble beginnings. But every time she visited Diamond, it was unavoidable. She'd tried to get Diamond to travel to her side of town, but Diamond refused.

Afraid to park her car in the rear, Ciara parked in front of the bar instead. Situated on the corner, the exterior of the Oasis was in desperate need of a coat of paint and some serious siding. As she pulled open the door, Ciara took a deep breath and steeled herself to prepare for another of one Diamond's dramas. She found the bar relatively empty except for a few lone patrons.

"Vince." She nodded at the barkeep, who just so happened to be dating her mother. Balding, middle-aged and overweight, Vince was loud and crude with a thick New York accent and he should have been every woman's nightmare; instead, he'd found solace in the arms of her ditzy mother. "Is my mom upstairs?" Ciara asked.

"Yeah, she's up there doing her nails or something. You be sure to tell her that she'd better call Suzy and make sure she's covering for Candy. Otherwise we'll be one short for tonight's show."

"I'll be sure and do that, Vince," Ciara said sarcastically, sauntering past him toward the dressing rooms. Who did he think she was—his secretary? Ciara climbed up the back staircase to the small apartment Diamond and Vince shared and knocked on the door.

"Coming," a voice rang out from inside. Diamond opened the door seconds later and Ciara was rewarded with a loud screech.

"Ciara! Oh, baby girl, it's so good to see you." Diamond kissed either cheek and squeezed Ciara's shoulders. A hug that Ciara did not return. "Where have you been? I've been waiting for you since yesterday."

Ciara looked her mother up and down and was embarrassed. Her mother was overly made-up, wearing a tight bustier that revealed her ample bosom. She'd paired the bustier with some tight leather capris. How did Diamond always manage to find clothes that made her look trashy? She was forty-five years old for heaven's sake. Why didn't she dress like it?

"I do have a life, Diamond," Ciara replied, walking inside. She looked around the modest apartment for a place to sit, but the tiny living room was cluttered with clothes and paper. Diamond didn't work and could easily clean up the place. What did she do all day? Ciara wondered as she stepped over clothes and brushed some newspaper onto the floor and off the couch to make room for a place to sit.

"Don't be a grouch." Diamond closed the door behind her daughter and plopped down in her recliner to watch *Judge Mathis*. Picking up her bottle of ruby-red nail polish on the coffee table, she returned to polishing her toenails.

"I'm not a grouch," Ciara said, throwing her purse on the side table.

"If you say so," Diamond huffed. She knew her daughter didn't approve of her, but she didn't care. As long as she was happy with herself that was all that mattered.

"Well?" Ciara raised an eyebrow. "What do you

want, Diamond? Because I'm on my lunch hour and have to get back to work."

"It's like I said when I called," Diamond replied. "I need to borrow a little cash."

"Why? Isn't Vince bankrolling you?"

"The bar isn't doing so good," Diamond replied, "as you can probably see from the lack of customers downstairs, and I need a few things. And Vince is being a real tightwad with his cash these days. He says I'm spending too much."

"Is that true?" Ciara asked. She was sure it was. Diamond went through cash like water.

Diamond smiled guiltily. "I suppose I may have overspent a little, but I just had to have a pair of these tall four-inch boots that were on sale at Macy's. Wait here and I'll show you."

Diamond rushed off toward the bedroom and minutes later returned carrying a pair of tiger-print leather boots with a four-inch heel. "So, what do you think?"

Ciara shook her head in amazement. Her mother would never change. She had no idea about the value of money because she'd never stayed in one place long enough. She'd always gone from one man to the next; moving her and a young Ciara from place to place after each one of her relationships had successively failed.

Ciara had hated each and every one of them. Every guy was usually only after one thing and poor Diamond never figured it out until it was too late and he was moving on to the next person. Until Paul Williams had come along. Nearly forty years her senior, he'd married Diamond and had later left her his fortune, which she'd had the bad sense to waste. "Diamond, how much did those boots set you back?" Ciara asked.

Diamond looked down sheepishly and didn't answer.

"Diamond, how much?" Ciara's voice rose an octave.

"Oh, two hundred dollars," Diamond whispered.

"Two hundred dollars! Are you insane?"

"I know, but I just had to have them," Diamond explained. "They fit my new knit jersey dress to perfection."

Ciara was so frustrated at her mother's lack of discipline. Every time she was low on cash, she came knocking on her door.

"And you want me to bail you out, I presume. Why do you always do this, Diamond? Do I look like your personal ATM?"

"Of course not," Diamond replied and on cue tears began to form in her dark brown eyes. "It's just, you know I haven't had an easy life. I grew up on the streets and had to raise you all on my own."

Ciara sighed. She'd heard this song and dance a million times. Diamond had run away from home at sixteen and had met up with some Las Vegas showgirls who'd taken her under their wing and taught her how to get by. Ciara understood all that because she'd lived through it with her, so she would not be made to feel guilty because Diamond was a spendthrift.

"It's not my fault you ran off with another man and didn't tell Daddy. He would have helped, you know. Taken care of the both of us." From what she'd heard,

her father had adored Diamond and when she'd become
pregnant, they'd quickly gotten married. Diamond
hadn't been content as a married housewife and mother,
but she'd been young and gullible and had run off with
the first smooth talker she'd met, leaving Ciara's poor
accountant father with a broken heart. And when that
relationship had failed, Diamond had returned to the
only thing she knew how to be: a Las Vegas showgirl.

"So, you blame me for your horrible life?" Diamond
questioned her.

"Who else should I blame? You are the parent.
Aren't you?" Of course, Ciara wondered about that
sometimes. Many a time, she'd had to help a tipsy
Diamond up the stairs after one too many or had been
forced to listen to her get it on with some stranger.

Diamond shrugged her shoulders. "What's done is
done, Ciara. I can't make up for it, baby girl. But you
are in a position to help your mama. You're a big-time
reporter now."

Little did she know, thought Ciara. Her reporter's
salary barely fed her. Ciara stood up abruptly. "I have
to go or I'll be late."

"And the money?" Diamond turned on the puppy-dog
eyes. Ciara shook her head. She should let Vince kick
Diamond out, maybe then she would learn her lesson.
Of course, then she would have no place to go and where
would she end up? At Ciara's doorstep. No, no, it was
better she give her the money and hope for the best.

"I don't have two hundred."

Diamond smiled and lightly touched her cheek.
"Whatever you could give me would be great."

Ciara leaned over, grabbed her purse and pulled out a hundred-dollar bill from her wallet. "How about one hundred?" Ciara held up the money.

Diamond quickly snatched it and stuffed it down her bustier.

"Thanks, kid, you're a real lifesaver."

Ciara glanced down and her watch read a quarter to two. "I've got to go, Diamond."

"Listen, Ci-Ci, I really appreciate your coming by. You always help your mama out when I need it." It meant the world to Diamond that even though her daughter had moved up in the world, she hadn't given up on her.

"Please don't get all mushy and sentimental, Diamond. It doesn't suit you," Ciara retorted, walking to the door. She may have agreed to help her, but Ciara didn't get the warm fuzzies from her mother.

"Okay, okay." Diamond knew a good thing when she had it and wouldn't push. "I'll see you later," she said, closing the door behind her.

Ciara breathed a sigh of relief and took the stairs two at a time to get out of the dingy bar. Thank God that was over, she thought rushing back to her car. Now she could look forward to her evening with Jonathan and all that implied.

Chapter 4

When Ciara arrived at Capital Grille, she found Jonathan waiting for her at the bar having a Scotch neat. Ciara was somewhat nervous about her attire. "I hope this is okay?" she asked, referring to her buttercup business suit. She hadn't had the time to go home and change.

"Of course it is." Jonathan grinned widely. "You look beautiful." From where he was, he liked everything he saw.

"Have a seat, you'll love this place. They make the best lobster bisque."

"Ooh, it sounds delicious," Ciara said. "And I'm starved."

"CG has excellent entrées and a great selection of wines."

"Sounds mouthwatering," Ciara licked her lips in anticipation.

Jonathan followed the tiny action, mesmerized by her mouth.

"Your table is ready," the hostess said, interrupting them.

"I'm curious as to why a guy like you would choose to get involved with me, a television reporter. I'm sure your family advised against it." Once they were seated, Ciara wasted no time cutting to the chase.

"True, they don't agree," he replied. "But I make my own decisions."

"In a political campaign, I doubt that's even possible," Ciara said aloud.

"So you think I'm a puppet and my father pulls the strings?"

"No, no, no," Ciara explained herself. "I merely meant that you probably have a lot of people telling you how to dress, how to talk, how to act. It must be extremely difficult. I'm sure they're the reason you didn't announce your candidacy today. I think that was a wise decision."

"Thank you." Jon smiled. At least someone appreciated his game plan. "I thought I might appear too eager to the public and not respectful of my father's tenure if I announced my candidacy five minutes after he resigned from office."

"I agree with you. The public can be somewhat fickle, but that's what makes the news so exciting and unpredictable."

The way she talked about her job with such passion

made Jonathan envious. It must be nice to decide for yourself the direction your life would take. For him, his life had been planned out since birth: private school, Harvard, law school, and now running for office. "Have you always known you wanted to be a reporter?" Jonathan asked. "Because you seem to enjoy what you do."

"Well, of course," Ciara replied as if the thought to do anything else had never crossed her mind. She'd always wanted to be a reporter. That was why she'd run her high school and college newspapers. "I love what I do. Being a journalist is in my blood. I live it, I breathe it, 24-7."

"Wow, say how you truly feel!" Jonathan said, over-whelmed by the sheer enthusiasm in Ciara's voice. He wished he knew what that felt like. Yes, he was good at being a lawyer and politician. He'd trained his whole life for it, but was it his true passion? He didn't know. He'd never been allowed to find out.

"Don't you love what you do?" Ciara asked.

"No, not always," Jonathan answered truthfully.

Ciara was surprised by his answer. Did the golden boy have problems like the rest of the human race? What troubles could someone like him, born with a silver spoon in his mouth, ever have that couldn't be solved by one flick of his father's wand?

"Why not?" Ciara asked. "From what I can see you're a natural. The camera loves you," she said. She wondered if she could get an exclusive interview for WTCF.

"Thank you." Jonathan blushed, causing Ciara's heart to go pitter-patter.

"You're welcome. But I'm sure I'm not telling you something you haven't been told before. You have the *it* factor, now you just need to show that you can back it up."

"Well, that's exactly what I intend to do. I intend to showcase issues important to my community like educating our children and taxes."

"Sounds like you know the issues and that's important. Because trust me, the press won't let you get away with a pat answer."

"Don't I know it," Jonathan replied.

The waitress came back with their lobster bisque and placed it in front of them. "This looks delicious." Ciara wasted no time in digging her spoon into the creamy mixture with chunky bits of lobster. She tore into the bowl and it was empty before Jonathan had hardly had a bite.

He'd been so busy watching her facial expressions as she devoured the soup, he'd barely touched his. She'd looked up several times and found him openly staring.

"Mmmm, was that good," Ciara commented. She placed her spoon in the empty bowl and peeled a nibble off the warm loaf of bread the waitress had brought to accompany the soup.

"I can tell." Jonathan leaned over and wiped some of the liquid off the corner of her mouth with his finger and licked it off with his tongue.

Ciara was the first to break their gaze and speak. "Enough about our respective careers. I'm curious as to what makes a man like you tick."

"What do you want to know?"

"C'mon, something tells me you're a man of many talents," Ciara replied flirtatiously. "You're surrounded by all that money and power, it must be intoxicating."

"Sometimes it is," he responded. And sometimes he wished for a moment of peace. Over the next three months he wouldn't have much of it with the special election coming up in November. That was why he'd been so hell-bent on keeping his date this evening. The women he typically dated were all the same.

Beautiful, well-bred socialites skilled in the art of conversation, parties and none of whom had the least bit of substance, which was why Ciara Miller intrigued him. He was sure he'd barely touched the surface of such a complex woman.

"And you're unattached because?" Ciara asked.

"I choose to be. And you? Why is a beautiful woman like you still single?"

"I'm not the settling-down type," Ciara stated. "I didn't grow up with a white picket fence with dreams of having a family. I was raised by a single mother and grew up poor with barely a roof over my head." Ciara drew her water glass to her lips and took a generous sip.

Jonathan's brow rose. Her statement revealed a lot about Ciara. Clearly there were some things in her past that had affected her deeply because hurt was etched across her face, but just as soon as it surfaced, the pain was gone.

"I can't wait for dinner," Ciara said, smiling again while she changed the subject. "Because if that bisque was any indicator, dinner ought to be darn good."

After a leisurely dinner and light conversation about their various interests, they shared a decadent chocolate mousse that afterward left Ciara feeling frisky. Could it be because Jonathan had removed his overcoat, rolled up his sleeves and unbuttoned his top button? Just that little bit of skin was making Ciara all kinds of horny. What was it they said about chocolate?

"Listen, I enjoy my freedom," Ciara said after regaling Jonathan with tales of her bad-girl youth. "No restrictions. You know what I'm saying. I like being completely uninhibited."

"I like uninhibited," Jonathan said, leaning in closer until their arms touched.

"Do you?" Ciara scooted closer and lightly rubbed his arm.

At the slightest touch of her hand, all the hairs on Jonathan's arm stood up at attention. He was more aware of her than ever.

"Yes, I do," Jonathan said. He appreciated a woman in touch with her sexual side and one so completely unpredictable. "So let's get out of here and perhaps we can get uninhibited together."

"No can do, sweetheart," Ciara replied and rose to her feet. "I have to work tomorrow and with the way my boss has been riding me I can't afford to be late again."

"Oh, you're no fun." Jonathan pouted.

"I'll make it up to you," Ciara replied, seductively leaving Jonathan no doubt of her intentions.

"Promise?" Jonathan raised a brow.

"I promise."

* * *

"I'm home," Ciara yelled later that evening as she walked inside the apartment.

Rachel poked her head out from the kitchen and wiped her hands against her flowery apron. "How was your day?"

"Oh, it was rough," Ciara said, kicking off her shoes and flopping down on the chaise on their sectional sofa. She tucked her legs underneath her and laid her head against the armrest.

"How about a glass of wine?" Rachel suggested.

"That sounds wonderful," Ciara said, massaging her temples.

Ciara smiled at her younger sister. Poor thing couldn't dress worth a darn. Rachel was more comfortable in a pair of jeans and a T-shirt than in Ciara's high-fashion wardrobe. Rachel was wearing a pair of old sweats and her long hair hung in a ponytail.

Rachel returned several minutes later carrying two glasses of red wine and sat beside Ciara. "Mine wasn't any better. My professor ripped apart my psychology paper."

"Guess who I saw today?" Ciara asked, taking a sip of wine.

"Please don't tell me it was Diamond," Rachel guessed correctly. Ciara nodded. "Asking for money no doubt?"

"Which I don't really have, but…"

Rachel turned and glared at her sister. "Please tell me you didn't give it to her?"

Ciara shrugged her shoulders. "Why do you let her

do this to you, Ci-Ci?" Rachel called Ciara by the nickname she'd come up with when she was two years old and hadn't been able to say her name. "You let Diamond run a guilt trip on you every time because she had a hard life. Well so did you, sis. That woman dragged you around the country. You don't owe her anything." Rachel had seen Diamond come time and time again to Ciara for a handout and she was sick of it.

"I know, I know," Ciara said. She hadn't forgotten being kicked out of their apartment because Diamond couldn't pay the rent or doing her homework in the back of some scummy bar. All because Diamond refused to grow up and keep a job. "But I can't just leave her hanging in the wind. She's my mother."

"Yes, she is. But she's a grown woman and quite capable of taking care of herself," Rachel replied. Every time Rachel saw her, Diamond had another man on her arm. So why was she always looking to her daughter for a handout? "I'm tired of seeing her use you, Ciara. You have to stand up for yourself and stop letting her walk all over you. She only does this because you let her get away with it."

Ciara stood up and walked over to stare out the window at the passing cars. "I know you're right, Rachel. But you just don't understand the bond Diamond and I share. Despite her shortcomings, we've always been there for each other through all the ups and downs. I don't know how to walk away from that."

Rachel jumped up, came over and squeezed her sister's shoulders. "Ci-Ci, I'm not asking you to walk away from Diamond. I just don't want to see Diamond continue to take advantage of you."

Ciara patted Rachel's hand and pulled away. "I know you mean well, Rachel, and I thank you for your concern, but I'm going to have to deal with Diamond myself."

Rachel threw up her hands. "Okay, okay. It's your funeral. I've spoken my piece. I told Dad I would have a talk with you and I did."

"So Dad put you up to this?" Ciara inquired. "I should have known." Diamond was Robert Miller's least favorite person, which was surprising considering they'd once had a grand love affair. But then again, her father had been young and naive and maybe somewhat of a risk taker. And of course now after twenty-five years with her stepmother, Pilar, Robert had become somewhat of a stuffed shirt. "Well you can tell him that I've been properly warned, but that I'll take it from here."

"Don't say I didn't warn you." Rachel couldn't resist delivering one final comment.

"Duly noted," Ciara said.

Jonathan began his Friday clashing with his father's expert opinion even though he'd rather have spent a leisurely morning making love to Ciara. He'd already prepared himself to hear about the dangers of dallying with the press because his father would have had overnight to think of an appropriate lecture.

True to form, when he arrived at his campaign headquarters, Zach, Reid and his parents were already huddled together in the conference room.

"Good morning," Jonathan said to the elderly woman serving as his receptionist. A retiree, she'd generously volunteered her time as a contribution to his campaign and she just so happened to make the best cup of coffee Jonathan had ever had.

He was dropping his briefcase in his office and walking toward the conference room when Dorothy handed him a mug. "Thanks, Dorothy, you're a doll."

Dorothy returned a generous smile right back at him. She just loved it when the young man showed his pearly whites.

Jonathan knocked on the door before entering. "Can anyone join in this conversation? Or should I make myself scarce?"

"Come on in, Johnny boy," Zach said, rising from his seat and shaking his best friend's hand, "because we have a lot to discuss." As Jonathan entered, Zach closed the door behind him.

His father didn't waste any time laying into him. "You can't get involved with a member of the press. Do you have any idea the damage you could do or might have already done? And the campaign hasn't even started yet." Charles Butler shook his head.

Jonathan took a seat at the head of the table. They must have thought he had never been in a campaign before. "I'm well aware of my actions, Dad. I'm not five years old."

"Then you must know how precarious this situation is."

"Jonathan, you know we only want what's best for you." His mother tried the maternal approach. "Perhaps you should end things with this Ciara Miller before it begins."

"So you know her name," Jonathan said. "I guess I shouldn't be surprised. But what all of you need to know is I won't be interrogated by any of you. This is my life and I choose how to live it."

"Once you become a politician and are in the public eye," his father said sternly, "you give up all rights to life solely as you see fit. I urge you to reconsider this behavior. It could be detrimental to your campaign."

"I have to agree with your father." Zach looked at Reid, who was sitting next to Jonathan. Reid stood up and moved to another chair down the table. "Listen, to me, Jonathan." Zach scooted his chair next to his friend. "How do you know this Miller woman isn't setting you up for some sort of scandal? That she hasn't been paid off by the opposition to bring you down?"

"I don't, but I will keep my eyes wide open," Jonathan said defensively. He didn't know why he was fighting so hard to maintain contact with Ciara; he barely knew her. Could it be because Ciara had completely surprised the heck out of him? Sure, they'd had great sex, but it was more than that—she excited him more than any woman ever had.

"Honey." His mother rose from her chair. She bent down and grabbed either side of Jonathan's face. "Your father and I have been in this business for twenty-odd years," she said, bending down farther until their faces were inches apart. "Your father came into office when racism was rampant." Dominique remembered the stress they'd been under, which would have broken up many a marriage, but she and Charles had endured and because of that their relationship was stronger than ever. "Believe us when we say we know the dangers of politics."

Jonathan appreciated his mother's honesty, but it still didn't sway his decision. "If you don't mind, Mother, I'd like to turn the attention away from my love life and back on the campaign where it belongs," Jonathan said, effectively dismissing all talk of Ciara Miller from the conversation.

"Excellent idea." Zach knew Jonathan well enough to know when to back off. Once he had his mind made up, there was no swaying him. If they continued to push, he would dig his heels in deeper. Zach just hoped he could help him avoid a public train wreck. "Because there's a lot of work to be done. As you all are aware, your announcement speech at the University of Pennsylvania is next Friday. I'd like to go over it with you now." Zach strode toward the door and held it open for Jonathan.

"If you'll excuse me, then." Jonathan stood up and followed Zach out the door, leaving his parents and Reid effectively out of the loop, which is how he wanted it.

After they'd gone over the fine points of Jonathan's speech, Zach broached the subject of a romance with Ciara Miller again. "Listen to me, Jonathan. I know you think what you're doing is right," Zach said. "I'm a man, too, and sometimes we are led around by our noses, but this is more than just bedding this woman. Your whole career is at stake. A career you've worked hard to achieve."

"Logically, I know you're right, Zach," Jonathan said, leaning back in his chair. "But Ciara is so real. She shoots straight from the hip. Maybe it's because she's a journalist. It's just so rare to find that kind of honesty these days." In the few short hours he'd spent in her company, Jonathan had felt more alive than he had in a long time. He wasn't walking the straight and narrow line for once in his life. He was finally living it and he wouldn't apologize to anyone.

"A reporter, honest?" Zach chuckled. "Now there's a contradiction. Jonathan, you have no idea if you can trust her."

"True, but isn't the game of life a crapshoot?"

"If you're such a gambler, why hire me?" Zach asked. "I thought you wanted a sure thing." Zach was well aware of his talents and he put people in office. He didn't spawn losers. Jonathan may want to sabotage his career, but Zach wanted no part of it. He'd successfully managed half a dozen campaigns and he wished to maintain that record.

Jonathan smiled at Zach's arrogance. He shouldn't be surprised though; that was what he liked about his best friend. "I do. That's why I have absolute faith that you can spin this to our advantage. I mean, Ciara's in the media. She could be a great asset."

"I guess I never looked at it like that before," Zach said.

"That's because you're all doom and gloom," Jonathan replied. "You're such a pessimist."

"And you're too much of an optimist."

"But isn't that why I'll make an excellent congressman? Because deep down I believe in people, heck, in the American public to make the right decision and choose me to replace my father."

"You go on dreaming, Jonathan," Zach said. "And in the meantime, I'll work on staging the best campaign I can. Speaking of which, you know we need to discuss your finances. We need a cash influx because you're running low on cash and you can't continue to finance the campaign out of your own pocket or you'll be ruined. It's time to step up our fund-raising efforts."

"What's the first step?"

"Your mother and I have discussed some event ideas. Let me finalize our ideas and work up a proposal for you." Zach glanced down at his watch.

"When can you have it ready?"

"Give me a day or so and I'll have it for you," Zach said, heading for the door. "Forgive me, but I have a luncheon appointment."

Jonathan nodded and breathed a sigh of relief once Zach had gone. He was thoroughly exhausted with hearing everyone else's opinion of whether or not he should date Ciara. Only his opinion counted and he thought she was adorable. Confident, poised, intelligent and breathtakingly beautiful, Ciara possessed all the qualities he wanted in a woman. Was it possible that Ciara Miller could be Mrs. Jonathan Butler?

"So, we're on for tonight?" Ciara asked from her desk in the newsroom the following week. She'd been eager to see him again and make good on her promise, but he'd been too busy preparing to announce his candidacy. He'd only called once to set up a date for Friday.

"Absolutely. I'm looking forward to it."

"Great." Ciara smiled. "I'll see you then," she said, then hung up the phone and swirled around in her chair. When she did, she found that she wasn't alone. Shannon was standing behind her. "Shannon, you startled me." Ciara clutched her chest. "Can I help you with something?"

Shannon smiled. "Well…I thought you might be interested in attending Jonathan Butler's announcement speech."

"Of course I would," Ciara's replied. It would give her the chance to see Jonathan in action. But what surprised her most was that Shannon was being so nice to her, of all people. Ciara knew she wasn't her favorite person of late.

"Good. Find Lance and go pull a story together."

"Thanks, Shannon. I really appreciate the opportunity."

A fake grin plastered on Shannon's face. "Just do a good job and perhaps more opportunities might await you." Shannon spun on her heel and walked away, leaving Ciara to wonder what had changed.

She and Lance discussed it on the way to the speech.

"I just don't trust that witch," Ciara said. "I know she has it in for me. So why is she being nice all of a sudden?"

"I don't know," Lance replied. "But I would watch your back. She could be setting you up for a fall."

"Then I'm just going to have to show her who she's dealing with," Ciara said feistily.

"Hmmm, and I bet she's not the only one," Lance commented.

"What are you talking about?" Ciara asked.

"Oh, c'mon. I know you went out on a date with Jonathan Butler. How did it go?" Curiously, Ciara had remained quiet about their date. Usually she was chatty, once she'd kicked another man to the curb.

"It was fine," she replied, trying to appear nonchalant.

"Oh please, Ciara. I know you, remember? And with the smile you've been wearing, Butler must have rocked your world," he teased.

"Lance!" Ciara punched him in the arm.

"It's okay. It's about time someone cracked the armor around that stone-cold heart of yours."

"Are you saying I'm impervious?"

Lance turned around and focused his dark eyes on her.

"If you want whatever you have going with Jonathan to work, you're going to have to open up your heart."

Tell Jonathan her fears, her hidden secrets? Never. Ciara didn't know if she could be that honest. Hell, she didn't think she'd been that honest with herself, let alone another person. Ciara chuckled. "Now why would I do a thing like that? Whose to say Jonathan Butler will last that long?"

Lance shook his head. He wondered when Ciara would stop being so afraid. He hoped it wasn't when she found herself all alone.

Chapter 5

Jonathan's announcement speech went brilliantly. He spoke of the issues that he thought were important to the people of Philadelphia County, such as education, health care, taxes and homeland security. He'd chosen the University of Pennsylvania's student union as the place to make his formal announcement.

It was Zach's idea that he come off as youthful and energetic, in contrast to his opponent, Alec Marshall, a fifty-year-old county commissioner. What better way than to announce at a college campus with hundreds of students gathered around? He could rally the youth about the importance of voting while making his bid for Congress.

He and Zach were speaking with the organizers of

the event, the University of Pennsylvania Democrats, at the student union, when his eyes suddenly flew to the doorway. Moments later, like a ray of sunlight, Ciara appeared and all clear thought escaped him as he struggled to return to the conversation at hand.

Zach's eyes followed his and he shook his head in disgust. The last thing Jonathan needed was a distraction.

"Look who's here," Zach whispered in his ear, testing Jonathan's resolve. He nodded in Ciara's direction.

"I'm aware of it," Jonathan replied.

"Good. Stay focused," Zach said, patting his back.

"Not to worry. I'm on top of it," Jonathan replied. Though pretty soon, he hoped to be on top of something else entirely. After the event was over, he hoped to steal a few minutes with Ciara. More than once today, his thoughts had turned to her and the incredible night of lovemaking they'd shared and those delectable little noises she made when she was on the brink of coming. He loved bringing her to the edge and then slowing the pace. It drove her mad, but he loved every minute.

"Jonathan, what do you think?"

Jonathan shook himself. "I'm sorry, I missed what you said." Zach glared at him. Once again, the reporter had caused him to lose focus.

Ciara smiled as she watched Jonathan from across the room. She'd heard his speech. He was a natural orator and would make a great congressman. She could just see him on Capitol Hill.

"Wasn't he magnificent?" Ciara asked, unable to hide her obvious appreciation for Jonathan's talent.

"Are we a little mesmerized by all the politics and power? I've heard it can be addicting," Lance replied, taking a canapé off the platter of appetizers the waiters were serving and plopping the entire pastry in his mouth.

"I suppose," Ciara said as she watched Jonathan sip on sparkling cider. Smart move, thought Ciara. He should avoid alcoholic beverages on the campaign trail. "But trust me, he isn't the first powerful man I've dated and I'm sure he won't be the last."

Ciara doubted Lance believed her one bit because he raised a suspicious brow. "If you say so," he responded. "Though I do wonder why the temperature level rose several degrees when he laid eyes on you," Lance added.

"Did it?"

Lance nodded.

"Well, I suppose you're right." Ciara fanned herself. "It is sort of hot in here."

"Why don't you go cool yourself off?" Lance pushed her toward Jonathan's towering presence. "Because it looks like your man is finally alone."

Ciara turned around and Lance was indeed correct— Jonathan was alone and walking straight toward her.

"Hello, beautiful." Jonathan looked down and smiled at her broadly. He gave Lance a look that said *get lost* and he quickly departed.

"You know we really have to stop meeting like this," Ciara replied.

"Our paths are certainly crossing more of late," Jonathan commented. "Is it fate or a coincidence?"

"Maybe both. So, what's on the agenda for tonight?" Ciara asked. Stepping away from their intimate circle, she headed to the coffee bar and ordered herself a chai tea.

"How about dinner at my place?"

"Are you sure about that?" she asked, handing the attendant a five and accepting the paper cup. "Because the last time we were at your place…"

"I know." Jonathan smiled. "So how about it?" he asked, leaning against the bar.

"Hmmm." Ciara thought about it as she sipped on her tea. "Oh," she said, wincing when the hot liquid nearly scorched her tongue.

"I could kiss it and make it better," Jonathan supplied.

Ciara chuckled. "That won't be necessary, but let's make it dinner at my place."

"Your place?"

"Yes, my place," Ciara replied. "Everything can't always be your way, Butler," she said and started toward the door.

"Where are you going?"

"I'm getting out of Dodge," Ciara said. "Your campaign manager is coming this way and for some reason, I have a sneaky feeling he's not all that eager to meet me." She'd seen him glowering at them, so she made a fast exit.

Leaving Jonathan to hope that more from their first night after the bar was on tonight's menu.

Later that evening, Ciara wished she hadn't opened her big mouth. She had to stay late at work and had no time to make dinner preparations, so she did the next best thing—she ordered in. A gourmet selection of Italian antipasto, Caesar salad, chicken carbonara and garlic bread arrived on her doorstep a short time after she'd arrived home. And it was a good thing, too, because Jonathan was due shortly.

She was laying out her wonderful feast when the doorbell rang. She glanced at her reflection in the foyer mirror. Not too shabby, she thought. She'd had just enough time for a quick shower and a light application of makeup. The multicolored silk lounge set she wore was comfortable with a hint of sexy. She opened the door with a flourish and found Jonathan leaning against her door frame holding a bottle of wine. His usual Armani suit had been replaced with trousers and a black T-shirt.

"Come on in." She opened the door for him to walk through, but instead he kissed her, swept her off the floor with one arm and shut the door with the other. Ciara had to curl her arms around his neck to keep from falling, but she needn't have worried because Jonathan had a strong hold of her.

He buried his nose in her hair, which smelled of a hint of coconut and avocado.

"Put me down," Ciara ordered. "Are you some kind of caveman?"

"No, I just missed you," Jonathan stated, lowering her to the floor.

Ciara softened and her mouth creased into a smile. He sure knew the right words to say to make her melt like butter. "Great comeback."

"I try, I try," Jonathan laughed. "Is that Italian I smell?" he asked, inhaling deeply. The strong aroma of garlic had greeted him when he'd first entered, along with Ciara's natural fragrance.

"Yes, it is. And before you ask me if I made it, the answer is no. I don't cook," Ciara said honestly. No sense in giving him false illusions that she was a happy homemaker.

"I remember." Jonathan smiled. "Here, I brought this for dinner." He handed her a bottle of white wine.

"Thank you. Now make yourself comfortable," Ciara ordered, "while I get the rest of the food."

"No rush," Jonathan said, taking a look around. It was a small two-bedroom, one-bath apartment with a large living area and an eat-in kitchen. Although casually decorated with mixed pieces of furniture, it housed all the essentials—flat-panel television, stereo and the like. Jonathan walked over to the mantel and perused her family photos while she set the table.

"You live here with your sister, right?" Jonathan called out to Ciara.

"Yes, it's much cheaper that way," she responded. "A reporter's salary isn't much to speak of." Everyone always thought television journalism was all glitz and glamour. Little did they know that it was hard work with very little rewards. Ciara returned carrying plates, utensils and a wine opener.

"Is this your mother and father?" Jonathan asked, fingering a photograph of a family of four on the mantel.

"Hmmm." Ciara glanced in his direction. "No, afraid

not. That's my father, stepmother, Pilar, and my half sister Rachel."

An O formed on Jonathan's lips. "I'm sorry, I didn't realize…" he began.

"Don't apologize. Anyone would draw the same conclusion," Ciara replied.

"You and your sister could be twins," Jonathan said, noting the similar features in the photograph: big bright eyes and dimples.

"Yes."

"And will I have the pleasure of meeting her this evening?" Jonathan wondered aloud.

"Why do you ask?" Ciara said coyly. "Do you want me all to yourself?"

"That's right," Jonathan said, swiftly pulling her into his arms. "I want you all to myself tonight without any interruptions." He bent down and nuzzled her neck with the tip of his nose.

"Mmmm…" Ciara moaned. "You have nothing to worry about. Rachel is staying over at a friend's tonight."

Ciara savored his embrace, from his big strong arms to his massive chest. Jonathan Butler was all man and she craved him. Throughout the day, her mind had wandered to their passionate night of lovemaking. Jonathan knew exactly what buttons to push to make her reel. She remembered calling out his name half a dozen times during their night together.

Jonathan smiled. "Excellent. So what do you say…" he whispered, brushing his lips across hers, "we take this to the bedroom?"

"What about dinner?" Ciara asked, nodding in the direction of the dining room.

"Later," Jonathan replied and gathered her in his arms. "I hunger for something else entirely."

Ciara saw the naked hunger and passion lying in Jonathan's eyes and responded by kissing him full on the lips.

"Which one?" Jonathan asked, stopping in the hallway.

Ciara nodded to the right and Jonathan kicked open her bedroom door with his foot and carried her inside. Once he lowered her to the floor, they threw off the pillows and comforter lining her bed before hastily undressing and climbing in between Ciara's blue silk sheets.

She was surprised when his eyes locked with hers and he lifted one foot to his mouth and sucked on her toes while massaging her calves.

"Oh, that feels marvelous," Ciara squealed with delight. She had never had a guy suck her toes before. It was highly erotic. When he was finished, he lifted the other leg and repeated the technique, and she purred and stretched languidly.

She was a willing captive under his skilled mouth, and when his tongue circled her nipple before taking the entire mound into his mouth, Ciara moaned, "Oh, Jonathan…" He took her response as a cue to continue his ministrations. He used his hand to massage her other full breast. His skilled fingertips brought the nipple to a rocky pebble within seconds.

His exploration of her body continued from her breasts and lower to the silken skin between her thighs.

When he heard her soft cries, his fingers explored her wetness. Extracting his finger, he sucked deeply of her juices.

"You taste so good," he said, groaning with pleasure. Lowering his head, his mouth began where his fingers left off. He doggedly sucked her, making her slick with moisture. The intimate stroking of his tongue caused her to tremble uncontrollably as wave after wave of pleasure washed over her.

Using his tongue, he opened her up like a lotus flower and teased the tiny nub until she whimpered and called out his name.

Ciara returned the favor by teasing his nipples with her tongue and massaging his buttocks with her hand. Then she surrounded him with her palm and stroked the length of him all the way up to his throbbing tip. She reveled when his eyes rolled back and he moaned aloud. Wanting to please him, she took his engorged shaft in her mouth, licking and teasing him until he pushed her head away.

She didn't stop though. Instead she reached into her nightstand drawer and pulled out a packet. She removed the latex protection and smoothed the condom over his heated flesh.

Jonathan couldn't take it anymore; he wanted to be inside her wet heat. He switched positions until Ciara was lying underneath him, and he swiftly entered her. Her muscles fastened around him like a vise and Jonathan heard himself groan.

"More, Jonathan," Ciara gasped. "Deeper…"

Jonathan grasped her hips and gave her everything she was asking for with fierce pulsing thrusts.

"Yes, oh…yes." It was exquisite torture feeling Jonathan planted deep inside of her and Ciara rose to meet his every thrust.

Jonathan's own need matched hers and he fought for control but lost the battle. When she came her body contracted around him and he came immediately.

The world became a blur as sheer pleasure coursed through their entire bodies. Jonathan wanted to hold her close and savor the moment, but once their breathing steadied, Ciara threw on her robe and went to the dining room to get them some food. She returned carrying two plates loaded with chicken and pasta.

After they had filled their bellies, their conversation surprisingly turned to politics. "Did you ever think about not getting involved in politics?" Ciara asked, studying him freely.

"You mean not become a politician?" Jonathan's eyebrows furrowed. "That's blasphemy to a Butler."

"C'mon, Jonathan," Ciara said, wiping sweat from his brow with the back of her hand. "Haven't you ever wanted to do something else? Be something else? Aren't you tired of living in the public eye?"

"Are you asking this as my lover or as a reporter?" Jonathan queried, his eyes darkening dangerously.

"As your lover," Ciara answered honestly. She was curious as to how Jonathan handled life under such constant scrutiny.

"Then the answer would be yes, I've wondered what it would be like to not be a politician, to be free to live my life as I choose."

"So why haven't you?" Ciara asked.

"Because politics is all I know," Jonathan replied truthfully. "I've been groomed to be a politician all my life."

"You're so intelligent, Jonathan. You could do anything. Be anything."

"That may be true, but I happen to love what I do." Jonathan grinned widely.

"A little cocky, aren't we?" Ciara said. "You haven't even won the election yet."

"But I will," Jonathan said confidently, rising on his elbow. "Just as long as I raise some campaign funds."

"Are you going to have some fund-raisers?"

"Yes, my campaign manager is working up a plan and we're going to meet tomorrow to discuss it."

"Well, from a voter's standpoint," Ciara began, "I think you need to show you're a man of the people. Do something fun like a softball or baseball game."

"You mean all-American."

"Yes," Ciara continued. "Gather some of your friends, associates, and, heck, even some of the aldermen down at City Hall and show the people that you are not afraid of getting down and dirty. That you're one of them and not some privileged rich kid born with a silver spoon in his mouth who just had the congressional seat thrown in his lap."

"Thanks a lot," Jonathan said.

"From someone who has never had anything, I'm telling you how the common man might view you."

"How you see me?" Jonathan wondered aloud.

"No," Ciara replied, caressing his cheek. "I think you have what it takes, you just have to convince everyone else." Those were the last words Jonathan remembered before he fell asleep.

When she awoke the next morning, Ciara found Jonathan sprawled out over her queen-size bed, with one hand draped possessively over her middle, preventing her from moving. Glancing at the alarm clock, she noted it read 9:00 a.m.

"Jonathan…" Ciara nudged his middle, but he wasn't budging. "Jonathan, wake up," she ordered, shaking his arm. He finally responded by rolling over onto his side and rubbing the sleep from his eyes with the back of his hand.

"Good morning, sunshine," Jonathan said, fingering Ciara's honey-blond tresses. Even in the morning light, she looked as stunning as the first time he'd seen her.

"Do you realize how late it is?" Ciara quipped, throwing back the covers. Naked, she grabbed her silk robe off the bedpost and covered herself.

"No, it's Saturday. And my meeting with Zach isn't until later," Jonathan replied, propping up several pillows and falling back against them.

"I do. I have a lot of errands to run today," Ciara replied, opening the French doors to her closet and reaching inside to pull out a velour jumpsuit. She was uncomfortable that he'd spent the night over.

"Well…" Jonathan replied, throwing back the covers, "that can wait. I say we enjoy the rest of the morning while we can." He grabbed her by the arm, opened the door and swept her into the hallway toward the bathroom. Ciara resisted, wrestling her arm away from Jonathan.

"Don't be a spoilsport. Imagine how much fun we're going to have," he suggested huskily while tickling her middle. ·

"No, Jonathan, I can't." Ciara was squealing so much neither of them heard the key in the lock or the footsteps on the hardwood floor.

"Well, well, well, what do we have here?" Rachel asked, leaning against the door frame and admiring Jonathan's naked form.

"Rachel!" Ciara said, quickly moving to stand in front of Jonathan. "What are you doing here? I thought you were staying overnight at Diane's."

"Didn't know I needed an appointment to come back to my own home," Rachel said, smiling at her sister's embarrassment. Ciara's cheeks were stained red.

"Nice to meet you," Jonathan said, leaning over Ciara's shoulder and offering his hand, which Rachel accepted.

"So you're the man that's been keeping my big sis out at all hours."

Jonathan grinned. "That would be me."

"And if you'll excuse us," Ciara interrupted their exchange and gave Rachel a nod, but instead of moving Rachel stood still, enjoying their discomfort. Ciara gave her sister the evil eye.

"All right, all right. But next time, you guys ought to be more careful. You wouldn't want to get caught with your pants down," Rachel replied. "No, make that *off*."

"Rachel!" Ciara cautioned. Smiling, Rachel hurried off to her bedroom.

Once Jonathan was safely back in her bedroom, Ciara apologized. "Sorry about that."

"Don't apologize. It's not your fault. She was right. You guys share an apartment, so we'll have to be a lot more mindful or stay at my place."

"So, you think *this* is going to become a habit?" Ciara asked.

"Hmmm." Jonathan rubbed his chin. "Two nights together in a week. I would say yes."

Ciara threw a pillow at him. "You're so smug."

Jonathan roughly pulled her toward him, causing Ciara to fall on the bed. "And you love it," he replied, pinning her down on the bed and hungrily covering her mouth with his.

It was nearly an hour later before Jonathan left her apartment, completely satiated from the night's activities. He'd always adored sex, but with Ciara he felt like a sex maniac. He had to have her morning, noon and night. Her appetite was equally insatiable. Smiling, he walked to his car with a pep in his step, oblivious to the world around him. He never saw the photographer behind the maple tree snapping a picture of him leaving Ciara's.

Later, after Jonathan had left, Ciara was beginning her Saturday workout when Diamond buzzed her on her cell.

Ciara was in no mood for her mother's theatrics today. Instead of answering her call, Ciara hit the gym for a brisk session with her personal trainer on weights and thirty minutes of cardio.

She was deep in her Saturday ritual of grocery shopping, dropping off her dry cleaning and filling up her car, when Diamond rang again.

Ciara sighed wearily. There was no escaping the woman, but this time Ciara was prepared. She had no money to loan Diamond to bail her out of one of her many escapades.

"Hello, Diamond," she said, flipping open her Nokia.

"Baby girl." Ciara heard the relief in Diamond's voice. "Boy, am I happy to hear your voice."

"What can I do for you today?" Ciara inquired, pumping gas into her Camry.

"Well, you see…" Diamond said, stalling.

"Just spit it out, Diamond," Ciara said, fast becoming annoyed with her mother's games.

"Vince kicked me out," Diamond blurted.

"He did what?"

"Told me I was too expensive and too much of a liability for him to keep me around. Can you believe that? After all I've done for that man."

Ciara quietly chuckled to herself. She doubted Diamond was slaving in the kitchen preparing his food, keeping the house clean or ironing his shirts. The only thing Diamond knew how to do was spend money.

"I mean, do you know the lengths I went through to keep a roof over my head, dealing with his potbelly and receding hairline. Yet, I did it because I thought he cared for me. And now this…" Her voice trailed off and Ciara could hear her sniffing in the background.

"And what pray tell do you want me to do?" Ciara asked.

"Ci-Ci," her mother said, using her childhood nickname. "I need a place to stay."

"No—" Ciara started, but Diamond interrupted her.

"You know I wouldn't ask you, but I don't have any place to go. Do you really want to see your mama out on the street?" Diamond sniffed. "Just give me some time to get on my feet and I promise I'll be out of your hair in no time."

Famous last words, thought Ciara. Why did Diamond always impose on her? Was this her cross to bear being her only child? Ciara shook her head in disgust.

"Diamond, you know I live with Rachel. Can't you stay with one of your girlfriends?"

"I would but they all have children and boyfriends. I can't impose on them." But she could impose on Ciara? When Ciara didn't speak, Diamond did what she did best. She whined. "Please, baby girl. Just help me out of this pinch."

"All right." Ciara gave in to the inevitable. "Listen, you can stay for a couple of weeks, but this is no long-term arrangement. You'll have to sleep on the sofa."

"I knew you wouldn't let me down, Ci-Ci. I'll meet you at your place in an hour."

The next thing Ciara heard was a dial tone. Thanks for the notice, thought Ciara, closing her phone. Now what was she going to do? Rachel hated Diamond and Ciara highly doubted she would appreciate sharing their small apartment with her. What had she agreed to? And more importantly, how was she going to get out of it?

* * *

Jonathan returned to his penthouse for a quick shower and to change clothes before meeting his paternal grandmother for lunch at her home in Society Hill. As a child, he'd always loved coming to the red-bricked neighborhood and cobblestone alleys that were rich in history and culture.

When he arrived, she was already in the sitting room with tea and petite cucumber and ham-and-cheese sandwiches waiting on the settee.

"Nana." Jonathan came forward and leaned down to lightly squeeze her delicate shoulders. Only five feet tall and with such a small frame, he nearly dwarfed her.

Ava Butler had weathered many a storm, first losing her daughter in childbirth and then the death of his grandfather five years ago. She was a strong woman and someone whom Jonathan respected a great deal.

"How's my handsome grandson?" his grandmother asked, beaming with pride. Her grandson was a fine-looking specimen, in tailored gray slacks, a polo shirt and Italian loafers. She was sure all the ladies probably fell all over his classic good looks and proud jawline.

"Doing fine, Nana." Jonathan took a seat in the high-backed chair across from her. His grandmother was still a beauty. At seventy-five, her caramel skin was still smooth and she remained active by walking five miles a day and eating right.

"So," his grandmother began, "I hear there's a new woman in your life." Casually, she leaned over and poured each of them a cup of tea. "Cream and sugar?"

"Yes, ma'am." Jonathan reached over and added

several tea sandwiches on a plate. He smiled at his grandmother's directness. She always got right to the point.

"To the cream and sugar? Or to the new woman?" she asked.

"Yes, to both," Jonathan replied.

A huge smile broadened her face. "That's good to hear, Johnny boy. I was beginning to feel like I'd never live to see you get married and start procreating."

"Whoa!" Jonathan held up his hand. "Who said anything about marriage and children?" He enjoyed Ciara's company and they were great in bed together, but his grandmother was ready to marry them off!

"I do," she responded evenly. "I don't think I've ever seen that glint in your eye before." Her grandson sparkled. There was an excitement that she had never seen before. Even when he'd graduated from Harvard University and Penn Law or won the race for alderman, she'd never seen that look.

"You're such a romantic, Nana," Jonathan commented, munching on a crustless ham-and-cheese sandwich. "You know my focus is my career." Even though he, too, had thought of marriage, but of course he'd never admit it.

"Johnny, you can't put all your eggs in one basket," his grandmother responded, lightly sipping on her tea.

He was surprised to hear her speak like this. Didn't she have any faith in him? "You don't think I can win?"

"Of course I do. You can do anything you put your mind to," his grandmother returned. "All I'm saying is all that success is meaningless if you don't have anyone to share it with."

"In case they haven't told you, Grandma, this woman you're rooting for-happens to be a reporter." Jonathan picked up another tea sandwich.

"And?"

"My parents, Zach, hell, even Reid are dead set against me dating a member of the press."

"I don't see you as a follower, Jonathan. You're a natural-born leader. Forget about the naysayers and follow your heart. It won't lead you in the wrong direction. What's her name?"

"Ciara Miller."

"Unusual name."

"For an unusual woman."

"She sounds promising."

"I doubt my mother would agree with you, Nana," Jonathan said, bringing his lips to the delicate, fine teacup.

"Dominique, oh please," his grandmother shushed him. "Your mother is one to talk. Did she ever tell you that I never approved of her? I did my best to try and break up her and your father."

"No!" Jonathan was shocked, but not surprised that his grandmother would resort to any lengths to protect her only son.

"But why, Nana? Mom came from a well-bred family."

"Even so, I felt that no woman was good enough for my Charles and the same case applies here. Your mother is not going to approve of any woman you're dating because you're her baby."

Jonathan had never looked at it that way before. Perhaps his mother was having a hard time letting go.

"My advice for you, my dear, is to be strong in the courage of your convictions like your father and let no one including your mother decide what or who is right for you."

Jonathan leaned over and gave his grandmother a gentle squeeze. "That's good advice and I'm going to put it to good use."

Chapter 6

When Ciara arrived home, she found Rachel under a pile of books. "Studying for an exam?" she asked, carrying her purchases into the kitchen and emptying several bags of groceries. She didn't relish the thought of telling Rachel that Diamond was moving in, however temporary it might be.

"Yes, girl. I have a psychology test on Monday."

"Oh," Ciara sighed. How was she going to tell her? Rachel and Diamond were like oil and water. They just didn't mix. It had all started when Rachel had begged their father to let her stay over with Diamond and Ciara one weekend when Rachel was twelve. Always curious about what Ciara did when she left their house, Rachel had wanted to see how the other half lived. After that visit, the rest, as they say, was history. Rachel had hated every minute of eating nothing but McDonalds and being stuck in the house watching television because Diamond was fawning over some man.

Her sister was the antithesis of Diamond. She was twenty-one and could have easily lived in the dorms and let their father subsidize her studies, but instead she wanted to live on her own. Do for herself. She even waitressed during her spare time. Ciara was immensely proud of her little sister.

"Rach…" Ciara began.

Rachel looked up from the psychology book she was reading.

"What's up?"

"Well, you see…" Knock. Knock.

Oh no, thought Ciara. Please don't let that be Diamond. She hadn't had a chance to prepare Rachel yet. Rachel stood up and headed for the door.

"Wait!" Ciara stopped her. "There's something I have to tell you."

"Can it wait?" Rachel asked. "Let me get the door first." She quickly walked to the door and swung it open.

"Rachel!" Diamond yelled, throwing her arms around a less than enthusiastic Rachel. "How good to see you." She kissed both of her cheeks before bending down and wheeling her suitcases right past Rachel and into the living room.

"What's going on, Ci-Ci?" Rachel asked, trying to remain calm. She had no idea why Diamond was bringing her suitcases into their home.

"I can explain," Ciara started.

"You mean you didn't tell her?" Diamond shook her long weaved locks. "Ciara's letting me stay here for a while."

"What!" Rachel gave Ciara a withering look.

"Rachel, listen. Diamond's going through some hard times and she just needs a place to crash until she gets back on her feet."

"And you told her she could stay here?" Rachel asked, fuming. "Without even asking me? How could you?" She stalked over to the dining room table and started packing her books into her book bag. When she was finished she brushed past Ciara and slammed the door to her bedroom.

"What's she so mad about?" Diamond replied, plopping down on the couch and making herself at home. She picked up a *Newsweek* magazine and started flipping through it.

"Are you just going to leave those in the middle of the room?" Ciara pointed to Diamond's suitcases lying in the middle of the living room floor.

"Of course not, baby." Diamond jumped up. "Where would you like them?"

"Just put them in my room," Ciara answered. "I'm going to talk to Rachel." Spinning around, she turned and walked to her sister's door. She hesitated before knocking. Rachel was clearly not pleased and Ciara saw no way out. Diamond was her mother, after all.

Finally gathering her courage, she knocked on the door. "Rachel, can I come in?" When she received no answer, Ciara entered anyway. She found Rachel packing clothes in a suitcase.

"Rach, what are you doing?"

"I would think that would be obvious," Rachel replied sarcastically.

"You don't have to do this."

"Oh yes, I do," Rachel fired back as she snatched several T-shirts off hangers. "I want no part of Diamond's shenanigans."

Ciara tried to explain. "She'll only be here a short time. I promise."

"Don't make promises you can't keep," Rachel said, stuffing more of her belongings into the suitcase.

"Rachel, you're being unreasonable."

"Diamond isn't trustworthy. And you know this, but what I don't understand is how an intelligent woman like you can be so stupid. You know she is just using you until the next man comes along." When she was done packing a few items for several days, Rachel shut the case.

"She's my mother, Rachel. If you were in my position and Pilar came to you, you would help her."

"The only problem with that scenario, Ciara, is that Pilar would never ask me, because she would never put herself in that kind of position." Grabbing the suitcase and her book bag, she stormed past Ciara.

"Rachel!" Ciara called after her, but Rachel didn't turn around. Instead she sped past Diamond without hazarding a glance and slammed the door behind her.

"Wow, what bug crawled up—"

"Not a word, Diamond," Ciara warned from the hallway. "I'm really in no mood for you right now." And with that comment, she walked to her room and shut the door.

* * *

Across town, Dominique Butler met with Reid at his apartment.

"I am so furious with my son," Dominique said, storming past Reid. "He is endangering his whole career by dating that reporter."

Reid shut the door behind her. He watched her pace the floor, wearing a hole in his carpet.

"I couldn't agree with you more, Dom," Reid replied. "Your son is being very careless with his future." He opened his refrigerator and grabbed a mineral water. He screwed the top off and handed it to Dominique.

"A glass and some ice, please." Dominique handed the bottle back to Reid.

He wasn't surprised that Mrs. Priss would never lift a finger to pour her own glass. He'd known the Butlers for a long time and Dominique Butler was used to running the show. Some said that if Charles Butler had not run for public office then Dominique would never have stepped down from the bench, where she'd served for five years as a juvenile court judge. Dominique felt she had to devote her energies to getting her husband elected.

"He may be careless, but I'm not taking any chances. I am not going to let some floozy come in and wreck my son's career before it's even started."

"And what would you like me to do?" Reid asked, plopping down in his recliner.

"Personally—" Dominique sipped on her water "—I think you should run a check on her, Reid. Find out who she is. Make sure she's who she says she is."

"So, if there's any secrets in her closet, you would like Jonathan to know about them?" Reid asked devilishly. He smiled inwardly. It would give him no greater pleasure than to see Jonathan get what he had coming to him, and his own mother might help him hang the noose around the golden boy's neck.

"Ah, now you get my drift," Dominique chuckled.

"I most certainly do, Dominique," Reid replied, rubbing his chin thoughtfully. He would show that snot-nosed kid that Reid was not to be messed with. "Don't worry about a thing—I'll take care of everything."

Jonathan met Zach at his campaign headquarters to discuss options for raising money for the campaign. Zach came with several ideas, including dinner with the candidate and coffee, but nothing interested Jonathan as much as Ciara's softball-game idea. Her idea was brilliant and Zach agreed to set it up.

Afterward, Jonathan telephoned Ciara. "Hey, beautiful," he said from the other end.

"Hey…"

"Is something wrong?" Jonathan queried. Ciara didn't sound like herself.

"No, everything's fine," Ciara lied through her teeth. No need to burden Jonathan with her family troubles.

"Doesn't sound like it."

"I just have some personal issues I need to deal with," Ciara replied, avoiding the issue. She did not want to discuss Diamond in any way, shape or form. The less Jonathan knew about her mother's checkered past the better.

"You know, you could confide in me," Jonathan stated. "Whatever is going on, I'll listen. I won't judge. Maybe I could even offer you some advice."

"I'm afraid there's nothing that can be done," Ciara replied honestly. "The situation is what it is." Rachel was upset with her because she'd allowed Diamond to move in, and there was nothing that could be done.

"Well, how about I take you out and cheer you up?" Jonathan suggested.

"You mean a night out on the town?" Ciara inquired.

"Yes. I received some free preseason tickets for the Philadelphia Eagles game. We can grab a bite there and then maybe grab a beer afterward. How does that sound?"

"Sounds great," Ciara replied. It had only been a few hours and already Ciara was ready for some breathing room.

"I'll pick you up at six."

Excited, Ciara slammed down the receiver and rushed into the hall closet where she stored some of her street clothes because her own closet was bursting at the seams.

"So, where are you off to?" Diamond asked. She'd been eavesdropping on their conversation and heard Ciara was leaving, on her first night no less!

"I'm going out with a friend," Ciara replied, pulling out her favorite pair of jeans. She did not want Diamond involved in her personal business.

"Sounds like he's more than a friend," Diamond replied knowingly from the couch as she popped some microwave popcorn in her mouth.

"Mind your own business," Ciara warned, heading to her room and closing the door.

She immediately stripped to prepare for a nice, hot shower. Ciara emerged feeling silky smooth and ready for her date with Jonathan. He aroused a passion in her that had long lay dormant. Sure, she'd been with other men and had had good sex, but none that made her feel so complete, so satisfied. And he did it not just with his body. He exercised her mind as well. He was constantly discussing his ideas for the future of the state, history, philosophy and more.

She shimmied into her fitted stretch jeans and pulled a gold tank top over her head. She admired the view of her backside from her pedestal mirror. The skinny jeans did wonders for her figure. Afterward, she applied a thin layer of foundation, followed by bold eye shadow and some eye-defining mascara. Ciara finished by applying broad streaks of mauve blush across her cheeks.

She casually pinned her hair with chopsticks. Inspecting herself in the mirror, Ciara felt like a winner, but something was missing. Opening her jewelry chest, she found what she was looking for in silver dangling earrings and a bangle bracelet. Applying a spritz of perfume behind her ears and wrists, her look was complete.

When she was ready, she swung open the door to her bedroom and found Diamond had changed out of her skintight jeans into a lounge set that was way too small for her, and revealed her ample bosom and the rather large tattoo over her left breast.

"Diamond, cover yourself for Christ's sake," Ciara stated.

"What's wrong with what I have on?" Diamond asked, looking down. "I'm home, for goodness' sake."

"This—" Ciara pointed around the living room "—is not your home. This is my home. Rachel's home."

"Well, I don't see Miss Rachel anywhere around," Diamond responded, glancing around with her hands folded across her chest. "Do you?"

"That's because you ran her away," Ciara said defiantly. "It's all your fault." Ciara grabbed her blue denim jacket out of the coat closet and slipped it on.

"Don't blame me," Diamond responded. "I'm the one with no place to go. Miss High and Mighty could have stayed. There was room for all of us."

"Cry me a river," Ciara replied sarcastically, walking over to the coffee table and grabbing her purse. There was no way Jonathan could pick her up. Diamond would embarrass her as she had done so many times before when she'd been a teenager. No, she would meet Jonathan at the stadium.

Flipping open her cell phone, Ciara dialed Jonathan's number. He answered on the second ring.

"Jonathan, it's Ciara."

"I'm on my way."

"Don't bother," Ciara replied. "I'll meet you there."

"Why? I'm already halfway to your place."

"I'd just prefer to meet you there," Ciara replied.

Jonathan scratched his head. He didn't understand why Ciara did not want him to come to her apartment. What was going on? Was she hiding something? Or someone? "If you say so."

"Yes, I do. I'll meet you in fifteen," she said, and

closed the cell phone. Ciara turned around and faced her mother. "All right, Diamond, try not to burn down the apartment while I'm gone."

"I'm not three, you know," Diamond snapped back. "And anyway, I don't cook."

Ciara reached inside her purse for her wallet and pulled out a twenty. "Here, order yourself a pizza. I gotta go." Ciara slung her purse over her shoulder and strutted for the door. "Don't wait up."

"Thanks for nothing," Diamond replied underneath her breath. Why did her daughter have to treat her with such disdain? Diamond would never understand it.

Once in her Toyota Camry, Ciara roared down the street while a black sedan followed at a discreet distance behind her.

Jonathan met Ciara outside Lincoln Financial Field. Dressed in blue jeans and a royal-blue polo shirt with one button casually opened at the top, Jonathan looked sexy, confident and every bit as delicious as the first time Ciara had seen him, causing her heart to speed up and her stomach to do somersaults.

Although he was as attractive as ever, Ciara couldn't shake the strange sensation that she'd been followed. The entire drive over, she'd felt as if someone was behind her. Was she imagining crazy scenarios? Surely, she had to be—what would anyone want with her? Instead, she would focus her energies on the handsome, extremely attractive man in front of her.

Jonathan was equally enamored with sultry Ciara. She was sassy and pretty close to irresistible. Jonathan felt his erection stir in his pants as she drew near. Ciara had a way of making him feel like a teenage boy, unable to control his desires.

"You look amazing," Jonathan said as he kissed her. "You ready?" he asked, offering her his arm.

"Absolutely," Ciara said, taking his proffered arm and walking to the entrance of the stadium.

Before they took their seats, Jonathan suggested they grab a drink at the concession stand. "A beer would be great!" Ciara replied.

"Two draft beers, please." Jonathan slipped the vendor a twenty. The vendor returned to the counter with two plastic cups filled high with Miller Lite. He handed Ciara a cup.

"Thanks." Ciara took a large gulp and followed Jonathan to the seats.

The tickets Jonathan had gotten were excellent. They were in the center of the stadium on the lower level near the green.

After the second quarter, the Eagles were down by two against the Green Bay Packers so Ciara and Jonathan climbed the stairs to the concourse in search of food. "So, what are you in the mood to eat?" Jonathan asked.

"A Philly cheesesteak," Ciara said excitedly.

"A cheesesteak," Jonathan said disdainfully. "Why don't we go to the Liberty Bell Tap Room or Liberty Grill?"

"That's no way to enjoy a football game," Ciara snorted. "A true fan eats food from the concession stands, not from a restaurant. You've got to loosen up, Butler."

"And you're just the person to help me do that," Jonathan replied once they'd reached the concourse. The line was long, but they eventually managed to get two Philly cheesesteaks with all the fixings: onions, peppers and mushrooms.

The Green Bay Packers were no match for the Eagles when Donovan McNabb rushed for a pair of scores and threw a pair of touchdown passes to Greg Lewis, leading the Eagles to a thirty-one to nine win over the Packers.

"That was a great game!" Ciara said as they rose from their seats. "Did you see McNabb? He was unstoppable."

"He sure was," Jonathan concurred. "No matter who they put to defend him, they couldn't stop him."

They followed the stadium crowd outside into the courtyard. "Where are you parked?" Jonathan asked, looking around.

"In the garage."

"Let's get a drink." Jonathan nodded to some of the bars on South Street. "You can get your car later."

"All right, one drink," Ciara replied, holding up her index finger. "Because I do have to drive home."

"Let's go." Jonathan put a guiding hand along the small of her back as they walked to a local bar down the street.

When they arrived, the bouncer recognized Jonathan, shook his hand, opened the rope and allowed them to pass.

"Come here often?" Ciara asked. She wondered if he brought other women to this bar to show his VIP status.

"No, not usually," Jonathan commented, "but I have been here before or after a game."

The bar was packed with other sports aficionados and couples on the dance floor jiving to R & B and hip-hop. The DJ was on fire, playing several old-school jams.

"What would you like?" Jonathan asked once they reached the bar.

"A sex on the beach, please."

While the bartender prepared her fruity concoction, Ciara bopped to the music the DJ was spinning. Jonathan handed Ciara her sex on the beach, while he drank a Corona.

"Cheers." He clicked his bottle against her glass.

"Cheers."

"Are you having fun?" Jonathan asked. "I hope I took your mind off your troubles?"

"Yes, you did, and yes, I am enjoying myself."

So was he. He was enjoying the soft curves of her body as it swayed to the music. The jeans she wore clung gloriously to her well-defined buttocks. Jonathan's brain immediately went into overdrive thinking about her luscious body underneath his, hearing her soft moans as he thrust deep inside her warm haven.

"Let's find a table," Ciara suggested, breaking his daydream and grabbing his left hand to pull him through the crowd. They found one spare seat at the far end of the bar by the dance floor. Being the gentleman, Jonathan stood while Ciara sat. "Looks like someone else's misfortune is my gain," she said, taking a seat in the high-backed chair.

Jonathan came around and stood next to her. "So did you get all your errands completed?"

"Just barely," Ciara replied. "That's before…" Then she stopped herself. What was she thinking? She'd almost spilled the beans about Diamond. It was just that Jonathan made her feel as if she could tell him anything. Almost anything.

"Before what?" Jonathan queried. "What aren't you telling me?" He had a feeling Ciara was keeping something from him. Something potentially damaging? he wondered.

"Nothing," she replied, a little too quickly for Jonathan's liking. Why did she feel the need to keep secrets? Couldn't she trust him? Or maybe some man had ruined her faith in the opposite sex? "Did Zach like my idea about a softball game?" Ciara asked, changing the subject.

Jonathan went along for now, but somehow he had to convince Ciara that she could confide in him, that he was worth the risk. "Yes, he loved the idea," Jonathan replied in her ear because the music was so loud.

"We're going to have a game in a few weeks, once I convince all the aldermen physically fit enough to play."

"That's great." Ciara smiled. It was nice to see that her ideas were valued. She wished her boss shared Jonathan's enthusiasm. "Maybe I can do a sound bite for the news."

"You would do that for me?" Jonathan asked.

"Of course." Ciara smiled, peering into Jonathan's dark brown eyes.

"I really appreciate your help and advice," Jonathan said, stroking her cheek. "It means a lot to me." In such a short time, Ciara Miller had become more important than a great roll in the hay. He'd come to care for the sassy reporter with the big opinions and even bigger mouth.

"Glad I could help," Ciara said, turning away. She wasn't sure she liked what she saw in his eyes. Was Jonathan developing feelings for her? And if so, how did she feel about that?

Before she could think further on the topic, Jonathan interrupted her thoughts. "Are you finished with that?" he asked, setting his empty bottle on the table in front of her. "Because I want to dance." He wanted to feel Ciara in his arms.

"Yes, I am." Ciara gulped the last of her drink and accepted Jonathan's hand as he pulled her to her feet. They found a small space on the crowded dance floor and started grooving to the beats. Jonathan was an excellent dancer. Ciara appreciated the way he moved his hips and how easily he gelled with her vibe.

When the tempo changed to a slow Maxwell ballad, "Fortunate," Jonathan swept her in his arms and pressed her firmly against him. Without the benefit of a bra as protection, Ciara felt her nipples immediately harden through her tank top as they came in close contact with his hard, masculine chest. When Jonathan bent his head down and rested it lightly on her shoulder, Ciara's breathing became shallow. He wasn't even doing anything to her and she was already turned on. She was closing her eyes and relishing the moment when she saw a flash of light from the other side of the room.

Peering through the crowd, Ciara caught sight of a photographer, hiding behind a crowd of people. Was that the flash she'd seen a moment ago? Had he been watching them the entire time? Was that why she'd felt as if she was being followed all the way over to Lincoln Financial Field?

"Jonathan." She poked him in the middle. "We have to get out of here quick," she whispered in his ear.

"Why?" He didn't want to leave. It had been ages since he'd been out dancing and he was enjoying himself.

"Because we're being watched," Ciara replied. Grabbing his face in her hands, she turned it in the direction of the cameraman trying to look inconspicuous in the midst of the crowd. "That guy is snapping pictures of us."

"Are you serious?" Jonathan couldn't believe it.

"Very," Ciara stated.

"Let's go." Jonathan grabbed Ciara by one arm and pushed his way through the crowd. She turned around and could see the photographer weaving his way through the crowd trying to catch them. Was that the WTCF logo? Had Shannon found out about her involvement with Jonathan? When they reached the bar, he yelled over to the attendant. "Where's your back exit?"

"Through the kitchen." He pointed to the back of the room.

"C'mon, Ciara."

Ciara could barely move her feet because she was so livid! How dare that woman invade her personal life? Who did she think she was?

Quickly, they ran through the room and into the kitchen. The kitchen staff didn't appear surprised to see their clientele running through. None of them made any effort to stop Jonathan and Ciara on their way out.

Once they were outside, Jonathan pulled her toward his Lexus. "Come with me," he ordered.

"But what about my car?" Ciara asked.

"We'll pick it up tomorrow," Jonathan said over his shoulder and clicked open the passenger door with his remote. He couldn't believe the press was already dogging him. Why would they care whom he socialized with? His father's voice echoed in his head. *You can never be too careful. Especially dating a member of the press.* Did Ciara have anything to do with this?

Ciara did as Jonathan requested and got inside, but she did not appreciate being told what to do. She was quite capable of getting home on her own. Matter of fact, she could use the time alone to figure out how she was going to handle ratings-crazed Shannon.

Jonathan rounded the car and jumped in the driver's seat. Within seconds, they were driving away from the club and the drama. Jonathan was so focused on the road while constantly looking in his rearview mirror to see if they were being followed, he didn't say a word to Ciara.

When they were a safe distance away, he finally spoke. "Are you all right?" he asked, glancing in Ciara's direction.

"Yes," she replied curtly with her arms folded across her chest.

"I'm sorry, Ciara. All I could think about was getting out of there with as minimum exposure as possible."

"Don't you think I understand that? I'm the one who noticed him. Matter of fact, I think he may have followed me."

Jonathan turned and sharply stared at her. "Why didn't you mention this before?"

"Because I thought I was imagining things."

"Clearly you weren't," Jonathan replied. "Ciara—" he turned to face her at the red light "—you and I both know that I'm a public figure now and my life is fair game. We have to be cautious. We can't get caught in situations like that."

"Situations like what? Dancing?" Ciara asked as her voice rose slightly. "That's hardly a crime."

Jonathan remained calm despite her tone and pulled off when the light turned green. "No, it isn't, but my opponent could make it appear like I'm a rich party boy with no morals or values. I have to be very careful of the image I present."

"I'm well aware of that, Jonathan. I am in the media." Ciara turned and faced the window. "Why don't you just take me back to my car? I'm sure the photographer is long gone."

"Or waiting for you back at your car," Jonathan replied. "Come home with me and I'll see that your car makes it here to my place."

"And how are you going to do that?"

Jonathan laughed. "I have my ways. I have my ways."

"All right," Ciara conceded. "I'll come home with you."

"Good, because I want you in my bed."

Ciara's brow rose. "Is that right?"

"Yes," Jonathan answered, smiling at her. "You're becoming addictive."

Ciara felt the same. That was why once they were in the foyer of his apartment, they lost all control and nearly fell over, kissing and touching each other. When Jonathan thrust his tongue inside her mouth and mimicked the movements he intended to make with his body, Ciara responded boldly and brazenly by returning his kiss and sucking on his tongue.

A loud groan echoed in the distance and Jonathan couldn't tell if it was his or hers because the tips of her breasts were pressing against his chest giving him a major hard-on.

They undressed in seconds, carelessly throwing their clothes to the floor as they made it to his leather couch. When Ciara stood in front of him wearing nothing but a silk thong, Jonathan nearly lost it. She kindled a spark in him that was raw and blatantly sexual.

Reaching out he grabbed a handful of her thick hair and lavishly ran his fingers through it. She was so volatile and fiery, she had him in flames after a few, hot wet kisses. He could already feel his erection thick and heavy between his legs. He needed to be inside her tight walls with a desperation he'd never known before.

Ciara was awash with desire as well. She wanted to get as close to him as humanly possible. She stroked his lips gently with hers, teasing the soft fullness of his lips, until he parted, allowing her entry. All the while, she caressed his wonderfully wide, deep shoulders, muscular thighs and well-shaped butt. Bending down, she flicked her wet tongue across one of his nipples and teased it until it puckered.

Jonathan let out a long torturous groan. Ciara was baiting him bit by bit, making him want her even more. With his rising desire, he didn't know how much longer he could continue playing by her rules. He quickly reached for his pants and pulled some foil packets out of his wallet. He sheathed himself while Ciara shimmied the tiny thong down her shapely legs and, when he could stand it no longer, he pulled her toward him and they fell onto the couch.

He plunged deep inside her, causing her to clench her thighs tighter. And when Jonathan lowered his head, took one nipple in his mouth and lightly grazed the hardened pebble with his teeth, Ciara arched off the couch, pulling him all the way inside her body. Sensations soon rocked through Ciara's entire body and Jonathan wasn't far behind. He felt the same amazing waves of pleasure as his entire body shuddered and the world exploded around them.

He inhaled, trying to catch his breath. Ciara was already gasping for air as they slowly separated from each other. She couldn't resist smiling broadly. "Wow! That was incredible."

"Yeah, it was pretty amazing, wasn't it?" Jonathan said. His big hands smoothed back her hair.

"I love making love with you, Jonathan," Ciara admitted out loud, wrapping her arms around him.

"And I love making love with you, too," he responded, squeezing her in return.

Chapter 7

The next morning, Ciara awoke somewhat disoriented. Wiping the sleep from her eyes, she glanced around at her surroundings. Had she actually slept over at Jonathan's? She never did that. She was always the first one to leave. But for some reason this time had been different. Was it the fact that the sex was exciting and unpredictable? Or the four orgasms she'd had during the night? They'd had sex on the floor, on his silky leather couch by the fireplace and twice in his bed once he'd finally carried her to his bedroom. He was truly the best lover she'd ever had and she had sore muscles to prove it.

Throwing off the comforter, Ciara stepped down from the platform bed and looked around for something to wear. She found one of Jonathan's shirts hanging off the closet door and grabbed it. Slipping one arm into the sleeve and then the other, Ciara wrapped his shirt around her the same way he'd wrapped his arms around her the night before. She remembered how warm and welcoming his arms had felt. She'd felt so safe. Why had she never felt that way before in a man's bed?

Ciara pushed open the bathroom door, but didn't find Jonathan. She was wondering where the stallion was when the smell of brewing coffee drew her in the direction of the kitchen.

Giddy relief flooded through her when she found him standing bare-chested, wearing a pair of pajama bottoms. Jonathan was in the midst of cutting up fresh fruit, making toast and juicing some oranges when Ciara walked in.

"Good morning, beautiful," he said, leaning over the counter and kissing her full on the lips. She looked absolutely sexy in his shirt. Now this was the way he'd envisioned their first morning together!

"Good morning to you, too," she said, lowering her head, somewhat embarrassed by her wanton behavior. What must he think of her? That she was a sex addict!

"How did you sleep?" Jonathan asked, pouring fresh-squeezed orange juice into a tumbler and handing it to her.

"Wonderful," Ciara answered, taking a seat at the breakfast bar and accepting the drink.

"You sound surprised," Jonathan said, looking up from his task of arranging a fruit platter.

"To be quite honest, I am," Ciara said, tossing her blond hair back. "I don't usually stick around for the morning niceties."

So she usually ran away? Jonathan wondered to himself. That would explain why she'd freaked out when he'd slept over at her place. Perhaps things were a little too close for comfort? What was she so afraid of? "That's a shame," he replied. "You never know what you might be missing."

Jonathan laid out the fresh fruit and whole-grain toast platter in front of Ciara, and handed her a plate and fork.

"Dig in." He grabbed the coffee carafe and held it up. Ciara nodded. She was useless without her morning cup of joe.

"All of this for me?" Ciara said. "And it's healthy, too. Are you for real or did I make you up?" She couldn't believe he was being so kind to her. She'd thought chivalry was dead. "Because I'm sure Prince Charming no longer exists. That's if he ever did," she added, forking up some fresh berries and adding them to her plate along with a piece of toast.

"I'm real," Jonathan replied. "But I most certainly am not Prince Charming. Breakfast is for both you and me." Opening his glass cabinet, Jonathan took a plate out for himself. He slid over the fruit platter and added fresh honeydew melon and cantaloupe to his plate.

Ciara laughed. "Touché." She brought the coffee mug to her lips and sipped the hot liquid before placing the mug back on the counter. Several minutes passed in which neither of them spoke. Ciara didn't know what to talk about because she'd never been in a situation like this before. Usually she was gone before daybreak.

Jonathan broke the awkward silence. "Ciara, I hope you know that I thoroughly enjoyed last night."

"So did I," she said, paying close to attention to munching on her fruit rather than look up at him. She wasn't embarrassed. She just didn't know where they went from here.

"But I really need to get going," she said, rising from the counter.

"Wait." Jonathan halted her with one of his big strong hands, hands that had stimulated every inch of her body the previous evening. "When am I going to see you again?"

Ciara shrugged. "I don't know—soon, I suppose. I have a big story to work on." She lied to avoid an awkward situation. She wasn't comfortable discussing taking their relationship to the next level.

"And I'm running for office," Jonathan replied, standing up and placing his empty plate in the sink. He walked over to Ciara and grasped her hands in his. "But let's not let that prevent us from getting to know each other better."

"Yes, but…"

"No buts, last night was pretty spectacular," Jonathan said, rubbing one seductive finger over her lips.

"As spectacular as our previous engagements?" Ciara asked coyly.

"No, better." Jonathan bent down and pressed his lips firmly over hers. Ciara couldn't help but respond and when his tongue slid inside her mouth, she opened up and allowed him entry.

"Oh, don't stop," she moaned. His lips traveled from her mouth to her neck and then up to her earlobe.

"And you taste so good," Jonathan whispered, pulling her into his embrace. "What do you say about taking this to the shower?"

"Jonathan, I need to be out of here in twenty minutes."

"Baby, that's all I need," he said, lifting her from the floor and carrying her toward his bathroom.

Jonathan had just returned home from dropping off Ciara when his phone started ringing off the hook. He picked up the phone on the last ring. "Hello," he answered.

"Have you seen the morning news?" Zach asked.

"No, why?"

"Why? Because you and Ciara are the main event," Zach responded evenly.

"God, I knew this would happen." Jonathan grabbed the remote off the cocktail table and sat down on the sofa. He turned on the television and began flipping through the local channels.

"What do you mean you knew this would happen?" Zach inquired.

"Last night, a photographer followed us and took some pictures of us at a bar."

"Did she happen to mention that it was her station that followed you?" Zach responded.

"What?"

"WTCF, the station where Ciara works, ran the story this morning. Insinuated that you were a playboy who liked to party."

"And my job as an alderman?" Jonathan turned to the station.

"All a smoke screen for what you really want, the congressional seat. But is Jonathan Butler ready to take on the federal government, they ask."

"What a load of hogwash!" Jonathan was furious. He had a clean record. Why couldn't they focus on the positive things he'd done in the community, like his work for GEAR UP, a program that partnered students from low-income schools with colleges and universities to help students realize their college dreams, instead of focusing on the negative?

"I warned you…" Zach started.

"Spare me the 'I told you so.'"

"Fine. I will. You made your bed. Now we're going to have to lie in it."

"That's the friend in you," Jonathan replied. "What is your opinion as my campaign manager?"

"Damage control," Zach stated. "End the relationship with Ciara before it ruins your chances."

"Not an option. What's next?"

"C'mon, Jonathan. You won't even consider the possibility that she's using you to get ahead?"

"Ciara had no idea what her station was planning," Jonathan said, defending the new woman in his life.

"Are you sure about that?"

Jonathan paused. Could he be sure? Ciara hadn't told him they were being followed. And she was really ambitious. Did she have an ulterior motive?

"Yes, I'm sure," Jonathan lied. He wouldn't give his best friend the satisfaction of admitting that he could be wrong. He would just have to wait and see.

"All right, if that's the way you want it." Zach

shook his head in dismay. "As your campaign
manager, we are not going to address this frivolous
story. Addressing it would give it credence. Instead
we are going to hit the campaign trail hard with
public appearances, radio and television spots. We'll
show the public that you are not just another rich
pretty boy."

"Fine, then that's what I'll do," Jonathan said. He'd
prove to the naysayers that he had what it took to be
congressman.

Ciara knew Shannon would be eager to break the
story and sure enough, when she went home to change
and turned on the television, she and Jonathan were in
the *Around Town* gossip report. She wasn't surprised.
Instead of flying off the handle and rushing over to the
station half-cocked, Ciara needed time to cool off.
Instead, she'd wait until Monday, but first she had more
pressing things to deal with and that was dinner with
her father, Pilar and Rachel.

She was sure they were all going to gang up on her
and tell her that she was a pushover for allowing Diamond to move in, but she would stand her ground. It
wasn't the first time and most certainly wouldn't be the
last. When she'd been a teen, they'd asked her to come
live with them, but Diamond had cried and pleaded
with her not to leave her, so she'd stayed and watched
Diamond go from guy to guy, all the while moving
Ciara from pillar to post and school to school.

She was sure she'd appeared foolish to her father.
Why not come and live with them out in the suburbs

and have a normal life? Ciara doubted she even knew what that meant. All she'd known was the hood.

During college, she had learned to assimilate. Dress better, speak better courtesy of her speech classes; but she had never been much good at making friends. Especially girlfriends—they were always jealous of her good looks. And men! Well, men she knew; she'd been raised at Diamond's knee and knew how to catch a man's eye, so she'd never had a shortage of dates during her college career.

These were the thoughts running through her mind when she pulled up in the driveway of her father's Georgian colonial-style, two-story home. True to his word, Jonathan had arranged for her car to be dropped off at her apartment. As she exited the car, she braced herself for what lay ahead.

She used her key and opened the front door. The smell of roast chicken filled the air. Since Pilar had gotten the new rotisserie machine several months ago, they'd had to bear roast chicken at every family gathering.

"Hello, hello," Ciara yelled to anyone within earshot.

"Ciara." Pilar was the first to greet her in the foyer. "How are you, dear?" she asked, giving her a warm hug and kiss on the cheek.

"Fine, Pilar. And you?"

"Doing well. Though I do wonder about you," Pilar commented. "Your father and I saw the news this morning over our cup of coffee. The piece on you and Jonathan Butler was hardly flattering."

"Oh that," Ciara laughed. "That's nothing." She tried to make light of the telecast.

"Now that might work with your father," Pilar said, escorting Ciara back into the dining room where she was setting the table for four. "But that will not fly with me. When did you start dating that hunk?"

Ciara smiled at Pilar's use of the word *hunk*. She was trying to appear hip while dressed in a two-piece sweater set and tweed slacks with her dark brown hair swept into a perfectly coiffed bun. She was the perfect picture of June Cleaver.

"A couple of weeks ago," Ciara answered.

"Hmmm, he is quite the catch," Pilar stated, placing linen napkins at each setting. "Comes from a good family, great background, you would do well to snag him before the rest of the women in this town wise up."

"Thank you for the commentary, Pilar. Where are Dad and Rachel?"

"In the family room watching football."

"Think I'll join them," Ciara replied, but Pilar halted her. "You know Rachel isn't too pleased with you for letting Diamond move into the apartment."

Ciara rolled her eyes. "I'm well aware of Rachel's feelings on the subject."

"And?" Pilar queried. "You both share the apartment."

"And nothing." Ciara immediately went on the defensive. "Diamond will only be staying in the interim. She'll land back on her claws like she always does."

"If you say so," Pilar said, leaving Ciara and going into the kitchen.

"I do," Ciara replied under her breath as she walked to the family room in search of her father and scorned sister. She found them spread out on the leather sectional with a bowl of popcorn.

"Can anyone join?" Ciara asked from the doorway. She didn't want to interrupt their bonding time.

Her father looked up from the couch. "Ci-Ci, how's my sweetie?"

"Good." Ciara bent down and gave her father a peck on the cheek, but when she looked over at Rachel, she was deep into the Eagles football game.

Robert Miller glanced at his youngest. "Rachel, aren't you going to say hello?"

Rachel gave Ciara a quick glance before uttering hello underneath her breath.

"Hello to you, too, Rach," Ciara threw back. Clearly speaking took too much out of her younger sibling.

"Is this how it's going to be all night?" her father inquired, glancing at both his headstrong daughters. "'Cause if so, you can both go home."

"Of course not, Daddy," Rachel quickly retorted. "But first Ciara must agree to ask Diamond to move out."

"Dad, you know I can't do that," Ciara returned, taking a seat on the couch beside him. "Diamond has no place to go. I'm all the family she has. I can't turn my back on her."

"But you can turn your back on me?" Rachel asked, jumping up into a seated position.

"*You* have someplace to go."

Embarrassed, Rachel hung her head low.

"So, is the air all clear?" their father asked. When

neither sibling said a word, he continued. "Rachel, you'll stay here for a while until Ciara helps Diamond get on her feet. Agreed?"

Rachel reluctantly nodded. She hated that Diamond was getting her way again.

"Now, Ciara, if you need any help covering Rachel's share of the rent," her father stated, "just let me know."

"Not again!" Pilar said from behind the sofa. "Robert, please tell me you are not going to lend that heifer a helping hand after everything she's done to you."

"Watch your language, Pilar," Robert warned. "Diamond is Ciara's mother."

"And you're my husband," Pilar replied. "I swear that woman causes this family nothing but grief." With that comment, she turned and stalked away.

"Why don't I just go?" Ciara stood up. "Since my mother is so repugnant to this family, then perhaps I am as well."

"Don't be ridiculous." Her father rose and grabbed her by the shoulders. "Don't let these two—" he looked down at Rachel and then toward the kitchen "—make you feel unwelcome. This is your home. You are a part of this family and by association so is Diamond. So, I will continue to do what I have always done and that's support you."

"Thank you, Daddy." Ciara gave him a bear hug.

"So—" her father sat back down "—now that that's settled, why don't you tell me why you're off gallivanting at some club with a politician?"

"Gallivanting?" Ciara inquired. "Dad, I'm a grown woman." She shouldn't have to defend herself.

"I know that, but you're dating a politician."

"I'm not the one running for office."

"No, but by association," her father continued, "you're in the limelight, too. All I'm saying, sweetheart, is that you need to be careful."

"Boy, do I know that," Ciara responded. She didn't know how her relationship with Jonathan had leaked to Shannon, but somehow it had. She was right when she'd told Chelsea the station's walls had ears. Now she was going to have to figure out how to deal with Shannon.

"Good, then I won't go on. That story was nothing but gossip and innuendo and I won't give it any more pause, just be on your guard."

"I will, Dad."

Her father rubbed his chin. "I'd like to meet this young man that has made you so reckless." He tucked a wayward strand of hair behind her ear. "You've always been so levelheaded, so unlike your mother."

"I met him," Rachel piped into the conversation.

"And what did you think of him?" he queried.

"Well…" Rachel began. "He was…" Then she made the mistake of glancing in Ciara's direction and saw the warning look. Ciara gave Rachel a harsh look that insinuated she not spill the beans about finding Jonathan naked in the hallway.

"Well?" her father encouraged.

"He was as handsome and charismatic in person as he appears on TV," Rachel replied.

Ciara breathed a sigh of relief from the opposite side of the couch.

"I figured as much," their father chuckled. "Ci-Ci has always had a way with young men."

"She sure does." Rachel smiled knowingly and Ciara blushed at the implication.

"Dinner's ready," Pilar called out from the dining room.

"I'm starved," Rachel said, jumping up and heading for the door.

As Ciara and her father walked to the dining room, she couldn't shake the sinking feeling that Shannon had more in store for her.

The following morning, Ciara was surprised that she still hadn't receive a telephone call from Jonathan. He had to have seen the telecast, and if he hadn't, she was sure his campaign manager had. So, was he avoiding her? Or perhaps he was succumbing to the pressure to end their relationship? She wasn't sure how she felt about it. When she'd originally met Jonathan, she'd wanted to use the relationship to her advantage. When had all that suddenly changed?

Those unanswered questions lurked in the back of her mind as she sat in on the morning meeting while Shannon doled out the day's assignments. Once everyone had their marching orders, they began to disperse. Ciara waited for everyone to leave the conference room before confronting her. Smoothing her suit, Ciara walked toward her.

Shannon was packing up her belongings when Ciara stepped in front of her. "May I have a word?"

"Of course." Shannon smiled smugly. She knew exactly why Ciara wanted to speak with her privately.

Ciara closed the door and took a deep breath before beginning. "Shannon, I realize—" But before she could finish Shannon interrupted her.

"Listen, Miller, I know what this is all about. You're in a huff because we ran that piece on you and Butler."

"Of course, I am," Ciara said. "Wouldn't you be?"

"No!" Shannon replied frankly. "If I were dating a politician, I would know that our relationship would be fair game."

Trust Shannon to see the situation to her advantage. "My life is not a game, Shannon," Ciara returned curtly. "I do not appreciate having my private life on public display or as fodder for your agenda."

"My agenda," Shannon repeated, looking Ciara straight in the eye, "is to bring this station's ratings up."

"Even if it means exploiting me in the process?" Ciara queried with her arms folded across her chest.

"If necessary, yes," Shannon warned.

"Then I guess the battle lines have been drawn," Ciara said, heading for the door.

"Wait!" Shannon called out to her. Shannon quickly thought on her feet. The station would fare better if Ciara was on their side; perhaps working with the little peon could be to her advantage. Maybe she should even throw her a bone. The girl was ambitious after all. "Listen, Miller," Shannon began. "There's no need to turn this into a war. We can work together on this."

"What do you mean?" Ciara asked, somewhat intrigued.

"Make sure WTCF is always the first to know about

Butler's campaign and I'll lay off your and Butler's personal relationship."

Ciara thought about it for a minute. That shouldn't be too hard, and the good press would certainly benefit Jonathan. "And what do I get in return for my good-will?" Ciara asked.

Shannon smiled. Ciara was a shrewd negotiator. "You get the weekend anchor spot."

Ciara was not easily fooled. "Monica already has that spot and I highly doubt she's ready to give it up." Did Shannon think she was born yesterday?

"What you don't know is that Monica's already accepted a new position with WMAU and has given her notice. She will be leaving in a few weeks." Shannon smiled.

"And you'd be willing to give me the position?" Ciara asked.

"You're a seasoned reporter. You've been doing general assignments for five years. You're solid. What do you think?" Shannon stuck out her right hand for Ciara to shake on it.

Ciara stared down at the pale hand in front of her. She didn't trust Shannon one bit; she'd renege just as soon as she got what she wanted. "Put it in writing and we have a deal," Ciara replied. She wanted a legally binding contract, something Shannon couldn't wiggle out of.

"Done," Shannon returned, still holding out her hand. Reluctantly, Ciara extended her hand and shook it. "Great," Shannon said, picking up her things. "I'll have Legal draw something up. Look forward to working with you, kid," Shannon tossed over her shoulder.

As Shannon walked out of the conference room, Ciara could only hope that she hadn't just made a deal with the devil.

Chapter 8

Later that week, Jonathan and Zach came up with a
sound plan to bring the focus back on the campaign.
The first step was an appearance at Children's Hospital
of Philadelphia. Jonathan would shake hands with the
chairman of the hospital and Rebecca Palmer, the
namesake of the pediatric wing, who'd given a chari-
table gift in her deceased husband's honor.

She was also good friends with Jonathan's father and
had given a sizable donation to Jonathan's campaign as
well. He appreciated her giving him the opportunity to
cut the ribbon at the opening ceremony. It was good PR
and he could use all the positive press he could get.

"What's next?" Jonathan asked.

"I have a few more appearances scheduled for you,

one of which will be the Labor Day parade, as well as a fund-raising dinner and the softball game your girlfriend suggested."

"She's not my girlfriend," Jonathan replied.

"Isn't she?" Zach inquired. "You're going out to dinner and to clubs and you're sleeping together. Why wouldn't I or the press think otherwise?"

Jonathan thought about it for a moment. Zach did have a point. As much as he and Ciara professed their relationship was merely casual, they sure were spending a lot of time together, in and out of bed.

He felt as if their casual relationship was developing into something more, but he wasn't sure of Ciara's feelings on the subject. She was so independent at times; he doubted she wanted to feel as if she needed anyone or anything. He could tell she was keeping something from him; he just wished she felt she could trust him.

"I suppose you're right," Jonathan finally replied.

"Glad you think so, because I'd like Ciara to be your date at the dinner and possibly make an appearance at the parade. You know, the whole woman standing by her man thing. Maybe we could even speculate that there is a wedding in the future."

"Marriage?" Jonathan asked. "Don't you think that's kind of jumping the gun?"

"Of course, but we need to present this relationship as if it's leading somewhere. The press loves a good love story. And your opponent is a happily-married father of three."

Jonathan sure hoped Zach was right, otherwise the election was lost.

* * *

"You and Butler are getting pretty close," Lance said on the drive to Children's Hospital of Philadelphia, where Jonathan was cutting the ribbon for the new pediatric AIDS wing.

"Jonathan and I are dating, yes," Ciara answered.

"C'mon, Ciara, it's me you're talking to," Lance chided. "You don't date."

"What are you talking about?" Ciara feigned ignorance.

"Your relationships have never lasted longer than a few weeks," Lance responded. "After you've tired of bedding them, you usually cast them aside like they're yesterday's trash."

"That's not true." Ciara attempted to defend herself. "It's just that none of them have piqued my interest."

"Like Jonathan Butler has," Lance finished where she left off. "Just admit that you're falling for the guy."

"I will admit no such thing," Ciara returned. "I happen to enjoy his company. He's a dynamic, charming, handsome man. We're bed buddies, nothing more."

"Call it whatever you want, but I know different," Lance stated, pulling into a visitors' parking space outside the hospital.

Was Lance right? thought Ciara as she exited the van. Was she falling in love with Jonathan Butler? No, no, no. She shook her head. She was no fool for love like Diamond, who constantly fell in and out of love. Jonathan was a means to an end. Because of her acquaintance with him, she'd already procured a weekend anchor spot. Who knew what was next? Or at least that was what she told herself, but in the back of her mind she had a feeling Lance could be right.

"You ready?" she said, coming around to the back of the van.

"Yes." Lance lifted the camera above his shoulder. "Let's rock and roll."

When they arrived on the third floor of the pediatric wing, they found a crowd had already formed around Jonathan. He was dressed immaculately as usual, in a gray Armani suit, black lace-up shoes, silver watch and cuff links. He looked every bit the smooth and persuasive politician as he shook hands and kissed babies. When he picked up one of the small children with HIV and held him close to his chest, Ciara's heart swelled.

Jonathan wasn't afraid of the child passing a disease to him. Instead, he offered comfort and support. She wasn't surprised. He was a kind, caring man and one that she could easily fall in love with, if she hadn't already.

Jonathan gave a short speech about the importance of AIDS research. He and Rebecca Palmer presented a check to the chairman of the hospital. After the ribbon-cutting ceremony and a photo op, Ciara waited until the throng dispersed before approaching Jonathan.

"Hey, handsome," she said from behind him.

Jonathan turned around and greeted her with a warm smile. "Ciara, I'm happy to see you. Sorry I haven't called the last few days. I've been doing damage control."

"I understand, you can't have your image tarnished

by hanging out with me," Ciara replied, a little too harshly.

"Far from it," Jonathan said, lightly taking her arm and leading her away from the crowd. "Actually my campaign manager thinks we should meet this head-on by going public with our relationship."

Ciara raised a brow. "How public does he mean?"

"Well...if you're up for it, perhaps a few appearances with me. It might ease the public's salacious curiosity."

"As the lady in your life?" Ciara asked, staring up at Jonathan. Was he asking her to be his girlfriend?

Jonathan responded by looking her directly in the eye. "Do you have a problem with that?"

"I...might," Ciara replied, flustered. She wasn't altogether sure she was ready to be Jonathan Butler's woman. Heck, anybody's woman. She was Ciara Miller after all. She was her own person.

"And what," he asked, leaning down to whisper in her ear so that only she could hear, "would convince you to turn that *might* into a *yes?*"

"Well, that would depend on what's required of me," Ciara returned.

"Publicly, Zach or my media consultant can answer that," Jonathan said.

"And privately?"

"Well, I've got that covered," Jonathan replied seductively. The husky softness of his voice sent shivers up Ciara's spine.

"Matter of fact, let's meet Friday night for dinner and we can discuss all that I require."

"Sounds good."

"It won't be until seven though. I have some meetings to finish up. Why don't I pick you up at the studio?"

"The studio?" Ciara inquired. "Do you really think that's a good idea?"

Jonathan shrugged his shoulders. "Our relationship is public knowledge now. What difference does it make?"

Ciara shrugged. He had a point. "None at all. I'll see you at seven."

She waved goodbye before returning to Lance, who was waiting by the elevator with a smug smile.

"Don't even start," Ciara said, pressing the down button.

"I wouldn't dream of it," Lance replied. He didn't need to. Ciara's desire to be near Jonathan at every possible occasion was revealing enough.

Across town, a deviant smile spread over Reid's face at the report just laid in front of him. The private investigator he and Dominique had hired to dig up dirt on Ciara Miller had given him the ammo to sink Jonathan's campaign. Sure, the sultry reporter was doing a fine job of that all by herself by keeping Jonathan in the spotlight, with the press focused on his love life rather than his message, but this was pure genius.

He couldn't wait to use this information as ammunition against that superior snot-nosed brat who thought he knew better than him, a thirty-year veteran in politics.

He intended to drop the bomb at just the right moment, when Butler least expected it. Reid would show Jonathan Butler exactly whom he was dealing with.

Dialing her number gave Reid immense pleasure. Dominique picked up on the third ring. "Reid, I've been waiting for your call," she said anxiously. "Did the investigator find out anything about Ciara?"

"No, not a thing, Dominique," Reid lied. "The investigation was a wild-goose chase. Ciara's clean. You have nothing to worry about."

Dominique breathed a sigh of relief. Thank God the girl didn't have any skeletons in her closet. Jonathan was all in the clear.

Jonathan made quite a stir when he came to the station to pick up Ciara for dinner. Of course, he had no idea how much of a celebrity he was until the television director, a Shannon somebody, came out to personally escort him to Ciara's desk.

The redhead was chatting away while he looked around for a glimpse of his sexy seductress.

"I'm sorry, Mrs....?" Jonathan searched his memory for her name, but it escaped him. He used to have a good memory, but with all the people he was constantly being introduced to lately, he'd become terrible with names.

"Please call me Shannon." She extended her right hand. "It's such a pleasure to have someone of your stature here at the studio." She stroked his ego. Men loved to be praised.

Jonathan was flattered, but he doubted he was the

first quasi celebrity to be at the studio. "Oh, I'm sure you've had dignitaries here, besides myself?"

Shannon shook her head. "Actually, not really," she replied. "We're such a small local station. Those interviews are reserved for the networks and the Barbara Walterses or Katie Courics of the world. Anyway, I'm sure you don't want to hear about all that. You're here to see Ciara."

"Yes, I am." Jonathan smiled, trying to appear cordial. Although, he didn't trust her one bit. She was probably the one responsible for the story on him.

"Well, it looks like Ciara is still in the editing room," Shannon replied after reviewing the sign-in sheet. "But you can wait for her at her desk in the newsroom."

"Thanks, I appreciate that."

Once they arrived, Jonathan was surprised just how open the newsroom was. Ciara had no privacy. Everyone could see and hear everything she did. Was this really a reporter's life? In this confined space with hardly any windows? How could anyone work with all the noise from the televisions and radios? And without any privacy?

He wasn't surprised to find Ciara's desk cluttered. It suited her personality. One photo particularly stuck out at him. It was of her and an older woman dressed in flashy attire. The woman looked like Ciara, unlike the woman in the family photograph in her apartment. Was she Ciara's mother? Jonathan wondered as Ciara flew in like a whirlwind.

After freshening her makeup in the restroom, Ciara was startled to find Jonathan's six-foot-three frame standing by her desk. "Ohmigod! You startled me," she said.

"Sorry, I didn't mean to," Jonathan apologized.

"Don't worry about it," she replied, opening her desk drawer and throwing her cosmetics bag inside. "I hope you haven't been waiting long?"

His presence threw her completely off-kilter. She had hoped to have a few minutes to gather herself before he arrived, but that was all shot to hell by his model good looks and dazzling sex appeal. Was it the Armani suit that made him appear so sexy?

"No, not at all. Your boss was kind enough to show me the way," Jonathan said, staring down at her. He was treated to another view of her eyes, except this time they had tiny golden specks in them. It was one of the many things he loved about her. Her constantly changing faces. She was a chameleon of sorts. "So are you ready to go?" He'd been anxious for her company since this afternoon.

"Yes, I'm starved."

Jonathan took her leather jacket off the back of her chair and helped her into it. "I know a great place."

Thirty minutes later, they were seated at Zanzibar Blue, an upscale restaurant and jazz club. Jonathan kept it simple and ordered a club soda while Ciara ordered Riesling. They listened to a native Philadelphian sing sultry jazz numbers while they waited at the bar to be seated.

"Ciara," Jonathan said.

"Yes?"

"Now that we're going public…" he began. "You can be my date at the fund-raising dinner."

"Did I agree to that?" she teased.

"How about I convince you?" Jonathan leaned over to her and lightly brushed his lips across hers.

"No need," Ciara replied. "I would love to be your date."

"That's fantastic." Jonathan smiled. "With you by my side the evening will be a success."

"You do realize that by going public, our relationship has moved beyond casual," Ciara commented, sipping her wine.

"And how do you feel about that?" Jonathan was curious to know the answer to that question. "When we initially met, it was all heat. And now…"

"Things are a lot more complicated," Ciara finished. "More so for you than me. Are you sure this is what you want?"

"I should be asking you that same question."

"Why?"

"Aren't you the one who always leaves before daybreak?" Jonathan asked, putting her in the hot seat.

"Your table is ready," the hostess interrupted them and led them to their seats.

Once they were sitting, Ciara had to admit he did have a point. She'd never been in a relationship for the long run, at least not until now. "True. And I'm not altogether sure I'm ready for a committed relationship."

"What are you so afraid of, Ciara?" Jonathan wondered aloud.

"I'm not afraid," Ciara answered defensively.

Jonathan didn't agree. He could tell the subject of commitment made her feel uneasy. "Ciara, I'd really like to see where *this* will all lead. Aren't you the least bit curious, too? You can't deny there's something between us."

Ciara didn't want to admit that she felt equally as strongly about Jonathan as he felt about her. She was used to fending for herself. She'd always had to look after herself because Diamond had always been too busy with one of her many boyfriends. Ciara wasn't used to letting anyone in.

"I admit that I find you sexy and attractive," she offered.

"Why are you hiding behind sex?" Jonathan asked. "Using it as a ruse to cover your true feelings."

"I'm doing no such thing," Ciara replied, lowering her lashes and avoiding Jonathan's direct glare. "I like sex. And you happen to satisfy me in that department. What's wrong with that?"

She did not want to become the kind of woman she disparaged. The kind of woman who needed a man. Men were only good for sex. They were only interested in your breasts, butt, hips, legs and mouth. It was all about sex. Nothing more. She'd seen how men behaved in the establishments where Diamond worked. Watched them paw at women. Ciara could not forget the time one of those drunken bastards had accosted her upstairs and had tried to force himself on her. She recoiled at the memory.

After that incident, she'd vowed to never ever trust a man. Men would say anything to get you into bed, but want you for your mind or your heart? Ciara doubted it. She didn't believe in fairy tales. And yet somehow Jonathan made her want to forget the past. He made her want to believe that a man could not only want her for her body, but her mind and her heart as well.

"Nothing," Jonathan replied. "If sex was all there was between us. I happen to believe that we have common interests, similar values and a mutual respect for one another, but if I'm wrong, please fill me in."

Ciara lowered her lashes. "You're not wrong, but…"

The waiter returned with their dinner plates and set them down. Everything smelled delicious. Ciara immediately sank her fork in and began eating, desperate to do something to hide her rising anxiety.

"Then let's stop playing games and confront it head-on. I want you, Ciara." He put his fork down. "And not just as a bed playmate. I want you by my side and, despite how you might protest—" Jonathan leaned over the table "—I know you want me, too."

Ciara's breath caught in her throat. It was all she could do not to choke on her food.

"Don't choke." Jonathan patted her back. "I want you alive and healthy for the fund-raising dinner."

Ciara reached for a glass of water and gulped it down.

"Now that I've made my intentions clear, I'll back off for now," Jonathan said. He'd seen the fear in Ciara's eyes and he didn't want her to feel pressured. "But know this, I intend to have you, Ciara. All of you."

Later, once they made it back to the studio, she quickly jumped out of the car. "Thank you for the ride back," she said. After everything Jonathan had said over dinner, she was eager to get out of such a confined space.

"No problem, I always show my woman to the door," Jonathan said smoothly, exiting the vehicle and following her inside.

She didn't realize he'd followed her in. "Well, would you like a tour of the station?" she suggested. "The ten o'clock broadcast is long since over, so it'll be relatively quiet with only the skeleton crew at the studio, at least for now."

Jonathan glanced down at his watch. "Sure, if it's not too late." Jonathan followed Ciara down the hall from the newsroom to the studio where the live broadcasts were shot.

When Ciara flicked on the switch, the room flooded with bright lights. Cameras and television monitors were everywhere, but what stood out was the main set, a beautiful mahogany news desk that shone center stage. "Creating a news program takes a lot of work," Ciara informed him as they walked in. "Typically a program manager decides what programs and promotions go on air after working with the producer, who writes the rundown and the script."

"How does a reporter know what to do?" Jonathan asked.

"A general assignment editor doles out the day's assignments or reporters can come up with their own ideas. Or we get stories from tipsters or stringers."

"What's a rundown?"

"That's a schedule of how the telecast will go. The anchors go to Makeup and Wardrobe while the stage crew gets everything in place. Behind there—" Ciara pointed to the dark glass enclosure "—is the studio control room. That's where the studio and technical director communicate with the stage crew.

"Over there is the audio booth." Ciara pointed to a small room. "They control the audio of the program, such as the sound effects and the mikes that the news team wears."

Ciara walked behind the anchor's desk and took a seat in the chair she would soon occupy. Once the lawyers finalized her contract within the next day or so, this would be hers. She felt guilty for not telling Jonathan but until it was a done deal, she had to keep the news to herself.

"So, what do you think?" Ciara asked, swirling around.

"I'm amazed, actually," Jonathan replied, "that it takes all these people to put the thirty-minute program together that we see on air every day. I have to give you your props."

"Thank you," Ciara said. "But where I want to be is right here." She pointed down to the anchor's chair. "I want to be an evening anchor."

"And I have no doubt you will be. You've got the drive and the ambition." There was a definite gleam in her eye that had not been there before. It made Jonathan wonder just how far Ciara was willing to go to make it to the top.

"You better believe it," Ciara replied.

"How's everything going with your hunky politician friend?" Diamond asked later, when Ciara had returned home after her dinner with Jonathan.

"Why do you want to know?" Ciara asked, kicking off her shoes and throwing her briefcase on a nearby chair. She plopped down in the plush recliner.

"Can't a mother be curious?" Diamond asked, putting down her *Cosmo* magazine. She was trying to forge a bond with Ciara, but her stubborn daughter would not cut her some slack. "You're spending an awful lot of time with the fella. Heck, you've even kicked me to the curb and I live with ya."

"Temporarily."

"I know that," Diamond retorted. "Why is it so difficult to believe that I want to share a little part of your life?"

Diamond cast her head low and Ciara felt bad. How did her mother always find a way of making her feel guilty?

"Things are going fine," Ciara tried again. "Actually, better than fine."

"So that news report was right? You guys are an item?"

"Yes, but not how they implied." Ciara turned to face her. "There's nothing illicit going on. We're both single and available."

"Yes, but that's not telling me much. How do you feel about him?" Diamond pressed Ciara for more information.

"I think he's an incredible man," Ciara replied. "Intelligent, kind, caring, extremely dedicated and did I mention incredibly handsome and sexy…" Her voice trailed off as she envisioned his chiseled frame.

"Sounds like he's the kind of man a woman could

marry," Diamond commented. "And if so, you need to snag him while you can. Rich ones like him don't come along every day and trust me, if he wins the election, women will be hanging all over him."

"I don't want to get married, Diamond," Ciara protested. "Unlike you, I don't want or need a man to complete me. I'm a whole person entirely on my own." She rose and went to the kitchen for a glass of wine after her long day.

Diamond ignored the dig and continued. "C'mon, baby cakes, this is your mama you're talking to. That tough-as-nails routine may work on some, but not me. I'm sure you don't want another woman coming in and snatching up your man. So, claim him, if he's yours. I would. His family is probably rolling in the cash. You'd never want for anything."

"Is money all you think about?" Ciara asked, sipping her wine at the doorway.

"No, but since you mentioned it," Diamond replied, "I could sure use some."

"Why? What do you need it for?"

"When I don't have any cash in my pocket, I feel uneasy."

"Then maybe you should find a job," Ciara responded, exasperated.

"As old as I am?" Diamond chuckled. "What could I possibly do? And who would hire me? The only thing I was ever good at was dancing and I'm well past my prime for that."

"So try something new," Ciara encouraged her. "You could go back to school, get a certificate in something.

Anything, just as long as it gets you out of the apartment. I'd even pay for it."

"You really are a poor excuse for a daughter," Diamond huffed. "All I needed tonight was a little handout and instead you make me feel worthless. Thanks for nothing." Diamond walked out of the room, leaving Ciara feeling two feet tall.

Frustrated, she threw herself on the couch. She hadn't meant to be hurtful, but Diamond had a way of bringing out the worst in her. Rachel was right. Diamond moving in was a really bad idea. Ciara needed to find her a job or a new man and quick.

The night of the fund-raising event, Ciara was excited at the prospect of being Jonathan's date. This was to be their first public appearance together as a couple since they'd begun seeing each other a few weeks ago. She wasn't nervous—she knew what questions to expect because they would probably be something she would ask. She knew how to keep her cool in intense situations. Life as Diamond's daughter had prepared her for the unexpected, such as getting kicked out of your apartment or having your gas turned off in the dead of winter.

But she would not dwell on the negative tonight. Instead, she dressed herself with great care for the evening. Her usual sexy hair had been replaced with a sophisticated French roll while her makeup was simple: a light dusting of powder, mascara and lipstick. Tonight, her natural beauty would shine through and for the finishing touch she slipped into a long silk charmeuse gown. It was the color of ginger and suited her bronze-toned skin perfectly. After another glance, she was ready. Grabbing her clutch, she walked out to the living room and waited for Jonathan.

He was punctual as usual, but what was more impressive was how good he looked in his hand-tailored tuxedo. His well-honed torso clothed in black and white was breathtaking. She could smell his expensive cologne and it caused her heart to race and her breath to run short.

"You look ravishing," Jonathan said. His eyes burned with intensity as they swept her face.

"You look handsome as well," Ciara returned, lightly kissing him on the lips so as to not ruin her makeup.

"Are you ready?" he asked. "The limo is downstairs waiting."

"Can't wait," Ciara replied. A few seconds later, they were seated in the plush limousine seats and off to the Four Seasons Hotel for Jonathan's fund-raising dinner. No sooner had they been seated, then Jonathan pressed his soft lips against her neck and nuzzled while his hands slid up the smooth expanse of her thigh.

"Hmmm," Ciara moaned, "you'd better not get started." She pushed his hand away. "Otherwise we won't be able to stop."

Jonathan laughed huskily. "I suppose you're right." He pulled away. He found it hard to control himself when she was near.

When they arrived, dozens of people had already filled the hotel banquet hall, milling around drinking champagne and chatting about the latest in politics and gossip. When she walked in, Ciara was sure she was going to be a source of public speculation, but instead, all of the attendees treated her cordially.

Jonathan was not shy about introducing her to everyone as his girlfriend, either. He kept a possessive arm around her waist the entire evening. Several people mentioned he was clearly besotted, to which he answered an emphatic *yes*. His parents remained distant, but they made polite conversation during dinner, asking Ciara about her job and her family. Ciara kept it simple, mentioning her father and sister. She left Diamond's name out of the conversation.

Ciara knew that neither of Jonathan's parents was pleased by her presence in his life, but they didn't say an unkind word. She supposed they had too much class to bring themselves down to that level.

Ciara tried to remain aloof and hide her growing feelings, but it was pretty hard to do in such close proximity to Jonathan. His powerful energy had an effect on her. Every time his thigh lightly brushed hers warmth flooded her entire being. When Jonathan needed a private word with a constituent, Ciara went off in search of some champagne.

She was enjoying herself until Reid joined her at the bar for a drink. "Hope you don't mind if I join you?" he asked smoothly.

She did, but she was much too polite to say so. Jonathan didn't like the man much and neither did she. There was something oily and shady about Reid. He reminded Ciara of all those losers Diamond had dated.

"No, not all," she said, plastering a fake smile on her face.

"Are you enjoying the evening?" Reid inquired.

"As well as can be expected," Ciara replied, sipping on her champagne.

"That's good," Reid said, "because perhaps it should be your last."

She whipped around and faced Reid. "Excuse me?"

"You must realize that your continued presence in Jonathan's life will cost him the election," Reid stated evenly.

"No, I hadn't realized that," she responded. She willed the fury that boiled in her veins to subside. How dare he tell her to break up with Jonathan? Who did she think he was? Jonathan's keeper?

"C'mon, Ms. Miller. Don't play stupid. You're a member of the press, you know as well as I do that every time a negative story appears about Jonathan, his poll numbers go down."

"And you think I'm the cause?"

"Aren't you?" Reid asked, leaning down so only she could hear him. "Why don't you do everyone a big favor and end this before you do more harm than good."

Jonathan was talking with his father when he noticed Ciara's obvious discomfort at Reid's presence. Reid had obviously said something to offend her because Ciara's face turned scarlet. Jonathan sprang into action and strode across the room.

"Is there a problem here, Reid?" Jonathan queried, circling his arm around Ciara's waist.

"Not at all," Reid replied. "Just making polite con-

versation," he said before walking away. He'd done
what he had to do. Made it appear that he was looking
out for Jonathan's best interest; all the while he was
secretly sabotaging him. Wait until Jonathan saw what
he had in store for him next.

"Are you okay?" Jonathan asked, tilting Ciara's head
so she could look up at him. "Was Reid harassing you?
Because if so…"

"No, no, no," Ciara replied. "I can handle myself
against the likes of him." She glanced at Reid's retreating figure. He wasn't the first slimy creature who'd approached her and he probably wouldn't be the last.
She'd come across many in her youth and had had the
courage to defend herself. Reid was no exception. He
was just better dressed.

Doubt crossed Jonathan's face. "Are you sure?"

"Trust me, I don't intimidate easily."

"Good. Would you like to dance?" Jonathan asked.
He'd been itching to take her out for a spin on the floor
the entire evening. He wanted to hold her in his arms
and wished the evening would never end. The dinner
had gone well. Actually, better than he had expected.

"I don't waltz," Ciara replied.

"Just follow my lead," Jonathan replied and twirled
her around. Once they were on the dance floor, Jonathan lightly pressed his hand into the small of Ciara's
back and led her across the floor. He was a smooth
ballroom dancer, but Ciara was not surprised—Jonathan was good at anything he did.

"Are you having a good time?" he asked.

"Yes, I am," Ciara said. Now that she was in his

arms. She didn't care for Reid Hamilton one bit. There was something about him that was oddly sinister and Ciara couldn't put her finger on what it was.

"Good, because I really wanted you here with me tonight."

"As a showpiece?" Ciara teased.

"Of course not," Jonathan replied. "As my girl-friend." He wanted every man in the room to know that Ciara was his, so they could be green with envy.

"I think I like being your girlfriend," Ciara said honestly. She'd certainly never been in a relationship long enough before to be one.

"I'm glad," Jonathan laughed, "because I don't like to share."

From the other side of the room, Reid seethed at the happy couple. Jonathan Butler was not hurting nearly enough. Sure WTCF had done the work for him by following them in the bar, but that wasn't nearly enough. Reid was going to have to turn up the heat.

So he watched in disgust as they danced the night away, but come tomorrow, he was going to use that ace up his sleeve.

Chapter 9

Jonathan, his parents, Zach and Reid were having a dinner strategy session several days later when a rap on the conference-room door stopped all conversation.

"I think you should see this," a campaign volunteer said, grabbing the remote on the nearby console and clicking on the television. He turned to WTCF, Ciara's news station.

"What's this about?" Zach said, turning to the volunteer.

"You'll see."

Jonathan watched in horror as his and Ciara's faces flashed across the screen. The story went on to say the new woman in his life had a shady past, having been raised by Diamond Miller, a Las Vegas showgirl. The station insinuated that dancing may not have been the only thing Diamond had been into because the establishments she'd worked were known for topless dancing, among other things.

In addition, the story revealed that Diamond had married an elderly financier, Paul Williams, and had inherited his estate, but had squandered all the money. Were these the kind of people the squeaky-clean Butler associated with? The report indicated that if Diamond was a gold digger, could her daughter, Ciara Miller, be far behind? The report ended with "Stay tuned to WTCF for more details on the scandal involving Jonathan Butler and Ciara Miller."

"I've heard enough," Jonathan said, grabbing the remote out of the volunteer's hand and turning off the television.

Reid saw an opportunity to turn the tide against Ciara. "Jonathan, don't you see that Ciara Miller is an opportunist?"

"What are you talking about, Reid?"

"First we find out her mother is a Las Vegas showgirl turned socialite who lost all her money, and Ms. Miller just happens to become weekend anchor at WTCF. Don't you in the least bit find that suspect?"

"Anchor? Ciara's not an anchor. She's a reporter."

"Now she is," Reid emphasized. "I did a little asking around and it looks like Ms. Miller has been promoted and will be anchoring the weekend news."

Was Reid right? thought Jonathan. Why hadn't Ciara told him about her promotion? Could she really be using him to further her own ambitions?

"C'mon, Butler," Reid replied. "Don't be so stubborn that you refuse to see the obvious. Miller is using you to get ahead."

"You're wrong. Ciara isn't like that. You don't know her." Jonathan doggedly refused to accept Reid's take on the situation.

"Isn't she?" Reid asked. "You saw the report. Saw how her mother used that man for his money and then had the nerve to blow it all. The apple doesn't fall too far from the tree, my friend. Clearly, you must see that."

Jonathan snorted. Reid was in no way his friend. There was no love lost between the two of them.

Dominique was fuming from her seat. She couldn't believe this was happening. She'd thought Reid had handled this. Well, if not, she was not going to let Ciara topple Jonathan's election.

"Enough is enough, Jonathan!" Dominique Butler stood up. "Reid is right. Ciara and her family are loose cannons. How long are you going to continue to let this woman undermine your campaign? Don't you even care anymore?"

"Do you even care that the story nearly indicated her mother could be a prostitute? Think about how Ciara must feel."

"I couldn't care less." His mother stood her ground. "You're my son and your future is on the line. You can't afford to get embroiled in a scandal. It'll ruin you."

"Everyone, calm down." Zach jumped into the fray. "Let's take a step back and let cool heads prevail."

"How can I be calm?" Jonathan shouted. "They are

crucifying the woman I'm falling in love with." Suddenly, the room became quiet as eyes fell on him. "That's right. I'm falling for Ciara Miller. And I refuse to let the press insinuate she's a woman lacking in morals and values. That's utterly ludicrous!"

"Well, what do you suppose we do, son?" Charles asked, being the voice of reason.

"Find me the person who is responsible for this story and bring me their head," Jonathan replied harshly. "That's what you can do."

Reid sat smugly back in his chair while Jonathan ranted and raved. He was immensely pleased with his handiwork. When he'd called up WTCF's news director, Shannon Wright, she'd been all too pleased to run the story. Better ratings for her. Forget that it would ruin her reporter's reputation. She was ratings hungry and jumped at the opportunity. He'd stuck it to Jonathan and that wily reporter, but he wasn't finished with him yet. He intended to ensure that Jonathan Butler would never see the inside of the Capitol.

Ciara's telephone rang while she attempted to cook dinner for herself before going to the studio. In an attempt to make chicken Parmesan, she had already made a mess of things. The chicken was burned and the spaghetti was overcooked. The only thing that had turned out right was the sauce and that was because she'd merely opened a jar of marinara sauce and poured it in a pan. She rushed to the phone in the living room and picked it up on the last ring before her answering machine came on.

"Ciara, turn on the TV. Quick," Lance said from the

other end. "You won't believe what Shannon has done this time."

"What are you talking about, Lance?" she asked, picking up the remote from the coffee table. She flicked through the stations until she found WTCF. She'd made a deal with Shannon. Her mouth dropped open when she saw Diamond's image on the television screen. Quietly, she sat and listened as they went on to report that her mother was a Las Vegas showgirl who'd married for money and when that money had run out she'd gone back to her former trashy lifestyle.

"That witch!" Ciara yelled into the phone. "She promised me that she would not run any more stories on me, so instead she goes after my mother! I could strangle her."

Thank God her mother was not back from the nail salon. Though she doubted much would faze Diamond—she was used to negative press, having endured plenty after her former husband's death. Many had said she'd used Paul Williams for his money, but Diamond had denied it. Claimed she loved the old buzzard with all her heart. But this time the backlash was affecting Ciara. They'd all but said her mother was a prostitute and opportunist and that Ciara was following in her mother's footsteps.

"What are you going to do?" Lance asked. He was worried about Ciara. She put on a tough facade, but he knew underneath that veneer was a vulnerable woman.

"I should sue the station for defamation of character," Ciara returned, her voice cracking. "Make them rescind that story."

"And what would that accomplish? The damage has already been done," Lance replied.

Ciara held back the tears that threatened to fall. "It would make me feel better," Ciara sniffed. She took a deep breath and tried to pull herself together. "Jonathan must think I'm total trash."

"When does Ciara Miller care about what other people think?"

"I don't care about other people," Ciara answered honestly. "Only Jonathan's opinion matters to me."

So, Ciara was finally admitting that Butler meant more to her than her average roll in the sack. Progress had definitely been made and Lance was glad for it. Ciara couldn't continue to live her life always closed up. Always afraid of being vulnerable. Never letting anyone in. If Jonathan could enable her to let her guard down, Lance was happy.

"Well, if Jonathan is any kind of man, he won't believe the innuendo."

"But not all of it is innuendo," Ciara replied. "Some of it is fact, Lance. Diamond was a Las Vegas showgirl and she did marry a rich old man and lose all his money."

"But you're nothing like her," Lance stated.

"No, I'm not."

"Then confront Shannon. You can't let her use you, Ciara," Lance retorted. He wanted Ciara to stand up for herself.

"And how do you suggest I stop her?"

"Not sure, but you have to find a way."

After she hung up with Lance, Ciara wondered how

in the world she could stop Shannon. When you saw a train wreck coming, how did you avert it?

All eyes were on Ciara when she came to the studio that evening to anchor the Saturday evening news for the first time. She was sure all her coworkers were wondering if there was any validity to the story that had run on her mother. Could Ciara be just as unsavory as her ditzy mother?

She put on a brave face as she walked to Wardrobe and Makeup, and tried not to let it bother her. Luckily, Chelsea was there for support as Ciara hiked herself up on the stool.

"Are you okay?" Chelsea asked, squeezing her shoulder. "I saw the story."

"Yeah, it was pretty bad." Ciara put on a stiff upper lip.

"Hey, you know, none of us who know you believe any of it," Chelsea replied, brushing Ciara's hair.

"Thank you, Chelsea. I appreciate that. But unfortunately, the voting public may think otherwise. This could hurt Jonathan's chances."

"You two have grown close?" Chelsea asked, applying some makeup to Ciara's flawless complexion. "Sounds serious since the last time we talked."

Gosh, that seemed like a lifetime ago to Ciara, when in fact it had barely been a month. Everything then had seemed so clear, so cut and dry, and now…

"Have you seen Shannon?" Ciara asked, changing the subject. A confrontation with that backstabbing witch was first on her list of things to do.

"For once, she's not around," Chelsea replied.

KIMANI PRESS™

An Important Message from the Publisher

Dear Reader,

Because you've chosen to read one of our fine novels, I'd like to say "thank you"! And, as a special way to say thank you, I'm offering to send you two Kimani Romance™ novels and two surprise gifts – absolutely FREE! These books will keep it real with true-to-life African-American characters that turn up the heat and sizzle with passion.

Please enjoy the free books and gifts with our compliments...

Linda Gill

Publisher, Kimani Press

Peel off Seal and Place Inside...

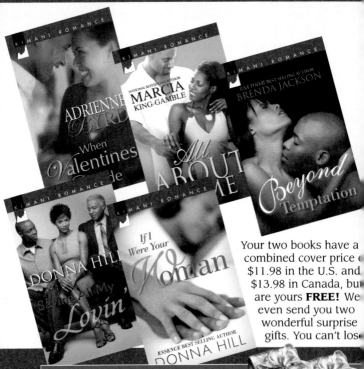

Two NEW Kimani Romance™ Novels
Two exciting surprise gifts

YES! I have placed my Editor's "Thank You" Free Gifts seal in the space provided at right. Please send me 2 FREE books, and my 2 FREE Mystery Gifts. I understand that I am under no obligation to purchase anything further, as explained on the back of this card.

PLACE
FREE GIFTS
SEAL
HERE

168 XDL ELWZ

368 XDL ELXZ

FIRST NAME

LAST NAME

ADDRESS

APT.#

CITY

STATE/PROV.

ZIP/POSTAL CODE

Thank You!

The Reader Service — Here's How It Works:

"Probably saw me coming and ran in the opposite direction," Ciara replied.

"So are you nervous?" Chelsea asked. "I know this is your first telecast." She applied a touch of blush to Ciara's high cheekbones.

"Quite frankly, Chelsea, with all that's been going on I haven't had the opportunity to be nervous about anchoring."

"Here's your dialogue." The studio director came through and handed her the script for the evening's telecast. Ciara quickly scanned the pages, becoming familiar with the lead stories. Before she could finish her makeup, the sound adviser came over, ready to walk her through what she had to expect and to wire her suit jacket with a microphone. Everything was happening so quickly, she didn't hear her cell phone ring until Chelsea handed it to her.

"Who is it?" she mouthed, not wanting to be interrupted.

"It's Jonathan."

Ciara accepted the phone. "Hi." She perked up.

"Hello, yourself," Jonathan replied.

"I suppose you saw the story Shannon ran on my mother."

"Yes."

"And?" Ciara was puzzled as to why Jonathan was not more furious. He sounded strangely calm on the other end.

"I hear congratulations are in order, anchorwoman," Jonathan said smoothly, even though he was furious with her for keeping the information from her.

Guilt immediately rushed through Ciara. She hadn't told him. That was why he was acting so strangely. He was upset that she hadn't confided in him. "Jonathan, I'm—"

But he cut her off, not giving her the opportunity to apologize, which made Ciara feel even more guilty. "I just wanted to tell you to break a leg or whatever it is they say in show business. Have a good night," he said, quickly ending the call.

"Thank you," Ciara replied to the air because Jonathan had already hung up.

Shortly thereafter, a florist showed up with a large bouquet of roses. The card read *Congratulations, Jonathan.*

Ciara felt like such a heel. How could she not have told him? Perhaps because she felt guilty at making a deal with Shannon? A deal that Shannon had already reneged on.

"Ciara, we need you at the desk for a run-through," the studio director said, interrupting her thoughts.

Reluctantly, Ciara put on a bright smile and did what she had been waiting seven years at the station to do: she anchored the news.

A couple of days later, Ciara had several errands to run before heading to the station. Her third stop was to take Jonathan out for lunch and make amends. She stopped by his campaign office around noon, praying that he was free.

When she arrived, his headquarters was a hub of frenzied activity. People were running around answering phones, stuffing envelopes and making coffee.

Campaign posters and boards were everywhere with Jonathan's picture.

"Jonathan Butler, please," she asked the reception- ist at the front desk.

"Do you have an appointment?" she inquired.

"No, I don't, but…"

"Oh wait, I know you," the older woman chuckled. "I saw you on the news." Ciara's cheeks flushed. Had everyone seen the telecast? "One moment, I'll let Mr. Butler know you're here." The receptionist buzzed Jonathan. "Ms. Miller is here to see you." And she knew her name! He must have said okay because the woman allowed Ciara to go in.

She walked in breezily, swept past Jonathan's desk and came and sat in his lap. There was only one way to deal with a man.

"Ciara…" Jonathan was in no mood for Ciara's an- tics and tried to push her away.

"Do you have time to grab some lunch?" she asked, kissing his neck and silencing his protests. "It's a beau- tiful day out." She wasn't altogether sure Jonathan would want to have anything to do with her, let alone speak to her after the broadcast on her mother. She would have to use all her feminine wiles.

Jonathan glanced down at his Movado watch. He didn't have much time. He was due for a photo shoot in an hour and a half. And he had no time for a long meal. "I'm afraid not." He attempted to push Ciara out of his lap, but she wouldn't budge. And if she continued squirming in his lap, she was going to give him a major hard-on.

"Pretty please," she said, pouting then covering his lips with hers.

Initially, Jonathan resisted. "I can't." He didn't appreciate Ciara keeping him in the dark about her promotion. It made him wonder if she was keeping more secrets from him.

He faltered when Ciara found that sensitive spot on his neck. On the flip side, they did need to talk.

"I don't have much time, maybe an hour." He finally managed to eke out the words.

"No problem," Ciara replied. "I have just the solution. Follow me." Ciara grabbed Jonathan by the hand, led him through his headquarters and outside into the warm August air.

"Where are we going?" he asked as they crossed the street. He was curious as to where they could possibly dine and dash within an hour.

"To the park," Ciara replied.

He was surprised when after a short walk she stopped in front of a hot-dog stand. "Hot dogs?" he inquired. He couldn't remember the last time he'd sampled one.

"Yeah, isn't it great?" Ciara asked, wide-eyed. "It's the best lunch in a pinch and cheap, too. What would you like on yours?"

"Ummm…" Jonathan floundered. For a moment he was rendered speechless. Ciara had a way of making him feel that way. She was completely unpredictable and that was what he loved about her. Any other woman would have insisted on a formal sit-down lunch, but not Ciara; she was in a class all by herself. "I guess I'll have ketchup, mustard and relish."

"Great combination," Ciara replied, turning to the vendor. "I'll have the same." The vendor prepared their hot dogs and handed them each one.

Ciara immediately bit into hers. She was starving, having not eaten the night before. Without Rachel around to cook her meals, she'd resorted to eating cereal for dinner. Boy, did she miss her sister!

They strolled through the park until Jonathan found an empty bench and they took a seat.

"Listen, Jonathan," Ciara began, wiping her mouth with a napkin. "I kind of wanted to get you away from all that—" she pointed back to his headquarters "—and have some time alone to say how sorry I am about all the trouble I've caused you."

"So this is one of the secrets you've been hiding from me?" Jonathan asked, glancing her way. "That your mother was a showgirl?"

Ciara nodded. "Yes, I was ashamed of her lifestyle and the way I grew up. I didn't want you to know about my past."

"Because you thought I'd judge you?" Jonathan asked, turning her chin and forcing her to look at him. "Do you really think that little of me? You must really think I'm a snob."

Ciara shook her head. "No. Of course not, Jonathan. I know you wouldn't judge me, but the press will, as well as your family." She was sure they were wringing their hands in despair at the disgrace her presence had brought to their family and Jonathan's campaign.

He grabbed Ciara by the shoulders. "I don't care about them, Ciara. I care about you. Don't you realize that by now?" he asked, searching her face. Jonathan spoke straight from his heart and he hoped Ciara could hear him. "Haven't I proven to you that I'm not going to walk away? That you can trust me. And then you don't even tell me about your promotion? How do you think that makes me feel?"

At his heartfelt plea, tears sprang up in Ciara's eyes. "I…" She was so flustered she couldn't speak. It was the first time in her life that someone had gone out on a limb for her. He was willing to risk everything to be with her? "I'm sorry," were the only words she could manage to say. What else was there? That she had no trust or faith in him?

"Ciara, you hurt me."

"I know and I'm sorry," she apologized. "This is all my fault."

"I don't blame you for your mother's lifestyle," Jonathan replied. "How can I? That was her choice. You were a child, for goodness' sake. I can only blame you for your actions and for not feeling that you can trust me."

"So I suppose you want to break up with me now?" Ciara asked, even though she already knew the answer. It was better they walk away now before things got even more serious. Although she'd come to care for Jonathan deeply, she was suicide for his campaign. Because of him, her career was thriving, but the same could not be said for his.

"Why would you think that?" Jonathan asked, frustrated. "Once again, you're selling me short, Ciara."

"I…I guess trust doesn't come that easy to me," Ciara responded.

"No kidding," Jonathan replied. What more would it take to convince her of his sincerity? "Why don't we take it from the top, okay? Because you haven't mentioned the other secret you've been keeping?"

"That my mother's been living with me and my sister moved out. You mean that secret?" Ciara supplied.

"For starters," Jonathan responded. "Is there anything else that you want to tell me?"

Ciara quickly shook her head. "No, that's it. I've no more secrets."

"Are you telling me the truth?" Jonathan asked. Because if he found out there was another secret, there would be no forgiveness.

Ciara nodded.

"Then, I believe you," he said, lowering his lips to hers. "No, make that I want to believe you, and to prove it I want you to come away with me, Ciara."

"What?" She was confused. Running away was the last thing they needed to do.

"My parents have a villa in Aruba. Let's go away for a few days and relax. Get away from all this negativity."

Ciara smiled hesitantly. A few days of fun in the sun did sound marvelous.

"How about it?" Jonathan asked as his brown eyes grew wide with excitement. "Imagine you and me swimming in clear blue waters and making love underneath the stars."

"Sounds marvelous, but I can't afford to leave now. I just started as weekend anchor. Can we go during the week?"

"Absolutely," Jonathan replied evenly. "I need some time away, Ciara, from all this drama."

"Then, let's do it." She leaped into his arms and he nearly fell off the bench.

"Great," Jonathan replied. "I'll set it up for next week."

Chapter 10

Aruba was the most beautiful place Ciara had ever seen. It was so peaceful and serene, they could forget about the potential pitfalls that lay ahead at home. The sun was shining brightly and the sky was so clear and blue that a cloud could not be seen on the horizon. As she stepped out of the limousine in front of the secluded villa at Arashi Beach, Ciara thought she had died and gone to heaven. It was every bit as luxurious as Jonathan had described.

"It's beautiful, Jonathan," she said, stepping onto the marble floor as the driver brought in their bags. The villa was bright, open and airy. The decorator had chosen cool shades to complement the cold marble, while the gourmet-style kitchen was top of the line:

stainless-steel appliances, maple cabinets and granite countertops.

Jonathan whispered something to the driver before handing him a tip.

"What are you up to?" Ciara asked, trying to read his mind.

"It's a surprise," Jonathan replied. "For later."

"I can't wait." She smiled.

Jonathan grinned knowingly. He had an exquisite romantic getaway planned for them.

"C'mon, wait until you see the view." He grabbed her hand and rushed her outside. A panoramic view of the white sandy beach greeted her from the large terrace. A tiki hut-style roof covered a portion of the terrace so she could cool off after several laps in the grand swimming pool that was surrounded by a tropical garden.

"It's lovely, Jonathan," Ciara sighed.

"Welcome to paradise," he replied, pulling her toward him and capturing her lips with his mouth.

"Hmmm," she moaned aloud.

"There's more where that came from," he stated.

"And this is all ours?" she asked when he released her.

"Yes," he answered. "My dad wanted a place he could come and turn off his phone, hide from the world and romance my mother." His parents had been none too pleased when he'd informed them that Ciara wasn't going anywhere and that he was whisking her off to their favorite getaway for some much needed R & R.

"He certainly found an oasis," Ciara said. "Who maintains it?"

"We have some locals who keep an eye on things when we or family or friends aren't using it. The maid service stocked up the refrigerator and will come in and tidy up every other day. There's a washer and dryer, too, if you need to do any laundry," Jonathan said as they came back inside by the living room entrance.

"Sounds like you thought of everything."

"Yes, I did." Jonathan's mouth curved into a smile. They stared at each other for a long minute before springing into action. Jonathan tilted her face upward and captured her lips. He kissed her again and again, letting his lips linger and coax a response from her. He cherished her mouth until her emotions swarmed and she clung to him for balance.

When he caught her bottom lip between his teeth, her lips parted to allow him to slip his cool tongue inside her mouth. He could kiss her forever and never tire.

Ciara moaned at the sweet intrusion and arched her body against his. When he lifted his head and withdrew his lips, his breathing was irregular and his eyes were clouded with passion. An electric tingle shot through her body and she wanted him. Right then and there.

She turned in his arms and sought his mouth again. She penetrated it with a deep thrust of her tongue until she felt a slight bulge in Jonathan's slacks. When her hands caressed his narrow hips and washboard-flat abs, Jonathan could barely stand the exquisite torture and ground himself against her.

They were both casually dressed in clothes that were

easily removed—Jonathan in linen pants and shirt, and Ciara in a halter sundress and sandals. She trembled as he loosened her dress straps and drew them down her shoulders. Her dress fell in a puddle to the floor. Her breasts spilled out of their restraints, leaving her bare-breasted and wearing bikini panties.

Jonathan sucked in a deep breath. Ciara's breasts were beautiful. So beautiful, he had to have a taste. Bending his head, he kissed the long column of her throat and the valley between her breasts. He drew one nipple into his mouth and suckled and then turned his attention to the other. He lavished the chocolate nipple with hot, wet kisses.

Ciara moaned and curled her fingers through his thick wavy hair. "Jonathan—" she called out to him, but he silenced her by crouching in front of her and, using his thumb, he unhooked her panties and slid them down her legs. She stepped out of them and he tossed them aside. He kissed her thighs and then those feminine curls between her legs.

"Ciara." He whispered her name and she parted her legs, opening up to him freely. He touched the exotic bud at her center with his tongue and worshipped her with his mouth. She moved and writhed against him, and when she wildly cried out loud, Jonathan felt exalted by her moans. Her surrender was glorious and the feel of her wet heat almost made him come. When he finally lifted his mouth, she was weak in the knees.

He rose to his feet, gathered her in his arms and headed over to the master bedroom. He swept back the comforter with one arm before gently laying Ciara on the bed. He clasped her face in his hands and kissed her mouth, her brow, her eyes and her nose, then returned to her full lips.

"Please, Jonathan," she pleaded with him to take her on a journey. "I can't stand it anymore, Jonathan," Ciara whimpered. "I want you inside me."

"I'll be right back," he said, rising from the bed. He was gone for what seemed several long torturous minutes before returning with protection. Swiftly, he placed a condom over his engorged shaft and then he was back in place as if he'd never left. His mouth was everywhere, kissing her lips, and his teeth grazed the curve of her jaw. His large hands roamed over her hips before curving over the generous swell of her bottom. He tugged her closer against his chest.

When she parted her lips, he licked them and traced the soft contours before slipping his tongue inside her mouth and savoring her sweetness. And when she thought she would die of wanting him, he slowly and deeply thrust into her silken heat, pulled back and then thrust in again. Ciara grabbed his biceps, holding on to him for dear life. He complied with her urgent demands and Ciara violently climaxed. Jonathan soon followed as several spasmodic aftershocks overtook his body.

The intensity of their climaxes left them both gasping for breath, bathed in sweat and spent. They fell asleep and later awoke in the cocoon of each other's arms.

Ciara rose on one elbow and stared down at

Jonathan. "I'm starved," she said. When he didn't answer, she ran her fingers over his dark curls. "Aren't you?" she asked.

"Hmmm," Jonathan groaned and stretched out. "I'm hungry for other things."

"And I thought I was insatiable," Ciara commented, kissing his hairless chest.

Jonathan pressed his lips against hers and stroked his tongue with hers. When she mimicked the lazy strokes of his tongue with her mouth, she could feel the resurgence of his arousal from beneath the sheets.

"Down, boy. You've got to give me a minute to catch my breath," Ciara sighed.

"How about a shower and dinner?" Jonathan suggested. "I know a fabulous place. Chez Mathilde has excellent cuisine with a Caribbean flair. I think you'll love it."

Ciara threw back the covers and jumped out of bed. Unashamedly, she started toward the master bath. "Sounds marvelous. Count me in."

Ciara used the spare bathroom adjacent to the master suite while Jonathan used the master suite. She wanted to look hot and sexy for him tonight, so she donned a gold lace halter dress and slipped on a pair of jewel-heeled sandals.

She swept her hair up in a loose ponytail and curled several tendrils along the side of her face. She added a pair of gold chandelier earrings and matching necklace to complete her look. When she was ready, she opened the door and found Jonathan leaning against the wall waiting for her.

"My, my," she said. "You sure do clean up nice." He was wearing a pair of white trousers and a peach polo shirt. He looked hot and smelled even better. The aftershave he wore tickled her nose.

"You're one to talk," Jonathan replied. "There are no words." Ciara looked like a Greek goddess in gold. The dress had an empire waist; it was formfitting and clung to her hips while the deep V gave him a tantalizing view of the swell of her breasts.

"I think it's time we left," he said. Otherwise, he'd be backing her up into the room and making sweet love to her all night long and they'd never leave the villa.

"Good idea," Ciara replied, taking his outstretched arm.

Jonathan had arranged for the limousine to return and take them to Chez Mathilde.

"Chez Mathilde is one of the oldest nineteenth-century residences still in existence today," he explained on the way to the restaurant. "In 1986, the restaurant was restored to its original architecture, based on Anna Mathilda Oduber's last dying wish. The restaurant is over 115 years old."

"Wow, that's some legacy," Ciara said. Seeing that Diamond had spent all of Paul Williams' money, Ciara doubted she'd be passing anything of value on to her, while she was sure Pilar would get the majority of her father's holdings.

Fifteen minutes later, they walked into Chez Mathilde without a reservation and were seated within a few minutes.

"How did you manage that?" she asked as they followed their host to a cozy table in the corner. Chez Mathilde was obviously a fine-dining restaurant.

"I have my ways," Jonathan responded as he helped her into the chair. The host seated them and went back to his post.

While they perused their menus, their waiter came and gave them a rundown of their wine selection. Jonathan chose the house white wine to accompany her Dover sole à la Meunière and his crispy duck breast. What followed was an impressive French five-course meal, the first of which was tuna tartar, followed by a delicious lobster tartlet filled with garlic butter, sautéed lobster tail and goat cream cheese.

When her entrée arrived, Ciara's mouth watered. The Dover sole sautéed in butter and topped with lemon was filleted at their table and served with roasted tomato, garlic sautéed spinach and herb boiled potatoes. Jonathan's entrée was even more extravagant. His crispy duck breast was served with passion fruit sage sauce, morels, sweet potato, Belgian endives and leeks.

After such an elaborate feast, when Jonathan suggested a moonlit stroll down the beach on the drive back to the villa, Ciara was more than on board. She could use the exercise after that fine French meal.

When the limo dropped them off in front of the villa, they walked around to the gate for their private access to the beach. Depositing their shoes, they strolled along the dark, moonlit beach. The shore was secluded. They were the sole lovebirds enjoying the warm night and cool breeze off the ocean. Quietly, they walked along, hand in hand.

The rush of waves against the sand and the full moon above were incredibly romantic. At some point during their stroll, when Jonathan abruptly stopped and turned to face Ciara, her heart leaped. She stroked his cleft chin and looked deep into his brown eyes.

His dark eyes searched her face and he looked as if he was on the verge of saying something profound, but instead, he merely bent down and brushed his full sensuous lips against hers.

"Let's go back to the villa," Jonathan rasped huskily. Back at the house, they quickly disposed of their clothes. Soon they were back in the king-size bed, making love in the moonlight.

Two days later, Jonathan arranged an outing for them after they had spent the previous day relaxing at the pool, cooking and making love all day.

"Yeah? What is it?" Ciara asked excitedly as the chauffeur drove them to Eagle Beach.

"Horseback riding," Jonathan answered.

"I've never been," Ciara replied. "Can't it be dangerous?" Her mind instantly traveled to actor Christopher Reeve.

Jonathan smiled. "There's nothing to worry about, baby. Horses are harmless. You'll see. It'll be a lot of fun."

And so it was. They joined several other tourists on the beach for an afternoon ride. Her horse, Princess, a beautiful palomino, was gentle and easy to maneuver.

Jonathan handled his black stallion like a seasoned jockey. When the hour and a half drew near its end, the tour guide allowed them to lead the horses into a full-blown gallop. With the wind blowing in her hair and the blue sky overhead, Ciara had never had so much fun. When they returned to the stables and dismounted, Ciara told Jonathan as much.

"Thank you, Jonathan. That was so much fun," she said, her face flushed with excitement.

"Glad you enjoyed it," he said. "But I'm afraid since you're not used to riding you're going to be sore tomorrow."

"Horses aren't the only animals I've ridden," Ciara said, lowering her voice so only Jonathan could hear.

"Ah yes, but this is different," he stated. "Trust me. I've arranged for us to have some spa treatments at the Bucuti Resort later this afternoon before dinner. How does a massage, facial and pedicure sound to you?"

"Like a taste of heaven," Ciara replied. She stopped suddenly and sat on a nearby bench. "But you've done so much for me, Jonathan. What can I do for you?" she asked, staring up at him. "I feel like you're being short-changed in this arrangement." She bit into her waffle cone.

"Just your being here with me is enough, Ciara," Jonathan replied, coming to sit beside her. "I wouldn't want to share this time with anyone else, okay?"

Ciara nodded in return. "Neither would I." The three-day break had been blissful and she didn't want it to end.

"Then, let's enjoy it and forget about tomorrow."

Jonathan stood and pulled her to her feet. "Tomorrow can wait."

The Bucuti Resort was for the wealthy and the privileged. Lush green landscaping, tropical plants and turquoise waters on a powder-white beach was the backdrop for their romantic afternoon. Bucuti lived up to its reputation.

Jonathan enjoyed watching Ciara's broad grin as she took in her luxurious surroundings. What she didn't know was that they were staying there after a candle-light dinner on the beach.

The Intermezzo Spa was located in a facility separate from the beachfront hotel, Ciara and Jonathan discovered as they walked through the pristine white sand and the palm tree-fringed pathway to the spa. When they arrived, their hostess greeted them and showed them to the locker room, so they could change out of their clothes into an Intermezzo robe and slippers.

"I invite you to have a Vichy Shower or dip in our Jacuzzi before your massage," she offered.

After they'd showered, Jonathan and Ciara met up with their masseur and masseuse for a couple's massage on the veranda. Unembarrassed, they each removed their robes and lay down on the massage table. Jonathan would be treated to a female masseuse, while Ciara would get the royal treatment by a male masseur. While they situated themselves, the masseur turned on some soothing nature music.

The moment the masseur laid his warm hands on Ciara's back and she heard the crashing of the surf in the background, she thought she had died and gone to heaven. She immediately closed her eyes and enjoyed the delicious sensation. The masseur knew the right amount of pressure and kneading to apply to achieve maximum relaxation. He started at her feet, but steadily moved his way up her legs, back, shoulders and neck. As he worked his magic, Ciara couldn't help but imagine that it was Jonathan's hand that was doing the kneading, and instead of stopping at her legs, he would work his way up her thighs.

Then she heard a moan. Was it hers? Had the masseur heard her? She popped open her eyes and looked over at Jonathan. That was when she realized where the moan had come from. His eyes were shut, but the masseuse was pounding his back with her fists, and the man was eating it up with a spoon. Ciara couldn't help but chuckle, which caused Jonathan to open one eye.

"What are you smiling at?" he whispered.

"Nothing, hot stuff." She gave him a wink.

When the hour was up, they finished their spa afternoon at Intermezzo with a signature facial and spa pedicure. Afterward, Ciara felt like putty. A potter could easily mold her into whatever shape they wished. When she was done dressing, she met up with Jonathan in the lobby.

She'd changed into a print chiffon dress with spaghetti straps and sandals. She left her hair straight and only bumped the ends with a curling iron.

Jonathan had changed into a lightweight cream-colored suit and a crisp peach shirt. "You look beautiful," he said, before handing her a scarf. "Put this on."

"Why?" Ciara inquired. She looked at him suspiciously. "Where are you taking me?"

"It's a surprise," Jonathan said, wrapping the scarf around her eyes. "And no peeking. Just trust me to lead the way."

Ciara was not used to trusting any man, but with Jonathan she felt safe and secure. She didn't have to worry. He was her safe harbor in a storm. He would always look out for her.

He took her by the hand and they walked for several minutes through the sand. Were they going back the same way they'd come? Ciara wondered underneath the scarf. She didn't have a clue.

Jonathan stopped several minutes later and removed the scarf, allowing Ciara to adjust her eyes to her surroundings. And what a sight it was.

On a secluded portion of the beach, laid out in the middle of the powder-fine sand, was a table set for two with a bucket of champagne chilling. The brilliant hues of a yellow, orange and lavender sunset was their backdrop.

"This is so romantic, Jonathan." Ciara was speechless. No one had ever treated her this well. Made her feel so appreciated. So wanted. So loved. Loved? Was Jonathan in love with her? His actions certainly indicated those feelings, but Ciara was afraid to believe them because then she'd have to acknowledge her own feelings.

"C'mon." Jonathan took her hand and helped her into her chair. He joined her while the waiter popped open their bottle of champagne. The waiter poured generously and handed them each a flute.

"Bonbini," he said.

"Bonbini," Jonathan returned. He gave the waiter a tip and he quickly scurried off into the distance. "Madame," Jonathan said, bowing ceremoniously. "To our last supper in Aruba." They clinked glasses and sipped their champagne.

Then Jonathan pulled off two silver tops, and jumbo Caribbean shrimp cocktail and assorted garden greens awaited them.

"There's more underneath the table in the picnic basket," he admitted. Ciara glanced underneath the table and saw a basket. "There's a vegetable bouillabaisse, beef tenderloins with béarnaise sauce, and chocolate-covered strawberries for dessert."

"You thought of everything," Ciara said. "If I didn't know any better I'd think you were in love with me." The moment the words were out of her mouth, Ciara wished she could erase them, but it was too late. "I meant…" She tried to backpedal.

"It's okay." Jonathan grabbed her hand from across the table and held it in his. "Because you're right."

"What… What are you saying?" she stammered.

"Can't you tell by now, Ciara?" he asked. He finally said what he'd been dying to say. "I've fallen in love with you, Ciara. With your passion, your determination, your independence, your beauty. All of it. I didn't expect it and I sure wasn't looking for love, but there it is."

Ciara couldn't believe her ears. "You love me?" she asked. "How can you after all the madness I've put you through?"

"Because I do," Jonathan stated.

"Are you sure you don't want to take it back?" she asked. "Because you can, you know. I wouldn't hold it against you." She smiled nervously at him.

"I don't want to take it back because then I wouldn't be true to my heart," Jonathan replied. "You're an amazing woman and I love you."

"I don't know what to say."

"Well if the answer isn't obvious to you…" His voice trailed off.

Ciara looked across the table at Jonathan and knew he wanted her to say the words back to him, but she couldn't bring herself to. She'd never said those words to another soul, except maybe her family. So she said instead, "Jonathan, I'm very fond of you." That was the best she could muster in this awkward situation, so she reached for her champagne flute and quickly gulped the remaining contents.

Jonathan was disappointed that Ciara couldn't repeat the same sentiment, but he wouldn't force her. She would say it when she was ready. So, he put on a brave front and smiled, even though he was wounded. "And I'm fond of you. There's no other woman for me."

"And there's no other man I want but you, Jonathan Butler," she responded. And she meant every word. These past few days had shown her that she wasn't an unfeeling shrew. That she was capable of feeling real emotion. She was capable of falling in love and she had with Jonathan.

"Then, let's eat." And just as quickly, the moment was gone.

They dined on the feast Jonathan had ordered, and later, they had one more magical stroll along the beach before returning to their villa, where they made love until the wee hours of the morning.

Later, when Jonathan drifted off to sleep, Ciara was still awake. She couldn't relax because she was questioning why she hadn't admitted how she felt. She'd known for some time that she was falling in love with him, but why were the words so hard to say? Tonight on the beach would have been the perfect moment, but she'd chickened out. She promised herself that next time, when the right moment came, she would tell him she loved him.

"Are you ready to go back?" Ciara asked on the flight to Philadelphia.

"No, not really," Jonathan said, "but we couldn't stay away forever." He'd enjoyed the time away in paradise and not having to worry about what curve was right around the corner. The time away with Ciara had shown him that she was an important part of his life. As a matter of fact, he could see Ciara as a permanent fixture in his life. She was everything he wanted in a woman. Beautiful. Smart. Sophisticated. Sexy. Independent. Brave. A real firecracker. He doubted he would ever find someone as rare as her.

"No, we can't. We have lives. An election. And our families to get back to." Ciara immediately thought of Diamond and hoped in her short absence that her mother had stayed clear of trouble. "Don't worry. Everything is going to be all right." Ciara gave Jonathan a reassuring pat on the knee. Or so she hoped.

Chapter 11

It was one of the last warm days of summer, the Saturday afternoon of Jonathan's softball game, or so the weatherman predicted. They'd been back for a week and it was back to the old routine. During their brief absence, Zach had sprung into action and engineered the event, including a full-court press. And surprisingly, Zach had invited Ciara's station, WTCF, in on the festivities—probably no doubt to show Shannon that Jonathan had nothing to hide. Suspiciously enough, every time Ciara was at the studio, the television director was MIA. She can't hide for long, thought Ciara.

Instead, she focused on what she could change, and to that effect, she sportily dressed in a sleeveless gray jersey and low-rise shorts that matched Jonathan's team's uniforms. She would cheer for her man with pom-poms while distracting the opposition with her skimpy outfit. His team consisted of a few close friends and associates while the opposing team was composed of several aldermen for the city of Philadelphia.

He looked devastatingly handsome as usual, but Ciara's mind couldn't stop focusing on his tight rear end. The standard gray uniform did little to hide his broad, deep chest and firm buttocks. Instead, it enhanced his sex appeal.

"Jonathan sure looks good," Rachel said at Ciara's side while nibbling on a pretzel.

"What was that?" Ciara asked, bringing herself back to the present. When she'd extended the invitation to Rachel, she hadn't been sure she'd accept. It was the first time they had hung out in weeks since Rachel had moved out. Ciara appreciated that Rachel was supporting her despite their difference of opinion.

"Looks like someone is in deep," Rachel chided, wiping her mouth when she was done. She'd never seen the love-struck look on her sister's face before. Ciara was a private person who rarely portrayed her innermost feelings. But since dating Jonathan Butler, Ciara had been completely different. More open. She even stayed the night at his penthouse.

"Love—no." Ciara shook her head. "Lust—absolutely. My man can really fill out a pair of pants."

Rachel blushed and inwardly smiled at Ciara's clever change of topic.

"It's so good to see you, sis." Ciara squeezed her

sibling's shoulders. "You really don't have to be a stranger."

"As long as Diamond's in the picture," Rachel replied, "I'll keep my distance. But it's good to see you, too. You have such an active social life with dinner parties and fund-raisers, not to mention Aruba."

"How did you know about that?"

"I called the apartment looking for you and Diamond told me you and Jonathan had escaped to paradise. Was it everything you expected?"

Ciara's thoughts immediately went to skinny-dipping in the clear turquoise ocean, the moonlit walks on the beach and making love until daybreak. "You've no idea," she commented.

"So, what's next for the two of you?"

Ciara didn't have time to answer because Jonathan ran up the bleachers and gave her a gigantic bear hug. "What was that for?"

"Have I told you recently what a great idea this was? With this turnout and the food." He swept his arm across the bleachers. He'd just hit a home run and was drenched in sweat, but Ciara didn't mind one bit. "Zach was able to procure free uniforms, softball equipment and free food, so we've raised several thousand dollars."

Ciara smiled. She'd known Jonathan would be great, a natural team leader because he excelled at everything he did. The softball game allowed him the opportunity to showcase himself in a different light to the press: an everyday man. The kind of man the average person could relate to.

"I knew you could do it, baby." Ciara laughed at Jonathan's enthusiasm. He'd forgotten all about the troubles before they'd left and looked truly happy.

"I'm curious to hear what other ideas you have," Jonathan said, "but I have to get back out there." With that, he went running back to the field.

"I'll be cheering you on!" Ciara shouted.

And cheer she did. She shook her fanny in front of the opposition and couldn't help but notice the pitcher's obvious infatuation. It worked to Jonathan's advantage because he threw an easy pitch, landing Jonathan another home run. When the teams stopped after the fourth inning for a break, she and several other wives did a short cheer for Jonathan's team, with Ciara completing several backflips and cartwheels.

She could hear whistles and catcalls as she went to the refreshment stand for a cool drink.

"I never knew you were so limber, my dear," Dominique Butler said disdainfully, sipping on her bottle of Evian. She didn't like the effect Ciara Miller had on her son.

Ciara swiftly turned around. She'd been waiting for Mrs. Butler's fangs to come out. Outwardly, she'd appeared cordial and polite, but Dominique was transparent and Ciara could tell Dominique Butler did not approve of her one bit.

"Well, there are many things I'm good at," Ciara replied.

"I bet," Dominique snapped. "Probably as good as your mother, I presume?"

That was a low blow.

Ciara maintained her composure, despite an overriding desire to haul off and smack the woman, but she stopped herself. This was Jonathan's mother after all.

"That's right," Ciara returned. "And you can bet Jonathan loves every minute of it." She spun on her heel and walked away, leaving Dominique aghast at the implication. Ciara would not be afraid of that broad. It would take more than the likes of her to make her crumble.

"Everything okay?" Rachel asked when she noted Ciara's flushed expression.

"Oh, just fine, just fine," Ciara said, returning her attention to the game.

Two hours later, Jonathan's team emerged the victors, winning eight to six. Ciara couldn't wait to celebrate later back at his place.

She waited as Jonathan went through a round of photographs with reporters. He'd treated them all to free hot dogs and soda to soften some of them up and it appeared to be working because Jonathan was sharing several laughs with the press. He'd even taken time out to take pictures and sign autographs with children and several members of the community. When he was done, he came and swept her off her feet, twirling her around in the air.

"Baby, you were great!" Ciara said, laughing uncontrollably. "Now put me down, before you make a scene." The press was already snapping photographs of them.

Jonathan lowered her to the ground. "Are you ready to go? Because I could use a hot—" he glanced at

Ciara's tight fanny in those low-rise shorts that snugly cupped her bottom "—no, make that a *cold* shower."

"Let's get out of here," Ciara said, pulling him toward the car.

Across the parking lot, Reid sat in his Mercedes fuming. His plan hadn't worked. Butler was flying high all because of that Miller woman. He'd thought that telecast would have neutralized her. Sullied her in Butler's eyes, but the man was besotted, led around by another part of the anatomy. Now, things were going to have to get ugly.

When Ciara returned home after leaving Jonathan's that afternoon, the sight that greeted her made Ciara's blood boil. Diamond had filled their living room with several shopping bags from Macy's. Had she used all the money that Ciara had given her?

"Diamond, what have you done?" Ciara shouted.

"Oh, I just had myself a little shopping spree," Diamond said, holding up a blouse.

"Where did you get the money?"

"Oh, c'mon, Ci-Ci. What's wrong with a little something nice every now and again?"

"I asked you where you got the money." Ciara was beyond annoyed.

"Oh, that," Diamond replied. "Well, I used the credit card on the top of your bureau."

"Diamond! How dare you use my credit card without asking me?" Ciara was exasperated. Perhaps it was time they parted ways. "When will you ever learn, Diamond? Why must you always go to the extremes? I brought you here. Let you live with me. Ran away my own sister and this is how you treat me?" Ciara shook her head in amazement.

"What have I done wrong?" Diamond asked, fingering her new outfits. She didn't understand why Ciara was making a big deal out of a few purchases.

"You've taken advantage of my kindness, time and time again," Ciara replied. "And I've had enough, Diamond."

On cue, Diamond turned on the waterworks. "You know I'm destitute," she replied. "How can you treat your mama this way?"

"I could ask you the same question, Diamond," Ciara replied. "How can you treat your daughter this way? When is enough enough? Why do you continue to test me?"

Diamond didn't care for Ciara's tone. "I'm not a child, Ciara."

"Then stop acting like one," she returned. "Grow up. And start looking after yourself and stop waiting for handouts."

"I'm not waiting for handouts," Diamond replied. "Is it too much to ask to expect one's daughter to help you after you've taken care of them for years, put food on the table and clothes on your back? It wasn't easy being a single parent, you know."

"Oh, please." Ciara didn't fall for that line. "Daddy always gave you money for me."

"Yeah, he did, but it was never enough!" Diamond stated. "Pilar hated me and the thought of my daughter having more than hers was too much for her to handle."

"So you're accusing Daddy of being a deadbeat father?"

"No, more like a patsy. Robert's been ruled around by Pilar for years and you know it."

Ciara paused. Diamond did have a point. Pilar most certainly ruled the Miller roost. As a teenager, she and Pilar had not gotten along, but over the years, they'd each gained a mutual respect for one another. But no matter her father's faults, Diamond had no right to continually abuse Ciara's kindness.

"Fine." Ciara conceded the point. "Daddy's no angel, but then again neither are you." As much as she wanted to cut Diamond loose, she couldn't put her mother out on the street.

"So, from now on, no more extra cash. You can continue to live here. Rent's free until you find a job. Agreed?"

Diamond thought about her options. She didn't really have much choice but to go along with whatever Ciara had in mind. "Agreed."

Several days later, Ciara finally caught up to Shannon in the studio as she prepared for the evening's broadcast.

When Shannon saw her, she tried to scurry out of the room, but Ciara yelled at her, grabbing everyone's attention.

"Shannon!"

Ciara rose from behind the set desk and rushed across the studio. "You're a hard woman to track down," she said, coming face-to-face with the woman who was systematically trying to ruin her reputation.

"I've been busy," Shannon replied shortly.

"So I'd heard. A word please." Ciara motioned toward the offices off the studio floor.

Shannon glanced at her watch. "You have a show in an hour that you ought to prepare for."

"That can wait," Ciara returned. "You and I have some long-overdue business to attend to." Ciara walked ahead of her and when Shannon didn't follow, Ciara turned and glared at her.

"My office," Shannon stated, brushing past Ciara.

She followed Shannon into the lion's den.

"So, what's this all about?" Shannon asked.

"You know very well what this is about. You and I had a deal," Ciara stated. "No more stories on me. And in return I'd keep WTCF in the loop on the campaign trail. And no sooner than we shake hands on it, you—" Ciara pointed at Shannon "—stab me in the back and run a hideously inaccurate story that my mother is some showgirl turned prostitute."

Shannon smiled. "WTCF said no such thing."

"No. But you damn well implied it!" Ciara's voice rose.

"And you have lost your objectivity," Shannon returned. "You are no longer impartial where Jonathan Butler is concerned. You've fallen for him and everyone can see it."

"You're wrong," Ciara lied. She could spit nails over the fact that Shannon saw right through her.

"If you say so," Shannon replied. "We received a tip about damaging information related to Jonathan Butler and we ran with it. He is a public figure after all, which means he's fair game."

"My mother is not fair game."

"She is because she's related to you," Shannon replied. "And you, my dear, are tied to Jonathan Butler's hip, which makes you and anyone who associates with you fair game as well."

"You're evil!" Ciara snapped.

"No!" Shannon replied. "Just practical. And you should be happy. Ratings for your broadcast are up twenty percent over Monica's show. I would say that all that bad press is certainly working in your favor. Everyone can't wait to turn on WTCF to see the infamous Ciara Miller."

"Oh!" Ciara fumed and stormed out of Shannon's office. She'd intended to read the woman the riot act, but instead she'd been run out of her office on a rail. Part of her was angry, but the other was secretly overjoyed. Could ratings really be up? Perhaps evening anchor was not out of her reach?

Later that evening, Ciara met up with Zach at Jonathan's campaign headquarters. Everyone else had gone and they were the only two people in the building.

"I was surprised when I received your call," Zach said as he locked the door behind Ciara.

"Why? Are you suspicious of all reporters?" she inquired, throwing her purse over her shoulder.

"Usually, yes," Zach answered honestly and walked toward the back of the office.

"But…?" she asked as she followed him.

Zach turned around. "I don't know." He rubbed his chin. "Something about you is just different. You know, genuine. Jonathan's not the only one who can see it."

Ciara smiled. "Thank you, Zach. I appreciate your faith in me. I know it's not shared by Jonathan's family. Which is why I'm here for some polishing up." Initially, she'd balked when the media consultant had tried to tell her how to act, but she'd had a change of heart. She was determined not to be a liability to Jonathan's campaign.

"Don't worry about them," Zach said, leading her into the conference room. "Charles is a teddy bear. Now, Dominique, she's a barracuda, but Jonathan's clipped her fangs and given her very little power in his campaign."

"Could be why she's so cranky," Ciara replied. "So," she said, pulling a notepad out of her briefcase, "what are you going to teach me?"

"First, we need to go over some of the issues Jonathan is focusing on," Zach said. He walked over to the credenza and pulled out several campaign brochures from the drawers. He threw them on the table. "You need to be able to give a sound bite at a moment's notice. Plus, we'll go over some general tips on how to behave with the press."

"I am the press."

"Yes, but it's not the same." Zach sat down beside her. "Now you're on the other side."

"I suppose you're right. So what do you suggest?"

"First off—dress conservatively in black, brown and navy. A smart suit with a below-the-knee skirt and pumps would be in order," Zach advised.

"Are you saying I dress too sexy?" Ciara queried.

He glanced at her current ensemble of vintage-print wrap dress and stiletto-heel black boots that fit her calves like a glove. "Do zebras have stripes?"

Ciara chuckled. "Touché."

Zach gave her several more pointers over the next hour, until Ciara changed the subject from fashion to careers. She couldn't contain her natural curiosity for discovering the unknown. She was curious to find out more about him. It was the reporter in her.

"So how did you get into politics, Zach?" Ciara asked.

"Well, I found that I loved the high-stakes gamble of politics," he answered. "Even more I realized I had a knack for winning. It started when I played sports and carried over into my professional life."

"I'm sure you have some juicy stories to tell." She grinned mischievously.

"I do, but they are best left a mystery," Zach said.

Ciara understood. In his profession, he could never be too careful. She rose. "Thank you, Zach, for all your help. I'm going to put your advice to work at the Firemen's Fund speech."

"Excellent idea. Show the press you're committed to Jonathan's campaign. Maybe it'll squash all the negativity surrounding you."

"Zach, you have to know that I had no idea WTCF would run with that story on my mother. She has always been a source of embarrassment for me. Not so much that she was a showgirl, but that she married Paul Williams and then squandered his money."

"It's okay." Zach patted her shoulder. "Jonathan doesn't blame you. He knows you would have never purposely run a story that would hurt your own mother. The man is crazy about you."

Ciara grinned from ear to ear.

"Ah, and from the looks of it, so are you," Zach said. Ciara didn't answer, but Zach knew. Despite her hard-nosed exterior, her love for Jonathan was written all over Ciara's face.

"Thanks again, Zach," she said, grabbing her briefcase and purse. "I'll see you at the speech."

"Your numbers are solid," Zach told Jonathan several days later over breakfast.

Jonathan breathed a sigh of relief. "So, the negative publicity hasn't hurt me?"

"Not thus far," Zach commented, sipping his mug of black coffee, "but you can't afford any more bad press because the next time, there'll be no stopping the bleeding."

"I think the softball game and my speech the other day at the Firemen's Fund helped show the community that I'm a man of the people and not just some playboy out to score the next big thing."

Zach agreed. He thought Jonathan had done an excellent job. Ciara had been in attendance as well and had fielded several questions gracefully. He was proud of her and had told her so.

"And we have to continue to build on that," Zach commented. "Like landing some high-profile endorsements."

"Set up some meetings," Jonathan replied.

"Sure thing." Zach jotted down several notes on his legal pad.

"Guess who I had a meeting with a few days ago?" Zach teased.

Jonathan furrowed his brow. He had no idea who it could be. "I don't know. Who was your mystery guest?"

"Your girlfriend, Ciara Miller."

"What?" Zach was confused. Why would Ciara want to meet with his campaign manager?

"She wanted some tips on etiquette on how to handle herself with the press."

"Why?" Jonathan was puzzled.

"Well, she doesn't want to be an embarrassment to you or your family."

"She could never do that," Jonathan stated unequivocally. "She's just as polished as I am. And articulate. She's an anchor."

"That's all fine and good, but clearly she has some underlying insecurities. Perhaps you should reassure her," Zach suggested.

"I don't know how much more I can reassure her. I told her I loved her." Jonathan didn't mind sharing his feelings with Zach. He was one of the few people Jonathan could confide in. He sure couldn't tell his parents.

"Love?" Zach inquired. "You admitted you loved her? When did you say that?"

"In Aruba."

"And how did she respond?"

"She said she was fond of me, but didn't mention love," Jonathan replied.

"Maybe she's gun-shy," Zach offered. "Give her time. She'll come around."

Jonathan sure hoped he was right because he was crazy in love with her.

The Labor Day parade went as planned. Jonathan made his appearance with the mayor and several aldermen. He stopped and shook hands with residents of his district and discussed the pressing issues facing Philadelphia County.

The weather was mild, so Ciara wore navy slacks, a teal camisole and matching wraparound cardigan with sleek peephole pumps. She had hoped to be standing by her man in a sophisticated Dior suit, but Shannon had made it clear that Ciara's presence at the parade would be in an official capacity as reporter for WTCF. Although she now anchored the weekend news, Shannon still expected her to cover the political beat a few times a week and since Ciara had made an unholy alliance with her to keep WTCF in the forefront, she had no choice but to do as she was told.

"I told you about making deals with the devil," Lance warned.

Ciara put up her right hand. "Please, no *I told you so.*" She already knew that Shannon could not be trusted. She just had no idea what else she had up her sleeve.

Ciara caught up with Jonathan after the parade. His parents and Zach had long since left and

Jonathan was still networking and talking to several constituents or supporters. When he was finished, he joined her by the WTCF van.

"Sorry I couldn't stand by your side at the parade," Ciara said with a down-turned mouth.

"Baby." Jonathan leaned down and kissed her full on the lips. "It's okay. Just knowing you were here was enough."

"Hmmm, you know exactly the right thing to say," Ciara murmured against his lips. They were so into each other that they didn't notice a swarm of reporters surrounding the WTCF van. Ciara noticed when several camera lights were shining directly on her.

"Guys, can you give us a minute, please?" Jonathan implored. He protected Ciara by standing in front of her and keeping the press at bay. "I promise I'll give you ten minutes later."

"We'd like to do that, Mr. Butler," one reporter said, "especially if you're willing to talk on the record about the allegations that WTCF just ran that your campaign manager, Zach Powers, could be involved with organized crime."

"Not again," Ciara groaned from behind Jonathan. The evil witch had struck again, but this time she and Jonathan weren't the target. Zach was.

A befuddled expression crossed Jonathan's face. "What are you talking about?"

"You mean you haven't heard?" Several reporters shouted at Jonathan all at once. "His former client, Senator Ken Hutcheson, was indicted earlier this morning by the grand jury for money laundering for the mob."

No sooner had the befuddled expression appeared on Jonathan's face than it was gone and replaced by a calm demeanor. He knew he couldn't let the press see him sweat, no matter what curveball they'd just thrown at him. "No, I hadn't heard," he returned.

"What does this mean for your campaign?" another reporter shouted.

"Are you going to keep Mr. Powers on?"

For once in his life, Jonathan was ill prepared. Zach was his right hand and usually fielded questions on his behalf. What would he do without him? His father had warned him how malicious the press could be and now they had gone too far.

"I…" Jonathan paused.

Ciara glanced at him. She saw how torn he was, so she stepped forward and spoke up on his behalf. "Mr. Butler has no comment on the indictment charges or the alleged accusations against his campaign manager," Ciara announced.

"Ms. Miller, are you speaking for Mr. Butler now?" one of her colleagues asked.

"Right now, I am speaking as Mr. Butler's friend," Ciara responded, squeezing Jonathan's hand. "He has no comment at this time. If you'll excuse us?"

Ciara turned her back to the press. The reporters took the hint and slowly began to disperse.

Jonathan breathed a sigh of relief. "Thank you, Ciara." He shook his head. "I don't know what happened. I couldn't get the words out."

"Probably shock," Ciara said.

"I don't know about Senator Hutcheson, but Zach is an honorable man. Above reproach."

"You know that," Ciara replied, "and I know that." She thought of Zach taking time out to help her. "But the press doesn't. They are just reporting the facts."

"So you agree with them ruining his reputation and dragging his name through the dirt, all in the name of truth?" Jonathan asked with his arms folded across his chest. He was disgusted at the thought.

Ciara didn't care for Jonathan's sarcastic tone, but dismissed it. He was upset, so she would let him have his say.

"No, I don't agree. But Zach, like you and I, is in the public eye and therefore subject to speculation."

"After what they've done to you?" Jonathan queried. "How can you possibly say that?"

"Jonathan." Ciara pulled on his blazer, so he could lean down and hear her. "Can we discuss this someplace else?"

Although the press had dispersed, several reporters were still across the street watching them and waiting. For what, Ciara didn't know, but she didn't want to give them any ammunition.

"Fine," he huffed and started for his car.

"Wait." She halted him with a hand on his arm. "Are we still on for dinner?"

"I don't know," Jonathan replied. "Right now, I have to do some damage control. I'll let you know."

"Okay." Ciara tried to mask her disappointment, but didn't do a very good job of hiding it. "Call me," she said to his retreating form. Once again, her station had caused trouble for his campaign. Was he upset with her? Did he blame her for what was going on with Zach?

"Is everything okay?" Lance asked from the sidelines. When he'd seen the press coming, he'd immediately hidden in his truck. He'd been afraid to get out for fear they'd start barraging him with questions. He preferred to be on the other side of the camera. Once the coast was clear, he'd exited the van.

"No," Ciara answered honestly. "Lance, everything is far from okay. In fact, it's falling apart. Ever since I met Jonathan, trouble has followed."

"Ciara, it's not your fault," Lance defended her. "You're not the one who ran these stories."

"No, but I am the reason Shannon is so obsessed with his campaign."

"I disagree," Lance replied. "Shannon is obsessed with ratings and with anyone who will help her achieve that goal."

"Why does that person have to be Jonathan?"

Lance shrugged. "Your guess is as good as mine. And if you knew, what could you do?"

"I don't know," Ciara replied, "but somehow I have to find a way to help Jonathan." Because if she didn't neutralize Shannon, their relationship did not stand a chance.

Chapter 12

Jonathan dialed Zach's number on the way to his car. He put on his earpiece and kicked his Lexus into gear. He quickly maneuvered the streets of downtown Philly on his way to the office.

"I already know," Zach said, answering his cell on the first ring.

Jonathan asked, "What's going on, Zach?" When he realized his speed, he slowed down. He couldn't afford to get pulled over for a speeding ticket.

"Senator Hutcheson, whose campaign I ran, was indicted by the grand jury today and now the press is speculating that I may have laundered money on his behalf. You know that's not true, Jonathan."

"Of course I do," Jonathan replied. He'd never

thought otherwise, but the timing of this stank to holy heaven! First, the attack on him and Ciara, and then her mother and now Zach. Someone was trying to ruin his campaign—but who? "We need to meet."

"I couldn't agree with you more," Zach said. "I'm already on it. Your parents and the consultant are on their way. We'll meet you at headquarters in thirty."

When Jonathan hung up, his first instinct was to call Ciara and apologize for his rude behavior, but he didn't. He was crazy about her, but he had nagging doubts. Why was WTCF always the station running negative stories on his campaign? What about his opponent? For some reason, he was the single focus. Why? Was Ciara involved in some way?

He sure hoped not. Ciara was always the one encouraging him and giving him advice. She wouldn't sabotage the very thing he'd worked so hard for. He just couldn't be that bad a judge of character. And as for Zach, well, Jonathan knew the allegations were a lie, but unfortunately his campaign couldn't continue like this or he'd lose for sure. Something had to give.

When he arrived, his parents, the media consultant and Zach were already in the conference room.

"This isn't good, son," Charles Butler began. "A connection with the mob will sink this campaign if Ms. Miller's presence hasn't already done it."

"Leave Ciara out of this," Jonathan replied. "She has no place here."

"Like hell she doesn't." Dominique Butler jumped up from her chair. "From the moment you met that woman, she's been nothing but a blight on your campaign. Rid yourself of her and you will heal your campaign."

"That's easier said than done, Mrs. Butler," Zach piped in. "The damage has already been done. The citizens of Philadelphia are going to wonder if I'm involved with the mob."

"But it is a lie," Jonathan said emphatically.

"Why hasn't anyone mentioned the fact that this story came from WTCF again?" Reid inquired. "They've been one step ahead of every other station in the city. And why is that, I wonder?"

Jonathan hated that Reid was verbalizing his fears, and he paced the floor.

Reid continued. "Ciara Miller has benefited from all of your bad press. She's now anchoring the weekend news. Not to mention the fact that her station has been number one in ratings for the last few weeks."

"It's true," Zach admitted. "WTCF's numbers have steadily risen over the last couple of months. But…"

"And didn't you meet with Ciara Miller a couple of weeks ago?" Reid asked.

"How did you know that?" Zach and Jonathan both asked in unison.

"It's my job as your adviser to know what's going on."

Jonathan didn't buy Reid's routine one bit. He knew he wasn't his biggest fan, so he highly doubted Reid would be looking out for his best interest.

"So why did you meet with Ms. Miller?" Reid pressed Zach.

"Why do you want to know?" Zach asked. He'd promised Ciara he'd keep their meeting a secret and he intended to do that. If nothing else, he was a man of his word even if the press didn't agree.

"Why?" Dominique jumped into the fray. "Why? Because that woman could have used you to bring down my son's career, that's what."

"That's ridiculous, Mother. You sound like Ciara has a conspiracy against me and I just don't believe that," Jonathan spoke up.

"Then you're blind," she returned.

"It's plausible, isn't it?" Reid asked. "That she met with Zach to pump him for information, trying to gain leverage for her station or perhaps she's been working for your opponent this entire time."

"You're wrong about Ciara," Zach said. "And that's all I'm going to say on the subject."

"Zach, you've known Jonathan for years," Dominique continued. "You're his best friend. How can you put that woman's image above my son's?"

"Stop ganging up on Zach," Jonathan yelled, silencing everyone in the room.

Reid sat back in his seat. So, Jonathan had no idea who was pulling the strings? Reid smiled inwardly. Well, he had one more final maneuver and they'd never see it coming.

"Why do you persist on sweeping Ciara's motives under the rug?" Reid said. "You realize you do so at your own risk."

"Is that a threat, Reid?" Jonathan queried, coming forward and staring Reid in the eye.

"Why would you think that?" Charles Butler replied. He was always Reid's staunchest supporter. "Of course it isn't."

"Charles, you don't have to speak for me." Reid plastered a smile on his face and rose from his seat. "I'm capable of standing up for myself."

"I know that," Charles said, "but my son is forgetting everything you've done for this family."

"I've forgotten no such thing," Jonathan replied. He didn't like his father's condescending tone.

"Why don't we all call it a day and regroup in the morning?" Zach said. "Clearly nothing will be solved today."

"That's a splendid idea, Zach." Charles Butler patted his shoulder. "You must know that no one in this family believes these false accusations."

"Thank you, sir." Zach shook the senior Butler's hand before they departed.

Ciara tossed and turned the entire night. She couldn't sleep because Jonathan wasn't beside her. She'd gotten used to sleeping over at Jonathan's place and her bed felt empty without him. More than that, her body ached; she yearned for his hard, firm body beside her.

She'd fallen helplessly in love with Jonathan Butler and he didn't even know it. She'd wanted to say those three little words in Aruba, but she hadn't had the heart. She'd felt like a fool. Instead, she'd said nothing and let the moment pass her by.

And now she wished she had revealed her true

feelings. Tonight, she'd picked up the phone nearly half a dozen times to call him, but put it back in the cradle. He hadn't called for dinner either. Was Jonathan starting to believe the hype? Was his family finally wearing him down? They'd probably convinced him that she was the devil incarnate and out to destroy him.

Several days passed and things went from bad to worse for Jonathan. WTCF was constantly rerunning the story, even though they had no new news to report. His opponent, Alec Marshall, was attacking his character. Ciara was MIA. But the worst was having the authorities come and question Zach at his headquarters.

As much as he wanted to get involved, Jonathan had to stay impartial and let the D.A. do his job. He couldn't be linked to some kind of cover-up, so instead he'd shut the door to his office and waited. Once the district attorney had gone, Jonathan headed to Zach's office.

"Zach, are you thinking what I'm thinking?" Jonathan asked, closing Zach's door.

"If you're thinking sabotage," Zach said, "then the answer is yes."

"Someone is out for my blood," Jonathan replied, pacing the floor. "First the story on me and Ciara and when that didn't work they went after Ciara's past and now this." Jonathan pounded his fist against the table. "Accusations that you're involved with the mob? Zach, we have to figure out who's behind this."

"First things first. I need to resign from your campaign," Zach stated matter-of-factly. He handed Jonathan a piece of stationery.

"What's this?"

"It's my letter of resignation."

"No," Jonathan replied and handed the letter back to Zach. "I will not give in to this maniac. Whoever he or she is."

"Jonathan, you're being really pigheaded," Zach replied. "When you announced your campaign, you were in the lead. Way ahead of Marshall in the polls. And now Marshall is gaining momentum. If you continue this stance, you will lose. I guarantee it."

Jonathan shook his head. "I just can't believe it's come to this."

"You have to cut me loose," Zach replied emphatically and handed him the letter again. He was under no illusions. He knew about winning campaigns and right now he was a liability.

"All right, all right," Jonathan conceded the issue. There was no way around it. The press had only speculated about Ciara's youth, but the idea of financial impropriety? He couldn't handle that. It just burned Jonathan to no end that he wouldn't be able to work with his best friend. Zach was the best in the business and whoever had it out for him was sullying Zach's good name in the process.

"I think you need to make a list of your enemies," Zach began. "Anyone that might have it out for you. Give it to me and I'll investigate. Strictly behind the scenes, of course. Can't have anyone thinking we're still working together. Matter of fact, you need to publicly fire me."

"In front of everyone." Jonathan nodded. "So you

think that whoever is behind these stories is someone I know?"

"Yes."

"Well, it would certainly throw them off track and…"

"And give us time to figure out exactly who the culprit is," Zach finished.

"Gotcha," Jonathan said, opening the door and raising his voice loud enough for the entire office to hear. "Get out, Zach!" Jonathan yelled. He watched several volunteer workers look in his direction, so Jonathan gave them a good show. If one of them was sabotaging him, he needed to be convincing. "I don't know what kind of shady dealings you're into, but I run a clean campaign."

"Jonathan, I'm your friend. You know I would never do anything to jeopardize your campaign." Zach walked toward the door and shouted back at him.

"I wish I could I believe that," Jonathan replied. "But I'm afraid I can't take that chance, Zach. I need you to pack your things and leave."

"If that's how you want it." Zach played along and lowered his head. Several pairs of eyes watched Zach as he went back to his office and packed up his belongings. Jonathan stood at the doorway to Zach's room and watched his best friend leave the building. How had everything gone so horribly wrong? And what was he going to do to fix it?

When Jonathan showed up to Ciara's apartment that evening with a bouquet of roses, he met her mother, Diamond Miller, for the first time.

"So you're the reason my past was spread all over the news," Diamond said from the doorway with her hands on her hips. She was wearing tight hot pants and a strapless tube top.

Jonathan knew she'd been a Las Vegas showgirl, yet he hadn't expected this. With big red hair, false eyelashes and bright lipstick, Diamond Miller was as loud as they came.

"Afraid so." Jonathan lowered his lashes. What could he say? The election had turned unbearably ugly. "May I come in?"

"Why?" Diamond asked, still holding the door in her hand. "I don't believe my daughter has heard one word from you in days and now you show up with flowers in hand as if all is forgiven?" Diamond had seen how Ciara had moped about the last few days because this joker hadn't called. She did not appreciate him stringing her daughter along. If he was going to break up with her, better to pull the Band-Aid off quickly rather than slowly.

"Ms. Miller, it has been a hectic four days," Jonathan admitted. "And I'm sorry if Ciara was upset. But I really need to talk to her."

Instead of getting caught up in the brouhaha, he'd decided to take a few days and evaluate the situation, which was what he did best. As a lawyer, planning and forethought was everything. He'd been in court many times, but now as he stood in the living room nervously waiting for Ciara while Diamond Miller stared at him over the rim of her Scotch glass, that experience did little to alleviate his anxiety.

Ciara was upset that he hadn't returned her phone calls. He'd been trying to salvage what was left of his campaign, but would she understand that? Perhaps she, too, realized that he had some residual doubt where she was concerned? His parents' and Reid's opinion were starting to gain validity.

On the other side of her bedroom door, Ciara let Jonathan sweat. Why should she come out and throw herself into his arms even though that was exactly what she wanted to do? She'd left several messages for him and he hadn't returned them. He'd totally ignored her, as if she didn't exist. Perhaps that was how he wanted it. So, she would go out there and play it cool and let him talk.

After a few minutes, Ciara finally appeared, casually dressed in a tank top and gaucho pants.

"Ciara." Jonathan's face instantly brightened when she walked into the room. Was that a good sign?

"Hey," she said from the doorway.

Jonathan attempted a smile. "I've missed you. I brought these for you." He handed her the flowers.

"Ummpph," Ciara replied, accepting the bouquet. Jonathan didn't seem to notice her less-than-enthusiastic response.

"So much is going on, Ciara," Jonathan began. "I think that someone is out to get me and so help anyone who's near me and gets in their path."

"So my daughter is in danger?" Diamond asked from the couch. "'Cause if so, buddy, you're not worth the trouble."

"Mom, please." Ciara motioned for Diamond to go

to her room. "Could you give us a minute?" But Diamond didn't budge.

Jonathan sucked in his breath. He was in no mood to get a lecture from Diamond Miller about putting Ciara's life in jeopardy. She was one to preach. From what he'd heard, she'd disrupted her life plenty enough. Present, case in point, but instead of saying how he truly felt, he did the respectable thing. "I understand your frustration, Ms. Miller. It matches my own. And I assure you I'm going to put a stop to this sabotage."

After she heard Jonathan's speech, Diamond finally left them alone.

"Maybe I can help?" Ciara replied. "All my resources are at your disposal. Such as they are." Ciara sat down and Jonathan joined her.

"No, no." Jonathan shook his head. "I need to do this on my own."

"I see." Ciara folded her arms across her chest. So he didn't want her help. Or maybe he just didn't trust her.

"Ciara, it's not like that." Jonathan reached out and grasped her hand in his, but she resisted. "Please don't be upset with me."

"Jonathan." Ciara tried to move away, but Jonathan kept a firm hold on her.

"Ciara, I had to fire Zach."

"What!" Ciara jerked away. "How could you, Jonathan? Zach is your best friend. Have you no loyalty?"

"Of course I have loyalty," Jonathan snapped, pulling his hand away. He was almost insulted that she thought otherwise.

Ciara realized how harsh she sounded and apologized. "I'm sorry, Jonathan, but you're letting all of this get to you."

"In case you haven't noticed, my image is already tarnished, Ciara. I can't afford the appearance of impropriety. Zach offered and it had to be done. At least until we find out who's responsible. Any ideas?"

"Well…" Ciara rubbed her chin. The first person that came to mind was Reid Hamilton, but he was a trusted family friend. He would never betray the Butlers, would he? She would have to do some digging before she made an accusation like that. Otherwise, she'd incur the Butlers' wrath.

"No, but there has to be someone you've ticked off in the past."

"I've racked my brain and I can't think of anyone." Jonathan shrugged. "I've always tried to be honest. You know, treat people fairly. I just don't understand, Ciara, why someone would have it out for me." Jonathan hung his head low.

"We'll find out who it is, Jonathan."

"I'm scared, Ciara." He took her delicate hands in his. "I can feel the election slipping away." It was the first time Ciara had heard defeat in his voice. Heard fear. He was usually so strong and powerful. So hopelessly optimistic.

"It's going to be all right." She squeezed his hand. She wasn't going to let him give up. "Listen to me, Jonathan." She grabbed his face in her hands. "You have what it takes to win, Jonathan. You've been groomed your whole life for this test. You can pass it."

"I don't know." Ciara heard the hesitation in his voice and it broke her heart.

"I feel like this is all my fault," she said. "If you had never started dating me, Shannon would have never gone after us and gotten fixated on you and none of this would have ever happened."

"If I'd never met you," Jonathan stated, capturing her gaze with his, "I'd have never known what it felt like to feel truly free to be myself. Ciara—" he cupped her chin to look at him "—because of you, I've felt more alive than I ever felt. My normal, boring, black-and-white life is now unpredictable and in Technicolor. I wouldn't trade that for anything."

"But look at all the upheaval I've brought to it," Ciara said.

"Upheaval I've needed," Jonathan returned. "I've always walked the straight and narrow, never veering from the path my family had chosen for me. Hell, without politics I don't even think I know who I am."

"Are you sure you want to win?" Ciara queried. Because to her it sounded as if he had doubts about the path his life was on.

That was a good question and it gave Jonathan several moments' pause. It was the first time someone had asked him if being a congressman was what he wanted. He guessed that was why he appreciated Ciara so; she didn't just tell him what he wanted to hear. She was always questioning him, making him think and reevaluate how he saw things.

"Of course I want to win," Jonathan answered finally. "It's all I know how to do."

"Listen, I know it might be scary, but perhaps politics isn't your calling. Maybe you should take some time to figure out what you want."

"Because I'm losing the election?" Jonathan said.

"No…"

"C'mon, Ciara, that's what you meant. And maybe if I lose, I'll take your advice, but until then—" he shook his head "—I can't accept failure."

"Then we will work together to fix this." She gave him a gentle squeeze. "We're a team. You'll see."

Although Ciara said all the right things, Jonathan wasn't so sure he believed her. He loved her but, try as he might, he couldn't erase the residual doubt creeping into his mind.

Chapter 13

"Lance, have you noticed anything different about Jonathan?" Ciara asked as they grabbed lunch at a local diner.

"Why? What do you mean?" Lance asked, perusing the menu.

"Did you see how he treated me earlier at the League of Women Voters' breakfast? He acted as if I was another reporter and not his girlfriend." She'd noticed he'd been distant.

"Well, it's good to see that you're finally admitting how much Butler means to you," Lance replied.

"Don't start," Ciara said. "I'll have the steak house chopped salad," she told waitress and returned back to her conversation with Lance. "It's just that he's been different the last week or so. Since he had to fire Zach, we've hardly seen each other and when we have, it's only been in a professional capacity. I'm starting to get the feeling he's avoiding me."

"I'm sure it's just your imagination," Lance replied evenly. "Didn't Jonathan tell you he loved you in Aruba?" When Ciara had gotten back from her trip, she'd talked of nothing else.

"Yes, but…"

"But what?" Lance queried. "Why are you looking for a reason to run? Can't you just accept that the man loves you and take that at face value?"

"I could," Ciara replied. "No, I should. You're right. It's probably just my imagination." She hoped her fears were unfounded.

Jonathan was exhausted. He'd had nearly half a dozen public appearances in the last week all in an effort to help his tarnished image. His opponent was steadily gaining ground in the polls and Jonathan was doing everything in his power to minimize it, but he was running out of time. He was so desperate, he'd allowed Reid to help him with the campaign and he had begun listening to his advice. Keep his relationship with Ciara out of the public eye. Focus on the issues. And that was exactly what he'd done, except that he could no longer avoid her. He'd promised he'd spend time with her later that evening.

He felt like such a heel, pretending that he was too busy to spend time with her. The problem was he was afraid Reid was right. It was too much of a coincidence

that her station somehow managed always to be the
first with breaking news concerning him or someone
connected to him. And although there had been a report
on Ciara's mother, that could merely have been a
smoke screen to cover up Ciara's true agenda. From
what he'd gathered, there was no love lost between
Ciara and her mother, so why wouldn't she throw her
to the wolves?

All those negative thoughts were playing havoc with
his mind. On the one hand, he knew he was head over
heels for Ciara; but on the other, he saw a woman desperate to be on top, after always being an afterthought
growing up. And so he'd kept his distance, choosing to
put his career over his social life, just as he suspected
Ciara had done. The only question was what would it cost
him?

"Are you sure you want me to attend the breast
cancer benefit?" Ciara asked Jonathan later that
evening when he finally stopped by her apartment.
She'd been anxious to see him. Their time together had
been limited of late. Ciara was thankful Diamond was
out on a night with the girls.

"Why would you say that?" Jonathan asked. "Of
course I want you to come."

"You haven't acted that way," Ciara replied. She
drew her legs up underneath her. Although he hadn't
said anything directly, she could feel Jonathan distanc-
ing himself from her. He hadn't asked her to accompany him to his last few public appearances. It was as
if he didn't want to be seen with her.

"I'm sorry, Ciara," Jonathan apologized. "That really wasn't my intention. I just needed to focus all my energies on the tasks at hand." Even as he said the words, Jonathan hated himself for being dishonest.

"Without me," Ciara added. "That's fine." She pressed her lips together in a straight line.

"Ciara," Jonathan admonished. He cupped her chin tenderly in his warm hand. "I love you. It's just that right now I'm under a great deal of stress."

"And I'd like to help you with that," Ciara replied. "Unless…" She paused. "You don't want my help?"

Jonathan didn't answer right away and Ciara had her answer. "So…you want my presence in your campaign to be minimal?"

"Ciara, I want you in my life."

"But not by your side," she finished.

Jonathan shook his head. "You're wrong," he said. "I want you by my side tomorrow night and, if I'm lucky, for the rest of my life."

"I don't know." Ciara shook her head.

She was unsure until he said, "I need you, Ciara."

She smiled. Those words were certainly welcoming, and she held them dear. "And I need you, Jonathan."

She stood up and pulled him to his feet. "Come with me," she said. She wanted to show him just how much she loved him even though she found the words hard to say aloud.

Once inside her bedroom, she slowly undressed and slid her naked body between the covers. "How about I cheer you up?" she asked, and reached for him.

"Hmmm, I'm kind of tired tonight, sweetheart,"

Jonathan replied, pulling off his tie. "Would you be terribly disappointed if I asked for a rain check?" He unbuckled his belt and dropped his trousers.

Ciara was puzzled. Since when did Jonathan turn down sex? He was always ready. "Well, no, I guess not." She shook her head in amazement. She reached for a gown on her nightstand and slipped it over her head. She never thought she'd have need for one with Jonathan.

When he was down to his briefs, he joined her in bed. "Good night, Ciara." He kissed her on the forehead, punched his pillow and turned over to his side, leaving Ciara feeling bereft and alone.

The night of the charity gala should have been all glitter and excitement, but Ciara felt particularly uneasy, especially after Jonathan wouldn't make love last night.

He arrived in a stretch limousine with his family to pick her up and take her to the benefit. Dominique was looking every bit the regal queen that she was while Charles Butler and Reid were dressed in tuxedos, but Jonathan was the only man she was interested in tonight. He looked dashingly handsome in a morning coat with tails. His hair had been clipped short in silky waves across his head.

Ciara was proud to stand by his side. She'd donned a one-shoulder silk chiffon gown and piled her hair high atop her head like a Greek goddess. Chelsea had done a wonderful job on her hair and makeup. Now, she looked every bit the sophisticated socialite she wanted to portray. Even though inside, she felt like a fraud. She'd never so much as tried on a dress that cost ten thousand dollars, let alone worn one.

When Jonathan had originally called and said he'd sent a package via courier, she'd had no idea what it could be. Shock had registered on her face when she'd opened the contents and it had revealed a Badgley Mischka original. She was extremely lucky to have a man like Jonathan in her life, which was why she was determined to tell him how she truly felt about him tonight. When it was just the two of them alone in bed together, she'd say the three little words she'd never been able to say to any other man. *I love you.* Perhaps it would ease the tension between them if he knew how crazy in love with him she was.

"Are you all right?" Jonathan asked, peering down at Ciara once they were seated in the limo. She had a strange look on her face.

"Oh, I'm all right," she said, snapping out of her daydream. "I'm just enjoying my surroundings. Thank you for asking me."

"You don't have to thank me," Jonathan replied. "There's no place I'd rather be than here with you." Ciara's heart skipped a beat at his sweet words. Perhaps she'd been judging him too harshly.

The rest of the evening was much like others they'd attended together. Politics. Drinking and socializing. Ciara was happy when it was finally time to take their seats and for the first course to come out.

They were midway through their desserts when Ciara excused herself to go to the restroom to powder her nose. She was on her way to the back to the ballroom when she spotted Shannon walking down the hall toward her with a news team.

Ciara had a sick feeling in the pit of her stomach that Shannon was up to no good. "Shannon, what are you doing here?" Ciara asked.

"There's a breaking news story here and WTCF is the station to deliver it."

"What are you talking about?" Ciara queried. "This is a charity benefit. There's no wrongdoing going on here."

"You're out of the loop, Miller," Shannon retorted.

"Then by all means, Shannon, why don't you fill me in?" Ciara said, grabbing Shannon's arm and pulling her off to the side.

"Fine." Shannon jerked her arm away. "WTCF received another tip. And this one is a doozy."

Ciara raised a brow. Yet another tip. This did not bode well for Jonathan. "What is it?"

"A source tells me that former Congressman Butler took illegal campaign donations."

"That's ludicrous," Ciara fired back.

"Our source is willing to provide us with detailed documentation to that effect."

"Documentation that could easily be manufactured. Do you have the proof with you?"

"Doesn't matter," Shannon replied. "I'm running with the story. And I'm going to call Charles Butler on it."

"In front of a roomful of influential people? That would be suicide for Jonathan's campaign," Ciara said. "Shannon, you can't do this."

"I can and I will," Shannon said, not backing down. "Matter of fact—" she paused "—I think you should deliver the final blow to the Butler campaign." Shannon handed her a microphone.

"I will not be a pawn in one of your twisted games." Ciara was tired of being made a fool of and pushed the microphone back toward her.

"Listen here, Miller." Shannon pointed her index finger at her. "You either get in there and confront Butler with this information—" she poked Ciara's shoulder "—or start looking for another job."

"Let me get this straight," Ciara replied. "If I don't do your dirty work and ambush my man, I'm fired? Are you insane?"

"No, I'm very serious."

"Well, let me tell you something, Shannon." Ciara circled around her. "Take your best shot. I have an ironclad contract. So, if you want to fire me, I'll see you in court."

"Fine! I'll do it myself."

"No, you will not." Ciara tried to block her path, but Shannon pushed past her, knocking Ciara off her feet.

"No, Shannon," Ciara yelled. Quickly, she rose from the floor, brushed off her dress and rushed toward the ballroom. She couldn't let Shannon hurt Jonathan.

Charging after her, Ciara burst through the ballroom doors. Jonathan had already stepped to the podium. As he looked out over the crowd and saw Ciara, he smiled. He was so lucky to have the woman he loved at his side tonight. Perhaps he'd been wrong to have doubts. Tonight, he was sure he'd seen love in her eyes.

Across the room, Ciara felt far from lucky. Shannon was already heading toward the stage with her cameraman in tow. "Mr. Butler!" Shannon yelled across the room.

Startled, Jonathan looked out over the crowd, trying to find the owner of the voice. Buoyed, Shannon stalked across the room.

As soon as he saw the WTCF logo, Jonathan cringed. "May I help you?" he said, trying to remain calm even though he had a terrible sense of foreboding in the pit of his stomach.

"Jonathan, don't say a word," Dominique Butler whispered in his ear as she jumped up out of her chair. Even in a Donna Karan dress, Dominique was a mother barracuda. "It's an ambush. I told you that Miller was behind all this."

Shannon continued loudly enough for everyone to hear. "A source close to the Butler campaign has alleged that your father took illegal campaign contributions while in office. What do you have to say about those allegations?"

Jonathan's face turned as white as a ghost. "That's a lie!" he shouted down at her. "My father is a man of honor, of integrity."

Shannon smiled. Butler was clearly unhinged by the allegations, so she moved in for the kill. She reached in her oversize purse and pulled out a folder. "Then how can you explain these?" She held up the folder.

From where Ciara was standing, the folder appeared to have damning evidence, and Shannon was running with it even though she hadn't received the information. Everyone was on their feet, all trying to get a view of the evidence, so Ciara had to push her way through the crowd.

"These would say otherwise," Shannon insisted.

"You, shut your mouth!" Jonathan roared across the stage. "I will not have you spreading lies about my father. Now, you take your news crew and get out of here. This is a private party."

"Thank you, Mr. Butler." Shannon smiled broadly. "You've just given me my sound bite."

Turning on her heel, she sashayed across the room, leaving chaos in her wake.

Jonathan's eyes traveled around the ballroom and landed on Ciara. The absolute contempt in his icy glare caused goose bumps to form on her bare arms. Surely, he couldn't believe that she had anything to do with this? After everything they meant to each other? No, no, he couldn't. Ciara rushed toward him.

When she finally made it to the stage, Jonathan, Reid and his parents were already huddled in conference while the other guests whispered among themselves about what to make of the latest tantalizing bit of gossip.

"It's over for Butler now," Ciara heard one man say.

"His cake is baked."

Ciara could only hope that was not the case.

"Jonathan," Ciara whispered up to him.

He turned and glanced at her momentarily before returning to his huddle. After several excruciating minutes, he returned, calm and poised, to the microphone.

"Ladies, gentlemen," he began. "I apologize for the disruption. Many of you know our family and have a long-standing relationship with us, which is why we know all of you will stand behind us as we get down to the bottom of these unfounded charges. That being said, I would like to return everyone's attention back to the cause at hand and that is breast-cancer research."

Jonathan continued the speech he'd intended to make, even though his heart was breaking. Ciara, meanwhile, removed herself to the sidelines. She would wait for a convenient time to speak with him after his speech.

Many of his supporters came to Jonathan's aid afterward and offered their support and assistance in disputing the charges, but Jonathan could hear none of it. All he could think about was the woman leaning against the wall, staring back at him with those beautiful hazel eyes, and how she'd completely betrayed him. She'd bewitched him with those eyes and that body until he'd been oblivious to what was happening right under his very nose.

Reid and his mother were both trying to calm his father down, who was extremely agitated by the unsettling accusations. This was the last thing his father needed. It was exactly the kind of stress he'd wanted to avoid by resigning from office. How could Ciara be so ruthless? So heartless?

Jonathan vowed from that moment to have nothing more to do with such a vile human being. Someone who valued ambition and her career above all else. Even above him? He guessed he was a convenient distraction. Or more like a means to an end.

Jonathan and his mother helped his father to the door. Charles was shaken up, to say the least. To have his good name soiled was beyond unbelievable. Reid was such a great help and it was the first time Jonathan appreciated his father's right-hand man. He knew the exact words to say to comfort his old man and Jonathan was thankful. Perhaps he had misjudged Reid. He and everyone else had sure been hip to Ciara's manipulation, while he'd had blinders on. He supposed love did make you blind.

Reid arranged for a car to pick them up in the alley to avoid the press, who were sure to descend like vultures, Jonathan had come to learn. They were leaving out of the side door, ready for a fast exit, when Ciara approached.

"Jonathan, we need to talk." She stopped him by touching his sleeve, but he backed away.

"I think you've done enough," Reid said as he led the Butlers out the door.

"What she needs to do is stay away from my son and our entire family," Dominique threw over her shoulder.

Ciara knew they held her responsible, but the venom in their tone made her blood chill.

"I agree with my family," Jonathan responded. His face was a glowering mask of rage. "You and I have nothing left to say."

"Jonathan, you must know that I had nothing to do with Shannon's stunt." Ciara implored him with her eyes.

"Why would I know that, Ciara?" he wondered aloud, turning to face her. "WTCF has done nothing but hurt me, my family and those closest to me." Raw pain glittered in his eyes.

"You weren't alone. Shannon came after me and my mother."

"How convenient," Jonathan replied, his eyes stony with anger. "C'mon, Ciara, why don't you admit that was merely a smoke screen for your true intentions?"

Every cold word Jonathan said was like a knife in her heart, but Ciara remained strong. She'd survived growing up with Diamond; she could survive this moment and the hate spewing out of his mouth. "And what were my true intentions, since you seem to know it all?" she asked sarcastically as a cold knot formed in her stomach. "What's my crime?"

"To get ahead," Jonathan replied evenly. He clapped his hands and applauded her. "You gave an Academy Award performance, complete with using yourself as bait. But I guess that comes honestly, seeing who raised you."

Before she even realized it, her right hand rose as if to slap him, but Jonathan caught it in his large hand. "How dare you say something like that to me? I don't deserve that from you, Jonathan. I've never given you a reason to doubt me." Tears streamed down Ciara's cheeks. "You know I would never hurt your family."

"I thought I knew you, Ciara, but I've come to realize that I don't know you at all." Jonathan kept his emotions in check. "It's all smoke and mirrors with you, isn't it?" he asked rhetorically. "And blind fool that I was, I fell for it. Even when you didn't tell me you loved me back. Because I believed you were scared and just needed to be loved and that in time you would say the words back. How wrong was I?"

"You weren't wrong, Jonathan," Ciara cried. "I do love you. I love you more than I thought possible."

"Ah, now you say you love me?" Jonathan laughed derisively. "When the stakes are high? Quite frankly, I don't think you're capable of telling the truth, even if your life depended on it. You're a woman of no morals and lacking in values and who uses people for her own advantage. And you know what? I'm done." Jonathan turned his back on her and reached for the door.

Ciara's face grew hot with humiliation. "Why are you doing this? How can you possibly throw my love for you right back in my face as if it meant nothing?"

"Because your love is worthless, meaningless." He spat out the words contemptuously. "Go find yourself another sucker," he said and stormed away.

"Jonathan, please!" Ciara cried out to him, but she didn't chase after him. She had too much pride and dignity to run after a man who thought so lowly of her.

Devastated, she slowly found her way downstairs to the lobby. The hotel doorman thankfully hailed her a cab and she was back in the safety of her own home within twenty minutes. On the drive home, Ciara realized she'd lost the only man she'd ever loved. Jonathan was gone forever. He believed she'd single-handedly sabotaged his campaign to get ahead. When the fact was her career could very well be over this minute if Shannon had anything to say about it.

When she turned the key in the lock, all Ciara

wanted to do was get under the covers and hide. She
felt bereft and desolate and struggled to choke back the
anguish that threatened to overtake her. When she
flicked on the light switch, she found her apartment in
utter chaos. Pizza cartons and beer cans littered her sofa
and cocktail table while various pieces of clothing were
strewn across the floor.

"Diamond!" Ciara growled and furiously kicked
empty beer cans on the floor. Even when she'd been
growing up, Diamond could never keep house. Ciara
had always had to pick up after her. "Diamond!" she
yelled. Where was her slob of a mother?

Ciara bent down and was picking up beer cans when
she found a pair of men's boxers. Surely Diamond
hadn't brought some strange man back to her apartment? She wouldn't go that far, would she? Glancing
around the room, Ciara had her answer.

She stormed over to Diamond's bedroom door and
banged on it. "Diamond, open up!" she shouted. When
there was no answer, Ciara turned the knob and burst
inside. She was disgusted by what greeted her. Diamond in bed with her ex, Vince.

"Ugh! What are you doing, Diamond?"

"Ci-Ci, honey, I didn't expect you," Diamond said,
pulling a sheet up to her chin. "Vince, cover yourself!"
She patted his flat behind. Vince pulled a sheet over his
naked form.

"Clearly," Ciara replied, turning her head. "Why do
you always do this? Why do you always shoot yourself
in the foot?" Ciara had reached her limit. "I tried to help
you. Give you a place to stay and you throw it back in

my face? I've had it, Diamond!" Ciara stalked from the room. "You're out!"

"Ciara, wait!" Diamond pulled the sheet around her, tucked it between her bosom and followed her daughter to the living room.

"Please don't be angry with me."

"I can't deal with you right now," Ciara said, heading to the kitchen. She opened up the fridge and pulled out a bottle of water.

"Why? What happened tonight, honey?" Diamond asked.

"As if I would want to confide in you," Ciara replied haughtily. "You've never been any kind of mother to me, so why should now be any different?" She took out her pain over Jonathan on Diamond. "I've never felt I had your love or that you ever wanted me at all. I was always an unpleasant inconvenience and you never let me forget it."

"That's not true, Ciara." Diamond used her given name. "I always loved you, wanted you. I just didn't know how to raise you. I know I wasn't a good mother, but I'm here now and if you want to talk to me and tell me what happened, I'll listen."

"You wouldn't understand," Ciara sniffed.

"Try me."

She thought about that for a moment. What did she have to lose? Now that Vince was back in the picture, Diamond wouldn't be sticking around for long. She would do what she did best and that was leave. "Fine." Ciara pulled out a chair and sat down.

"Give me a few minutes to put some clothes on and

I'll be right out." Diamond returned several minutes later but not before Ciara heard her whispering to Vince and saw the front door close.

"So, what did that politician do to my baby?" Diamond asked, reaching for her pack of Newports and lighting one.

Ciara didn't even care that she was smoking in the apartment because it symbolized her entire life going up in flames. First her job and then Jonathan. "He kicked me to the curb," Ciara replied. "He cast me aside like…" Her voice caught in her throat and she gasped for breath. Her chest felt as if it would burst. "Like… like I was yesterday's trash."

"Why would he do that? He's done nothing but stand by your side despite everything."

"Because this time, Shannon went too far. She didn't just attack him or me." Ciara patted her chest. "She attacked his father. The man Jonathan respects the most. Hell, idolizes. Worships. And she did this in front of everyone at the gala."

"I see." Diamond blew out a puff of smoke.

"No, it's worse," Ciara continued. "Mr. Butler's health has been poor. He has a heart condition. He resigned from Congress to relieve his stress, not add to it."

"Ah." Understanding dawned on Diamond's face. "And now he thinks you had something to do with all this?"

"Yes." Ciara faced Diamond with wide-eyed wonder. "He believes that I let WTCF ambush him onstage. After everything we've been through. Why would he lose faith in me now?" Ciara shook her head and rocked herself. "I l-love him and he just threw it back in my face. I don't understand, Mama."

"I don't understand it either, baby doll." Diamond scooted closer and wrapped her arms around Ciara's shoulders. It had been a long time since her baby had called her Mama. "But it's going to be okay because you're a tough cookie, ya hear me? You've had a lot of knocks in life and still got up fighting and now will be no different."

"I wish I believed you," Ciara cried.

"Believe it," Diamond replied. "You're not like me, Ciara. You don't need a man to support you. You want a man who complements you. And if Jonathan isn't the one, then he's missing out."

Ciara turned and smiled. For being such a lousy mother, Diamond was giving a darn good imitation of one. "Thanks." Ciara hugged her. "But you do realize that despite your sage advice it's time for you to move out?"

Diamond nodded. "I know. I know."

"No hard feelings?" Ciara voice rose an octave.

"None, baby doll." Diamond kissed her cheek. "It's long overdue."

Chapter 14

Jonathan spent the night at his parents' home. He was in no mood to go back to an empty apartment, especially now that Ciara would no longer be there. The penthouse would hold too many memories of the many evenings they'd shared.

He awoke the next morning and padded downstairs on the plush Berber carpeting to the tiled cherrywood kitchen. He found his father at the breakfast table drinking a cup of coffee and reading the morning paper.

"How bad is it?" Jonathan inquired.

"You don't want to know," his father replied, folding the paper in half.

"You're taking it surprisingly well this morning," Jonathan said.

"Well, I had last night to mull it over and realized that perhaps we all might have overreacted."

"Overreacted? To Ciara ambushing us? I don't think so."

"Actually," Charles continued, "Ciara didn't ambush you. Wasn't it her television director?"

"Same difference." Jonathan pulled a mug from the cupboard and poured himself a cup of coffee from the carafe on the counter. When he was done, he joined his father at the table.

"Are you sure about that?"

"Dad, I've had a chance to think, too…and it all adds up. Ciara's the only person that has benefited from all this bad press."

"But the other woman went for your jugular. Do you really think the woman you're in love with would hurt you this way?"

"Honestly, I don't know, Dad." Jonathan couldn't say for sure. "Ciara's so ambitious. She wants so badly to be on top. I wouldn't put it past her." He'd seen her in her element at the station and had heard the hunger in her voice when she'd spoken of doing anything to reach the top. "I think if someone dangled the right carrot, I think she's capable of anything."

"I'm sorry to hear that, son. I know how much you care about her."

"It's more than that. I love her, Dad. I love her," Jonathan emphasized. "I'm just not sure I can trust her, which is why this hurts so badly."

"Then a relationship between you two would never

work. Trust is the foundation of any good relationship," Charles said.

"I couldn't agree with you more. That's why Ciara and I are over."

"Welcome back, sis." Ciara gave Rachel a big hug. "I've missed you."

She could sure use the company. Diamond had moved back in with Vince the day after Ciara had found them together, leaving Ciara alone with her thoughts and her memories.

She'd hoped that once the dust settled and Jonathan had time to analyze the situation, being that he was a rational man, he would realize he had overreacted and apologize, but that day had never come. So, she'd swallowed her pride and called him herself, but he'd refused each and every one of her calls. That was when it had dawned on her that he was truly gone.

She'd called in sick the last few days because she hadn't had the heart to go in and face the music. So, she'd stayed in her pajamas and hadn't eaten much in days. Who could have an appetite at a time like this?

"It looks like it," Rachel said, noting Ciara's unmade face, sweats and bare feet. "I've missed you, too." She dragged in her suitcase from the hall. "And my own place. As much as I love my parents, I missed being on my own."

"Are those all your suitcases?"

"Yes," Rachel huffed and shut the door. "So, what did Diamond do to get herself evicted?" she asked. "Because I know she had to do something."

Ciara had a flashback of Vince and her mother in

bed, and recoiled. No, she could never tell Rachel about that encounter or her sister might burn her bed. Instead, it would have to remain her and Diamond's little secret.

Ciara dismissed the notion. "No, it was just time. Diamond knew she had overstayed her welcome and decided to move on."

"I hope now you've learned your lesson where she's concerned."

"Actually, Diamond and I have come to an understanding," Ciara defended her wayward mother as she sat beside Rachel. "I admit that she's lazy, messy and a spendthrift, but Diamond's got a heart and you can never fault her for that."

"Then if it's not Diamond, then what is it?" Rachel asked. She could see that Ciara was obviously upset about something or someone.

"It's me and Jonathan. We're over," Ciara replied abruptly.

"No." Rachel was shocked. "I can't believe it. Everything was going so great between you. What happened?" she asked, tucking her feet underneath herself.

"Jonathan thinks I'm a liar and a cheat."

"What?" Rachel was confused. "How could he think that?"

"Because Shannon ambushed his family at a charity gala. Didn't you see the papers?"

"No, I've been at the library. I had several papers due," Rachel replied. "And the last thing I wanted to do was read a newspaper."

"Well, Shannon put on quite a show. She confronted

Jonathan with allegations that his father accepted illegal campaign contributions."

"No." Rachel was flabbergasted. "And what did you do?"

"I tried to stop her and she pushed me out of the way," Ciara replied. "By the time I got to the ballroom, ·the damage was already done. Rach, if you could have seen the look Jonathan gave me. It was a look of such disappointment and utter disgust. He truly thinks I set out to hurt him and his family."

"How could he think that?" Rachel asked. "You would never hurt his family. Let alone yourself and your own mother."

"I know that and you know that, but Jonathan seems to think otherwise. To him, I've gained the most from all of his misfortune."

"Then he really doesn't know you at all," Rachel replied. Rachel knew her sister better than most and she would never do the things Jonathan accused her of. "And you're better off without him."

"That may be true, but I can't let him think the worst of me. Even if we're through, I need to know the truth. I need to find out who's been sabotaging his campaign and our relationship in the process."

"Are you sure that's a good idea, sis?" Rachel inquired. "Because whoever this is sure isn't taking any prisoners."

"You may be right, but I have a sneaking suspicion we know the culprit." She'd had a nagging feeling from the get-go about Reid Hamilton; now she just needed the proof to back it up.

* * *

She returned to work the following day much to Shannon's chagrin, but she didn't come alone. Once she'd called her father and had told him what had happened, he'd insisted she take his lawyer and good friend Martin Bennett with her in case Shannon followed through on her threat to fire her.

Shannon was shocked when Ciara knocked on her door. Ciara didn't wait for a response; instead she stormed in with guns blazing.

"Excuse you!" Shannon stood up and then she noticed the man behind Ciara. "And who are you?"

"I am the attorney representing Ms. Miller."

"I see." Shannon sat back down.

"And just so there's no misunderstanding," Martin cut to the chase, "if there is a hint of termination on your part, Ms. Miller is prepared to sue this station for breach of contract."

Shannon laughed. "So, you're pulling out the heavy artillery, huh?" Shannon glanced at Ciara. "Well, in case you didn't read the contract, let me enlighten you. There is an ethics clause, which states that Ms. Miller must abide by journalistic integrity, which she failed to do by failing to confront her lover with damning information. I'd say her ill-conceived relationship with a congressional candidate is enough."

"And are you calling that clause into play?" the attorney asked. "Because if so, I assure you, we are prepared to go to the mat in court, so you'd better be able to prove my client acted unethically."

Shannon thought about it for a moment. She didn't

even have proof yet from her source, so she would have to back down. "I guess your client is free to continue her job for now."

"Ciara?" Martin turned to her.

"I'll be fine," Ciara replied. "I've learned to swim with sharks." Martin nodded and left the room. Once he did, Ciara turned to Shannon. "As you can see, Shannon, you haven't won and I'm still standing," she said, slamming the door behind her.

It reverberated long after she'd gone, leaving Shannon to wonder just how far Ciara would go to dig up the truth. Would she learn that Reid Hamilton was Shannon's informant? She would just have to make sure that didn't happen. Picking up the phone, she dialed Reid's number.

When Ciara returned to her desk, she immediately started dialing several colleagues, trying to learn if anyone else had heard allegations against Jonathan's father. Why hadn't she done this sooner? Why did it take her losing her man to seek answers? But after several phone calls, she came up empty. None of her colleagues knew or had heard anything.

They were all in shock that a television director had stumbled across what they, investigative reporters, had not. So, where was Shannon getting her information? Somehow, Ciara had to get into Shannon's office and see if she could find anything. But how? Shannon was dedicated and worked twelve-hour days. How was Ciara going to get in that office without her knowing? She would have to wait a few days and when Shannon least expected it, when she thought the pressure was off, Ciara would strike.

* * *

As he walked through the WMAU station doors, Jonathan did not look forward to the debate with his opponent. Alec Marshall would attack him not just on the issues, but about his personal life as well, from Ciara to Zach to his own father.

"Don't worry, Jonathan." Reid patted his shoulder. "You're prepared. You know the issues important to Philadelphia County." The golden boy was sweating, as he should be. Because of Reid, Jonathan was in the hot seat. With all the negative press surrounding his campaign, Reid was sure he was going to lose, but to cover his tracks, he'd graciously accepted Jonathan's offer to oversee his campaign after he'd fired Zach.

Reid would have liked to spit in his face and tell him exactly what to do with his job offer. When he'd wanted the job, Jonathan had scoffed and given it to that pretty boy Zach Powers, and now that he was faced with losing the election suddenly he needed his help? Oh no, Jonathan was due a comeuppance and Reid wanted a ringside seat.

"It's not that I don't know the issues," Jonathan said. "I've prepared endless hours for this debate, but you just never know what the other guy is going to throw at you. It's how Nixon lost the election. After his debate with Kennedy, the viewing public didn't trust him."

"You're far from Nixon," Reid said, stroking Jonathan's ego. "You're much more similar to Kennedy. You come from a political family of great social standing. You're handsome. Charismatic. Articulate. You're who the voters of Philadelphia want to see, not some middle-aged, balding commissioner."

"I hope you're right."

"Of course he's right," Dominique Butler said, coming beside him and kissing him on the cheek. "The voters will love you."

"Where's Dad?" Jonathan looked over her shoulder.

"He wasn't feeling well," his mother replied, a little too quickly.

He searched her face, but his mother looked away. "Why don't I believe you?"

"All right," Dominique came clean. "Your father felt it best he stay away and keep the focus on you and not him."

"He didn't have to do that." Jonathan wanted his father by his side.

"Don't worry, he's at home, cheering you on." Dominique squeezed his hand. "Now go. I think you need a little makeup. You're looking a little pale." Instead of radiant, his usual buttermilk complexion was looking rather pallid.

Jonathan allowed the makeup artist to put on a little pancake makeup while the sound tech checked the microphones at the podium. His opponent had arrived with his wife and children in tow, presenting the perfect family unit, while Jonathan stood alone, without his father or Ciara there to support him. He missed her terribly. He'd thought of her often over the last week and had hoped that things could be different, but alas, that was not to be. Ciara Miller was a woman out for number one and he had no place in her heart.

When the makeup artist finished, Jonathan walked away and paced the floor, desperate to clear the cobwebs and return his focus to the debate and not a certain golden-haired beauty. When the director announced it was time and asked both candidates to take their places, Jonathan smiled over at his mother, who stood along the sidelines with Reid. She was giving him an enthusiastic thumbs-up.

The debate began with brief statements by both candidates about the issues they felt were important to Philadelphia County. After that the moderator stepped in for an hour-long question-and-answer session with the audience. Initially, they debated the issues, but near the end, his opponent made a snarky comment about Jonathan's family in an effort to lure him into a personal debate, but he did not rise to the bait.

"You're a public figure, how can you not address these rumors?" his opponent asked.

"Because they are not relevant to the issues, Mr. Marshall. My father's campaign was simply that—his campaign. I am not responsible for my father or anyone else's actions except my own," Jonathan responded, facing the television camera.

"What about your own?" his opponent countered. "Hasn't your focus been on clubbing and women these days?"

The moderator stepped in and asked a question. "That brings us to a relevant question in this campaign. Where do we draw the line with the press? Because they have been a dominant presence throughout the campaign."

"I'm not afraid of the press looking into my family life," his opponent replied. "I'm a family man commit-

ted to my wife and children. Can he say the same?" His
opponent turned and glared at Jonathan.

Several television cameras focused their lenses on
Jonathan, waiting for his response. "Yes, I can," he
answered without missing a beat. "I am a man committed to my family—the Butler family that has served the
great people of Philadelphia for twenty-five years—and
I hope to continue that tradition."

From the other side of the TV screen, Ciara sat in-
tently, watching Jonathan. She was happy that he hadn't
allowed himself to be railroaded into discussing the allegations against his family or address his personal life.
He didn't flinch or appear uneasy. Instead, he focused
on the issues and, despite how he'd treated her, Ciara
was still immensely proud of him. He'd made his
opponent appear spiteful and vengeful instead of calm
and reasonable. She just hoped it would make a difference come election day in two weeks.

Relief washed over Jonathan when the debate was
over, and he poured himself a glass of water and drank
generously. He'd been afraid to take more than a sip
because he didn't want to appear as if he were avoiding
hot topics. All in all, it had gone well.

"Congratulations." Dominique smiled broadly. "You
did a wonderful job, Jonathan. You reminded the public
about your father's excellent service. He would be
proud."

"Time will tell, Mother. Time will tell."

Ciara hid out in her car until well after midnight,
waiting for Shannon and the ten o'clock evening crew

to leave. When she was sure the coast was clear, she entered the studio. Better to have no witnesses to her break-in attempt.

Quickly, Ciara walked to Shannon's office and turned the knob. It was locked. So, she had something to hide, did she? Well, Ciara knew a thing or two about picking locks. Thanks to Diamond's poor financial planning, several times they'd been evicted and had had to pick the lock so they'd have a place to stay until the following morning. She pulled out an ice pick and deftly opened the lock in a few minutes flat.

Ciara looked down the hall in both directions before entering. She didn't turn on the lights for fear someone would see her, so she pulled a tiny flashlight out of her purse and went straight for Shannon's desk. It, too, was locked, but luckily Ciara found the keys underneath Shannon's desk mat.

She opened the drawer and was rifling through several folders when she came across the goods. In a folder labeled Jonathan Butler, Ciara found several tapes. Smart cookie. Shannon had taped her conversations.

Ciara, like any good reporter, had a mini-recorder in her purse and she inserted the tape. There was a male voice on the recording saying he had information that might be useful to WTCF. Despite how muffled the voice sounded, it was oddly familiar.

Ciara clapped her hand over her mouth. It was Reid. It had to be. He was the only one close enough to the Butlers to say he had information on Charles Butler's campaigns. Stopping the tape, Ciara placed another in the recorder. Once again, Reid was telling Shannon whom she could contact for information on a certain Diamond Miller, mother to Ciara Miller, who was dating Jonathan Butler. Ciara smiled. The last tape indicated Shannon had set up a meeting with Reid, so Ciara would have to beat her to the punch. Gotcha, Reid!

This was exactly the proof she needed to convince Jonathan that she had nothing to do with Shannon's attacks on him and his family. And when she was finished, he would see how horribly wrong he'd been about her.

He would never come to her of his own volition, so she would call him and reveal that if he came to see her, he would find the culprit responsible for all his bad press. Jonathan wouldn't be able to resist confronting the person responsible.

She'd heard that the Federal Election Commission had approached Charles Butler with search warrants to review his records. Mr. Butler had had no choice but to submit to the humiliation and watch as they'd carted off all his financial records. Ciara wanted to confront Reid with this information and clear Charles Butler's spotless reputation, and not just for Jonathan but for herself. Reid's scheming had disparaged her and Diamond. Payback was long overdue.

She took the entire folder of tapes and locked Shannon's desk and office before leaving the studio. When she finally made it to her car, she let out a long sigh. No one had seen her! Thank God! Now she could make her move.

* * *

"Your poll numbers rebounded after the debate," Reid said to Jonathan. "Now, mind you, they are not what they once were..."

Jonathan remembered how great the numbers had been three months ago. "But?"

"But it's cause for optimism," Reid replied.

"That's fantastic!" Jonathan grinned. "It's the best news I've had in weeks."

His receptionist knocked on his door. "Dorothy, come on in. What do you have for me?" he asked, nodding to the envelope in her hand.

"This envelope was sent by courier, so I figured it must be important." Dorothy handed Reid the envelope. Jonathan watched Reid tear it open and quickly read the contents. An eerie expression crossed Reid's face.

"What's it say?" Jonathan asked.

"Oh, nothing!" Reid dismissed it and maintained his composure even though his scheme could be unraveling in front of his very eyes. Apparently, WTCF's television director wanted a face-to-face meeting with him at the studio and for him to bring proof in hand of illegal campaign contribution or she might have to run a retraction. He'd told her over the phone he'd send it over. Why was she so anxious all of a sudden? Reid was going to have to neutralize Shannon Wright once and for all.

Jonathan was next. Ciara placed a private call to him on his cell phone so that he would have no idea she was the caller. He answered on the second ring.

"Jonathan, it's Ciara," she began. "I know that you don't want to have anything to do with me, but…"

Jonathan's heart leaped at hearing her voice even though it changed nothing between them. "But what? Why are you calling, Ciara?" he queried.

"If you want to find out who's been sabotaging your campaign, you will show up to the studio at twelve-fifteen."

"Why the station?" Jonathan asked. "Is this a trap of some kind, Ciara? What scandal are you setting me up for now?"

"There's no trap," she said, exasperated. "If you ever cared anything about me at all, you will show up tonight and I promise you all will be revealed."

"You're sounding very cryptic, Ciara. This can't be good. Are you in some kind of danger?"

Ciara chuckled. He actually sounded worried about her. "And if I were, would you care?" she asked. When he started to speak she interrupted him. "That was a rhetorical question."

"Yes, I would," Jonathan answered anyway. Despite everything, he still loved her and wished her no harm, whether she believed him or not.

"Then show up," Ciara said, terminating the call.

Jonathan looked at the receiver strangely before placing it back in the holder. What was Ciara up to? Had she really found the saboteur? And if it wasn't Ciara, then he had made the biggest mistake of his life by accusing her.

Chapter 15

Ciara had finished the ten o'clock broadcast some time ago. Now she was waiting for that slime Reid to show up so she could confront him, with Jonathan as witness. She glanced at her watch—it read a quarter to midnight. Butterflies did somersaults in her stomach. It was just nervous excitement, she told herself.

But could she really be sure? With a man like Reid, who knew what he was capable of, which was why Lance was nearby and videotaping their meeting. He would keep an eye on her and let Jonathan into the station so that he could hear and see for himself the person responsible for all the bad press inflicted on his family—and her, for that matter.

Ciara jumped when she heard Reid's menacing footsteps on the tile floor as he found his way to the semi-lit newsroom.

Reid was eager to get this business with Shannon over with as soon as possible. He was prepared to do whatever was necessary to silence the witch. That was when he saw a person lurking in the shadows. "Ms. Wright, why do you want to meet here?" he asked. "This isn't the least conspicuous place we could meet, you must realize."

Ciara stood in the shadows so Reid wouldn't see her. "True, but isn't that kind of ironic?" she chuckled.

"This is no laughing matter, Ms. Wright," Reid replied harshly.

Ciara knew that, which was why she glanced up in time to see Lance ushering Jonathan into the control room. That was when she came out of the shadows.

"No, it isn't," Ciara replied, finally revealing herself. She watched a look of horror spread across Reid's slimy face.

He wasn't sure what to make of the reporter's presence, so he decided to play it close to the vest. "What's this all about, Miller?" he asked, annoyed. He didn't have time to play with this silly little reporter. He had more pressing business at hand.

"Don't play coy," Ciara said. "I know it was you, Reid. You've been sabotaging Jonathan's campaign. And I have the proof to back it up." She cut to the chase. She saw no reason to prolong the conversation.

"That's utterly ridiculous," Reid laughed. "I'd never do anything to jeopardize the Butlers. I'm one of the family after all, while you, my dear, are an outsider."

"That's the way you wanted it, didn't you?" Ciara asked. "You set me up to take the fall for you because you hated Jonathan. What's the problem, Reid? Did you envy Jonathan? Crave the life he had? Felt it should have been yours?"

"Obviously I would crave what that spoiled brat had," Reid returned. "I, like you, have had to scratch and claw my way out of the gutter for everything I've ever got, while he's had it handed to him on a silver platter. I'd think you, better than anyone, would understand what that's like."

"Don't turn this around, Reid," Ciara replied.

"Oh, c'mon," he said. "Haven't you had to do the same, coming from your humble beginnings? Especially with a mother like Diamond Miller."

"This has nothing to do with me." Ciara refused to let him turn the tables. "You wanted to get even with Jonathan, isn't that right?" Ciara pressed him.

"You're a tenacious little tiger." Reid walked toward her and instinctively Ciara took a step backward. "I can see what Jonathan sees in you."

Ciara watched Reid undressing her with his eyes and instantly wanted to take a hot shower to wash off his filthy glare. As he circled around her, a wave of apprehension flowed over her, so much so that Ciara didn't dare turn her back on him.

"Just admit the truth, Reid Hamilton."

"The truth?"

"Yes, the truth would be nice, seeing how it's just the two of us here," she said.

That's true, thought Reid. The Butlers would never

believe a word coming from this lying tramp's mouth. He could tell all and never fear repercussion.

"Okay, I'll play along. Yes, I wanted to get even," he replied. "I wanted him to suffer. Suffer for all the times he treated me like I was nothing better than the gum on the bottom of his shoe."

"So, you admit you were behind everything? The reporters at the club, the stories on my mother, Zach and Charles Butler of all people? How could you do that to someone who calls you a friend?"

"Friend, oh please." Reid laughed sinisterly. "Charles Butler has treated me like nothing more than a gofer. A loyal servant to do his bidding. I owe him nothing."

"How did you do it?" Ciara asked.

"Oh, I had a hand in some of it, but not all. The investigation Dominique Butler paid for was priceless. It gave me all the ammo I needed to put the first nail in Jonathan's election coffin and, as for Charles, that was all a fabrication. I manufactured the whole story. But the press catching you and Jonathan at the bar, your mother's unsavory past and the ill-fated timing of Zach's previous employer's indictment, well that was just dumb luck that played right into my hands, but you'll never be able to prove any of it."

"You don't think?" Ciara asked and motioned to Lance to cue the tape. When he did, Reid's voice came blaring through the studio speakers. Ciara played the tape of his conversation with Shannon about Charles Butler first. She wanted Jonathan to know what a lying scum Reid Hamilton really was.

"How the hell did you get that?" Reid said, taking a disarming step toward her.

"How do you think?" Ciara asked. "Shannon taped every one of your conversations."

"She wouldn't."

"She's a journalist."

"So," Reid laughed nervously. "Now you know it was me. But who'll believe you? Those tapes could have been doctored. I've been a loyal friend to the Butlers and they'll never believe you."

"I think you're wrong about that." Ciara pointed to the control room and Reid whirled around to see Jonathan glaring down at him. She hoped he now realized how terribly he'd misjudged her.

From the other side of the glass, Jonathan recoiled from what he'd heard. The man his father cared for and respected had stabbed him in the back, and worse yet he'd set up Ciara to take the fall for his callous behavior. He must have truly hated his family to do something so evil. But even more troubling was how would Jonathan ever repair the damage that had been done to his and Ciara's relationship?

"See how wrong you were about Ciara?" Lance said, flicking on the light and flooding the control room with light. "Ciara would never have harmed your family. I admit she's ambitious, but she's not ruthless. He's ruthless." Lance pointed to Reid who was frozen in place in the middle of the studio floor. Probably trying to figure out how he was going to talk himself out this mess, Jonathan thought. As if that were even possible.

He'd heard the venom spewing out of Reid's mouth

and, courtesy of Ciara, there was now not only the taped conversations with Shannon, but also video footage of Reid's confession. His father would be unable to deny the truth. It would sting, but at least they would finally have closure and Reid Hamilton out of their lives once and for all.

"You're right," Jonathan said. "I made a mistake. Do you think she'll ever forgive me?"

"I can't answer that," Lance replied. "You'll have to ask her yourself."

Jonathan turned back around to look for Ciara in the studio, but she was gone. She'd disappeared as if she had never been there. He had to find her and somehow convince her to give him a second chance. He didn't know how, but he had to try. First though, he had to deal with Reid. He stormed out of the control room and down the stairs to the studio floor.

Jonathan was surprised Reid didn't scurry off into the night like the rat that he was. Instead, he stood in front of the set ready to take his beating like a man. And a beating was what Jonathan would have loved to give him, but that would be giving him too much power. Plus, Reid would only use it to have him arrested and finish his congressional hopes for good. No, Jonathan had no intention of playing his game.

"Congratulations, Reid." Jonathan clapped his hands. "I have to commend you on a fine performance. You fooled not only me, but my father. And for twenty-five years? Wow! That has to be some sort of record."

"What do you intend to do, Jonathan?" Reid inquired.

"Well, for starters," Jonathan said, "I want your sorry butt out of our lives. Make sure your belongings are out of my office before morning. I want all traces of you wiped completely out of the picture."

"And after that…"

"After that, I'm sure the police might want a word with you. I'm sure you've committed some sort of crime. And if not, maybe I can fabricate it. Oh, wait…" Jonathan paused. "That's your department."

"You're awfully calm, Butler, for a man on the cusp of losing an election that once was a sure thing," Reid chuckled.

"You would like that, wouldn't you?" Jonathan asked.

"For you to fall on your rear?" Reid replied, raising a brow. "I would love nothing better than to see you get what you have coming."

He said the words with such venom, Jonathan could make no mistake about Reid's true feelings. "Then you'll be disappointed," Jonathan stated, "because despite your best efforts, I *will* win this election."

"Good luck," Reid replied, "because I've all but sunk your chances and your loss now is a foregone conclusion."

"You wait and see, Reid Hamilton. The Butler family has more power and more connections in this community than you know."

"Well, I guess we'll find out come election night, won't we?" Reid laughed. "But in the meantime, you keep dreaming, Johnny boy. Perhaps it'll help you get over the loss of your hot little reporter because I'm sure she's lost to you now."

Jonathan grabbed Reid by his sports coat's lapels and slammed his back against the wall. Reid was so taken aback, his breath caught in his throat. He'd never seen Jonathan lose his cool. He tried to push Jonathan off, but he was several inches taller and more athletic than Reid.

"If I lost Ciara because of you, Reid, I promise I will make you pay." A sudden thin chill hung on the edge of Jonathan's words.

"Is that a threat?" Reid asked shakily.

"You can count on that." Jonathan stared Reid dead in the eye. He didn't blink, but Reid sure did. He was afraid of him. "And after I'm done with you, you'll have my father to deal with." When Jonathan released Reid, he fell back against the wall.

"And what can Charles do? He's nothing but a fragile old man. A shell of his former self."

"Ha, that's what you think," Jonathan laughed. "You had better run and hide, Hamilton, because there's no place in Philly where you'll be safe."

Jonathan turned and strutted out of the room, leaving Reid quaking in his shoes. Jonathan was on his way out when he found Ciara leaning against the door of the station. Waiting for him? He guessed it was his turn to be in the hot seat.

Startled, he said, "I thought you had left."

"Oh, no." Ciara wagged her finger in front of his face. "You don't get off that easy, buster. I have something to say to you and you're going to listen."

"Ciara, I'm sorry."

"Don't!" She put her hand up to stop him from

speaking. "Don't you dare try to stand there and apologize to me after what you've done."

"Ciara…" Jonathan began.

She cut him off. "You accused me of not just hurting you, but your family. You said horrible things to me. Accused me of betraying you."

Jonathan could only stand there and take the tongue-lashing Ciara was giving him because he deserved it. "I know, I know."

"Do you? Do you know how much you hurt me?" Ciara asked. "You said you loved me and when it was put to the test you bailed at the first sign of trouble. You refused to see me or take any of my calls. You were willing to think the worst of me, without even the possibility that you could be wrong."

"Ciara, I'm so sorry. You have no idea how much I regret my behavior. If I could take it all back, I would."

Ciara shook her head. "But you can't," she replied. "There's no going back, Jonathan. Reid didn't destroy our relationship, you did."

"Can't we try and work this out?" Jonathan opened his arms, but Ciara shook her head.

"No, we can't. You can't undo the damage that's been done. It's irreparable."

"Ciara, please give me a chance to make it up to you." Tears sprung in Jonathan's eyes. "I made a horrible mistake and I'm so sorry. Please forgive me. I love you so much."

"The ironic part is I love you, too, but what is love without trust?" Ciara asked.

Jonathan didn't have an answer because she was

right. Trust was the very foundation of any relationship. Without it, they were doomed.

When he didn't answer, Ciara walked out. And not just out the door. She was out of his life forever.

Although Ciara felt vindicated by Reid's confession, she still had one person left to deal with and that was Shannon Wright. She'd set up a meeting with WTCF's station manager and program director the next morning to bring to light Shannon's unsavory behavior.

Ciara was discussing her actions with them when Shannon burst through the conference room's door.

"What is this I hear about a meeting I'm not invited to?" she asked, taking a seat at the conference table.

"Because you weren't invited," the station manager replied.

Shannon glanced back and forth between the two men and then at Ciara. She didn't like the smug expression on the reporter's face. "What's going on, Bill? What lies has Miller told you?"

"Lies?" Bill asked. He pushed the power button on the remote, and the television on the credenza sprang to life. It showed the video Lance had taped of Reid and Ciara, in which Reid revealed that he'd been sabotaging Jonathan Butler's campaign from day one.

"What…" Shannon could hardly form the words. "What is this, this video? Did she—" Shannon pointed to Ciara "—bring this to you? Because if so, it's fabricated."

"Shannon, how could you run a story without verifying the facts?" Bill replied. "That's Journalism 101. Substantiate your story."

"Oh please, Bill," Shannon laughed derisively. "You didn't care about the 'facts' when the ratings were blowing through the rooftop, now did you? You asked me to deliver and I did."

"Yes, you delivered," Ciara replied. "But at what cost? You dragged the Butlers' reputation through the mud. And now it's up to this station to rectify it. Isn't that right, Bill?" Ciara glanced his way. "A retraction must be put on air."

Bill rubbed his chin. "I don't know, Ciara," he replied. "I admit Shannon's actions were unethical and she will be dealt with accordingly." He glanced her way. "But it's too late. The damage has already been done."

"You mean you don't want to plummet in the ratings by showing WTCF's lack of credibility." Ciara stood up. "I thought by bringing you this information you would do the right thing. I guess I was wrong." Ciara walked over and stopped the tape.

"You're right," the program manager replied and turned to Shannon on his left. "It's why we're letting you go, Shannon."

"What? You can't do that!" Shannon raised her voice. "After everything I've done? All the blood, sweat and tears. Not to mention hours I've given this station."

"I can and I just did," Bill replied firmly. "Pack your things and clear out, Wright."

"But…"

"Not a word, Wright." Bill pushed his chair back and stood his ground.

He turned to Ciara. "Listen, Ciara. I know you feel

WTCF treated Butler unfairly, but sometimes it can't be helped."

"Oh, no," Ciara returned, "this could have been helped." She snatched the tape out of the VCR. "You could have ended this, but…"

"But what?"

"Now, I quit! That's what," Ciara replied, grabbing her briefcase and walking toward the door. "I don't want to work for a station that doesn't value truth and integrity in journalism. I hold myself in too high a regard."

"And I take it the tape goes with you?" Bill asked.

"You better believe it!" Ciara said, tossing her hair and exiting the conference room.

She met up with Lance in the hallway on her way to clear out her desk. By the murderous expression on Ciara's face, Lance assumed the meeting had not gone as planned. "Shannon?" he asked.

"Fired!"

When Ciara stalked down the hallway to the newsroom, Lance followed in hot pursuit. Lance didn't understand. "Then why aren't you ecstatic?"

Ciara whirled around. "Because the station refused to run a retraction and admit negligence on their part and that they ran inaccurate information." She glanced around the newsroom for an empty box. When she found one, she took it with her on her way to her desk. "I gave them the opportunity to come clean and they refused. So, I quit."

"You did what!" Lance exclaimed.

"I quit," Ciara replied, haphazardly throwing items

in the box. "I can't work for those ratings-hungry scavengers. Lance, I want to succeed but not at the cost of my dignity and self-respect."

"I'm proud of you." Lance hugged his best friend. "Now you know I can't let you leave without me? I'm going to quit, too."

"No, no, no, Lance." Ciara shook her head. "Stay here and collect a paycheck and I promise you when I get to my next station, I'll bring you with me. You know me and you are a package deal." She smiled, poking him in the chest.

"We sure are, kiddo. We sure are."

As Ciara walked out of WTCF's doors for the last time, she didn't have any regrets. She'd come a long way in five years and her hard work and determination had paid off: she'd made anchor. She had what it took to be successful and in her heart of hearts, she knew she'd find another job—one that she could be proud of.

Jonathan's father was devastated by the news that his trusted confidant had betrayed not only Jonathan but him in the process.

"I can't believe Reid was behind this all along." Charles shook his head in amazement. "Reid, of all people. I trusted him."

"I know, Dad," Jonathan agreed. "But there was no mistaking the hatred in his voice while I stood behind that glass. It must have been eating him up for years. Constantly living in my shadow. He saw me as the golden boy."

"I'm to blame as well," Dominique Butler revealed.

"You see," his mother began, "I asked Reid to hire a private investigator to look into Ciara's past."

"Yes, I know," Jonathan replied, folding his arms across his chest. "Mother, how could you?"

"I don't know, son." Dominique hung her head low. "I was just desperate to find out anything that would put you at risk."

"You mean ammunition to get Ciara out of my life."

"Yes." Dominique nodded. "I suppose that was what I was looking for, but Reid told me he found nothing. And I believed him. I had no idea that Reid would use that information against you."

"And you think that makes what you did all right?" Jonathan queried.

"No," his mother answered. "I admit I was wrong and I'm so sorry for all the trouble this has caused you, Jonathan."

He rubbed his temple. Not only was Reid twisted, but he'd used Jonathan's own mother to play out his own sick revenge.

"This was not okay, Mom," Jonathan said.

"Son, your mother is sorry for her part in this." His father spoke up for his wife. "Aren't you, Dominique?"

"Of course," she replied. "Because you know I would never do anything to deliberately hurt you, honey."

Jonathan sighed. He was sure she felt awful enough about her part in this nightmare. But how could he blame her? He, too, had begun to believe the lies Reid had told. "Of course I know that." Jonathan hugged her. "But you have to promise me you're going to stay out of my personal life."

Dominique nodded.

"I just wished I had believed Ciara."

"Do you think she'll take you back?" his father asked.

"I highly doubt it," Jonathan replied. "After the way I treated her, I doubt Ciara Miller wants to have anything to do with me ever again."

"I hate him!" Ciara wailed to both Diamond and Rachel, who surprisingly could stand to be in the same room together since Diamond had moved out.

"*Hate* is a strong word, Ci-Ci," Rachel said. "And I doubt that it really applies here."

"I mean every word," Ciara huffed. "After the way Jonathan treated me, I hate him."

Suddenly, the doorbell rang. Ciara strode over and swung it open. "Yes?" She was surprised to find a flower deliveryman standing in front of her.

"Are you Ciara Miller?" he asked.

"Yes, I am."

"Then these are for you." He stretched out his arms to hand her the flowers, but Ciara shook her head.

"I don't want them."

"Excuse me?"

"I said I don't want them," she repeated. She knew they were from Jonathan. He didn't get to just send her flowers and think all was forgiven. "Donate them to the AIDS pediatric wing."

"Ciara, are you sure?" Rachel stood up and walked over. She perused the bouquet. It was a mixture of roses, carnations, lilies and irises. "They're lovely."

"Yes, I'm sure," Ciara responded. "Please take them away," she told the deliveryman.

He shook his head. He sure didn't understand women. "All right, miss."

Ciara closed the door after he left.

"If you ask me, that was going a bit overboard," Diamond commented on her daughter's rash behavior. "You see, Ci-Ci, hate is the flip side of love."

"That's not true."

"Trust me, honey child. I know about these things. As much as I hated Vince, I loved him all the same. And the same applies to you."

"Well, I'm not like you, Mama," Ciara said. She'd started calling Diamond by that endearment since the night Jonathan had broken up with her. "When someone hurts me, I don't go back for seconds."

"People make mistakes," Diamond replied. Lord knows she had and Ciara had forgiven her. "Can't you forgive Jonathan?"

Ciara shook her head. "No," she stated emphatically. "Sometimes there's no going back."

"How can you say that, sis?" Rachel queried. "You and I forgave each other."

"Can we stop talking about this?" Ciara didn't want to talk about Jonathan, let alone think about him. "I know you're both trying to help, but I need to find a job." She'd only been out of work a few days and already she felt antsy. She pulled out the Classifieds section of the Sunday paper.

"Haven't you made some friends in television?" Diamond asked. "Maybe one of them knows about a job."

Ciara smiled. Sometimes her mother wasn't too bright, but other times she hit the nail right on the head. "That's a darn fine idea, Mama." Ciara sauntered over to her desk by the bay window and pulled out her telephone book.

Thirty minutes later, she had an interview set up with WMAU. Monica, the ex-weekend anchor had informed her they were looking for a general-assignment reporter at WMAU and, although it was a step down from weekend anchor, beggars couldn't be choosers.

"See," Rachel said. "Things are looking up."

"From your lips to God's ears," Ciara replied, looking heavenward.

Chapter 16

Later that week, when Ciara met up with Andrea Logan, news director of NBC's WMAU, she was pleasantly surprised when the director offered her the afternoon news anchor spot. Sure, it wasn't the evening news, but at least she'd be in front of the camera daily. Was it possible to be this lucky? First, Monica had transferred and now the afternoon anchor had decided to stay at home and be a full-time mom.

"Ciara, WMAU would be very lucky to have a reporter of your caliber."

"Then I accept wholeheartedly," Ciara replied, vigorously shaking her hand. "But I do have two requests."

"And what would that be?"

"I'd like to run an exposé on the Butler campaign."

"That would not be wise," Andrea stated, "given your close relationship with the candidate. WMAU has to appear impartial."

"What would you say if I told you that I have a videotape along with voice recordings in my possession which clearly shows that Jonathan Butler and his family were set up?"

"I would say that would be the story of the year," Andrea replied excitedly.

Ciara pulled out a manila envelope. "Andrea, if you would give me the opportunity to run this story on the evening news, I promise you WMAU will not be disappointed."

"I'd have to see and hear the evidence first, before I approve," Andrea commented, folding her arms. "Because it's not just your butt on the line, Miller, it's mine, too."

"Agreed."

"Then let's watch it," Andrea replied. Reaching for the remote, she clicked on the television. "Go ahead, stick it in." She pointed to the VCR under the console.

Ciara walked over and inserted the tape.

"I'm curious about something though—if this tape is evidence that clears Butler's name, why didn't WTCF air it? I assume that is why you resigned?"

Ciara nodded. "Yes, that's exactly why. I believe in honesty and truth and integrity, and the station's management didn't share my high moral standards."

"Then this is the place for you. WMAU prides journalistic integrity above all else."

After they watched the tape, Andrea was enthusiastic over Ciara moving forward with the story. "I think this will be an excellent piece, Ciara. Let me look it over when you're done."

"About that other request," Ciara began. "I know a certain cameraman that would make an excellent addition to this station."

"Ciara…"

"I know I'm asking a lot, but if there's any way you can squeeze this in your budget that would be fantastic."

"Let me see what I can do," Andrea returned, "but I make no promises."

"Understood." Ciara smiled.

Afterward, she breathed a sigh of relief. Not only did she have a new job, but she would finally get justice for the Butler family—and right before the election!

"Have you spoken to Ciara?" Zach inquired after he and Jonathan finished playing a vigorous game of tennis at the country club.

They had showered and changed and were now seated in the dining room ordering lunch.

"No, I haven't," Jonathan replied. He turned and gave the waiter his order of blackened chicken Caesar salad. "I sent her a bouquet of flowers as an 'I'm sorry' and she refused them. Asked that they be sent to the new AIDS pediatrics wing at the children's hospital."

"Well, I can't say that should come as a surprise," Zach remarked. "I'll have the barbecue chicken salad." Zach handed the waiter the menu.

"Thanks a lot," Jonathan laughed. "You're supposed to be my friend."

"Yeah, well, a good friend will tell you when you've screwed up," Zach replied, reaching for his water goblet and taking a generous sip. "And, you, my man—" he playfully slapped Jonathan on the shoulder "—screwed up big-time." Zach sipped his water again.

"I know, but what do I do to fix it?"

"I'm sorry to say that I'm not sure if you can fix it," Zach said honestly. "You accused Ciara of not only hurting you but your family. That stung and Ciara is still feeling the burn. But maybe, just maybe if you give her time, she'll come around."

"Do you really believe that?" Jonathan asked, desperate to hold on to any shred of hope.

"Only time will tell, my friend," Zach replied.

Time did tell several days later when Jonathan watched the six o'clock news in his penthouse. WMAU promised a report by Ciara Miller on the special election between Jonathan Butler and Alec Marshall.

Jonathan was on pins and needles during the telecast until he saw Ciara's beautiful face come across the screen. In her report, she showed clips of the video in which Reid revealed he'd sabotaged Jonathan's campaign. Surprisingly, she'd been edited entirely out of the video, leaving Reid Hamilton solely holding the bag. Ciara commented about the damage done to Jonathan's campaign and asked the public to be the judge.

After the report aired, Jonathan exhaled. He didn't even realize he'd been holding his breath until the telecast ended. His cordless phone immediately started ringing after the broadcast.

Zach was the first to reach him. "We're back in business. Let's meet tomorrow and discuss a press conference."

"You mean you're back in charge of the campaign?" Jonathan asked.

"You better believe it. And you can thank Ciara Miller."

"I most certainly will," Jonathan replied. He intended to make amends to Ciara for the damage he'd done. He just hoped that she would take him back.

When he arrived at Ciara's new station the next day, Jonathan sat in his car afraid to go inside. What could he say to convince her to give them a second try? He'd misjudged her and now he expected forgiveness. He just hoped Ciara could find it in her heart to forgive him.

WMAU was much busier than WTCF. Jonathan had to show identification, sign in and be given a visitor's badge while the receptionist announced Ciara had a visitor over the intercom. When the young woman behind the desk suddenly smiled at him, he knew he'd been recognized. "Are you Jonathan Butler?" she asked.

"None other."

"Would you autograph my magazine?" She handed him a copy of *Vogue*. There was hardly any space to write, but Jonathan managed to scribble his signature. He was returning the magazine to the receptionist when Ciara walked down the hall.

She stopped mid-step when she realized who her

visitor was. "Go away, Jonathan." Ciara spun on her heel and started walking in the other direction.

"Wait!" Jonathan rushed after her and caught up to her at the entrance to the studio.

"You can't come in here," Ciara stated, but Jonathan followed her inside anyway. He didn't care that he was breaking the rules.

"I'm not leaving here until we talk," he stated matter-of-factly.

"I have a newscast in an hour."

"And I need less than that to tell you how sorry I am," he replied.

"Now is not the time and the station is not the place." She nodded to several coworkers who were watching their encounter. "Haven't you had enough bad press? Heck, I did you a favor and revealed Reid's sabotage. You're back on track now. Don't mess it up."

Ciara tried to walk away, but Jonathan halted her by grasping her elbow. "We are going to talk right now. Where's your office?" he demanded.

Ciara glanced up at him, and the serious look on his face told her he was not taking no for an answer. "All right!" She snatched her elbow out of his grasp and strode down the hallway to her office. It was small, with no window, but at least there they would have some privacy. Ciara shut the door behind Jonathan.

"All right, we're alone now. Speak," she countered icily.

"Okay…" Jonathan paused. He needed to take a moment to gather his words. He needed to say the right thing to win Ciara over, but right now, when she glared at him so vehemently, it seemed impossible. They were like two large land masses that used to be one continent, and he could see the place where they split apart. The question was how did he bridge the gap?

Ciara smiled inwardly. Usually Jonathan was so articulate. He was a lawyer after all, but today he couldn't seem to get the words out.

"I'm waiting." Ciara glanced down at her watch.

"Ciara, I'm sorry," he began. "I was a fool to ever believe the worst in you."

"True."

"But you must admit it was a logical assumption?"

"Logical?" Ciara asked. "How can you say that? Reid's sabotage not only hurt you, but me and my mother."

"I understand that, but you had the most to gain," Jonathan explained. "For all intents and purposes, you gained. Didn't you?"

"You're talking about my promotion to weekend anchor," Ciara offered.

"Of course I am." He stood up. "You didn't even tell me about that promotion. I had to find out from Reid that you were keeping things from me."

"But…"

"C'mon, Ciara, let's be honest here. You did give me a reason to doubt you."

Jonathan may have made "logical" sense, but Ciara wasn't buying it. "I may have given you a reason, but you should have never believed it."

"Why?" Jonathan asked. "You never gave me a reason to believe otherwise."

"What!" Ciara fumed. "How can you say that? I was right by your side at every event. I was in your bed. How could you believe otherwise?"

"Maybe if you'd told me you loved me," Jonathan replied honestly, and at that comment, Ciara lowered her head. "Yes, that's right. I said *I love you* in Aruba and yet you said nothing. Told me you were fond of me." Just remembering how much that had stung made Jonathan feel sick to his stomach.

"I do love you, Jonathan," Ciara said.

"Yes, I believe you do." Jonathan nodded. "Now I do. But you chose the worst possible moment to tell me. Why couldn't you have told me then instead of at the charity gala?"

Ciara shook her head. She'd asked herself that very same question. "I don't know. I guess I was afraid of being vulnerable. Of being that emotionally attached to anyone."

"Have you always felt this way?" Jonathan asked. "Haven't you ever been in love before?"

"No, I haven't," Ciara replied. "I never allowed myself to fall for anyone. Even in school, I relegated myself to short-term relationships. It was always about sex, nothing more. I never wanted to be like my mother, so needy for a man's affection. So, I put on a self-confident, self-assured face that I didn't need anyone or anything and eventually it stuck."

"Ciara, that's no way to be."

"I know that now," Ciara responded. "And do you want to know how I learned that?"

"How?"

"Because of you, Jonathan. With you I felt complete, whole for the first time. You made me believe in love and that I could be loved. Deserved love. That's why it hurt so much when I finally said the words aloud and you rejected them."

"I was upset, Ciara. Not thinking clearly." Jonathan tried to reason with her. "Ciara, I made a mistake. Can't you please forgive me?" he pleaded and dropped to the floor on one knee. He grasped her small delicate hand in his large masculine one. "I love you so much. You're an integral part of my life and I want to share that life with you. Please don't let Reid Hamilton win. He wanted to hurt me in the worst possible way. He gave me the noose to hang myself with and, boy, did I do a bang-up job of it. But I'm begging you, don't give up on me. Can't you please forgive me and give us a second chance?"

Ciara thought about everything Jonathan had just said and she knew her answer. Without a shadow of a doubt she knew she loved him. She'd never stopped. And maybe, just maybe she, too, had played a part in their downfall.

Knock. Knock. Knock.

The door to Ciara's office swung open. It was the floor manager. "Ciara, I need you on the floor, now." He stood waiting at the doorway

"But…" She glanced at him and then at Jonathan.

Jonathan implored her with his eyes not to leave until they had this resolved. "Ciara, please…"

"I'm sorry, Jonathan." She extracted her fingers from his. "I have to go." She rose from her chair and fled the room. As she walked into the studio, she was fitted with a microphone and earpiece. The makeup artist quickly worked on her face as she walked to the anchor's desk on set. While she perused the script for the afternoon telecast, she watched Jonathan walk into the studio. But instead of leaving, he stayed along the sidelines and watched her work.

Initially, Ciara was uneasy at his close proximity, but eventually her nervousness dissipated and she began to feel comforted by his presence. When the thirty-minute broadcast was over, Jonathan strode through the studio and right up to her at the anchor's desk.

"Sir, you can't be on set," the floor manager said, but the studio director shook his head. He knew who Jonathan Butler was even if the floor manager did not.

"Let it be," he whispered in his ear.

Jonathan didn't hear a word; his eyes were on Ciara only. In front of the entire studio, he bent down on one knee.

"Jonathan…" Ciara started.

"Don't." He put a finger over her mouth. "Ciara, I love you more than anything in this world and if you can forgive me, I would like you to do me the great honor of becoming my wife." He pulled out a black box from inside his suit breast pocket.

The studio director motioned to his floor manager to start taping.

"Ohmigod!" Ciara was stunned and covered her mouth. She paused for several moments as all eyes in the studio waited for her response. Although she hadn't seen that coming, she leaped out of her chair and into his arms. "Yes! Yes! Yes!" She furiously kissed Jonathan all over his face.

"Yes to what?" Jonathan asked.

"Yes, I can forgive you. And yes, I absolutely want to marry you, Jonathan Butler. I love you more than I could have ever possibly imagined and I want to spend the rest of my life with you."

"Thank you, thank you." Jonathan bent down to kiss her. "You've just made me the happiest man alive!"

The day of the special election, Ciara joined Jonathan and his parents to vote at the polls. The Philadelphia press was calling the congressional race too close to call. With the breaking news of Charles Butler's former campaign manager Reid Hamilton's sabotage, reporters were predicting that Jonathan could bounce back after the drop in numbers over recent weeks to defeat his opponent, Alec Marshall.

Ciara and Jonathan waited with bated breath at his campaign headquarters with his staff. Ciara had taken the day off to stand by her man and hold his hand. When the polling places closed at 6:00 p.m., Ciara and Jonathan both changed into what they hoped were victory suits. Ciara wore Dolce & Gabbana while Jonathan wore Armani. A short while later, they took a limousine over to the Four Seasons Hotel with his parents. His grandmother would be watching the results from home. As was their customary tradition, his parents had booked the penthouse suite for them to wait for the final election results. The suite housed two large bedrooms and huge living quarters.

As soon as they arrived, Dominique turned on the flat screen to watch the results. Only ninety percent of the precincts were in and it was still too close to call. Jonathan had forty-six percent of the vote to Marshall's forty-four percent.

Jonathan couldn't bear watching the results any longer and retired to the spare bedroom to pace the floor. Ciara followed close behind him. He was on pins and needles, and Ciara tried to reassure him as best she could. "Win or lose, baby, you fought a fair fight and you can be proud of how you carried yourself."

"I know, Ciara. It's just that I want this so bad," Jonathan replied, wringing his hands. "I never knew how much I wanted this until I realized it could be out of my grasp."

Ciara squeezed his hand. "Then I hope you win it!" Ciara's eyes brightened with tears and Jonathan wiped them away with the back of his hand.

"With you by my side, I'm already a winner," he said.

Hours later, Zach knocked on their door. "Ninety-six percent of the polls are in," he said excitedly.

"And?" Jonathan jumped up off the king-size bed.

"Come see for yourself," Zach said, opening the door.

Jonathan rushed past him and into the living room where his father stood with his chest out, beaming with pride, while tears streamed down his mother's face. Had he lost?

Jonathan glanced at Ciara first, who gave him an encouraging look, and then he looked at the television screen and that was when he saw it. With ninety-six percent of the precincts in, he'd beat Marshall, fifty-one percent to forty-five.

"Yes!" Jonathan balled a fist and brought it to his side. He rushed across the room and lifted Ciara off her feet, swinging her in the air.

"Congratulations, baby!"

"I did it, Ciara! I did it!" Ciara laughed at Jonathan's enthusiasm through her happy tears. Eventually, he returned her to solid ground and turned to Zach.

"Congratulations!" Zach shook his hand and gave him a pat on the back. "You, my man, are now a United States congressman for Philadelphia County. How do you feel?"

"Great!" Jonathan beamed.

"Good," Zach replied, "because now it's time to go downstairs and make your acceptance speech."

Afterward, when Ciara looked back at the moment, she would remember the joy, the laughter and the tears, the balloons and fireworks, but more importantly she wouldn't forget Jonathan's last words as she stood blissfully by his side at the podium when he made his acceptance speech.

"I want to thank all of my supporters and the voters of this great county for voting for me. I'd also like to thank my campaign manager, Zach, my parents, Charles and Dominique Butler, and my grandmother, Ava Butler, for their tireless enthusiasm and unwavering support, but most of all I'd like to thank my fiancée and soul mate, Ciara Miller. Without her I wouldn't be where I am today."

A barrage of balloons and confetti fell over Jonathan as he leaned down and kissed Ciara full on the lips. "I love you, Ciara Miller."

"And I love you, Johnny boy."

From boardroom to bedroom…

Brenda JACKSON

In Bed with Her Boss

Though D'marcus Armstrong is a demanding, cranky
boss, he's the star of Opal Lockhart's fantasies. But
what chance does a buttoned-up, naive secretary have
with this self-made millionaire? A pretty good one
actually…when Opal's sisters come to the rescue
with a makeover and some attitude adjustment!

THE LOCKHARTS
THREE WEDDINGS & A REUNION

*Available the first week of August
wherever books are sold.*

KIMANI™
ROMANCE

www.kimanipress.com KPBJ0280807

The negotiation of love…

A Cinderella AFFAIR

Favorite author
A.C. ARTHUR

Camille Davis is sophisticated, ambitious,
talented…and riddled with self-doubt—except
when it comes to selling her father's home.
No deal, no way. But Las Vegas real estate mogul
Adam Donovan and his negotiating skills are
leaving Camille weak in the knees…and maybe,
just maybe, willing to compromise?

*Available the first week of August
wherever books are sold.*

KIMANI™
ROMANCE

www.kimanipress.com   KPACA0310807

Sometimes life needs a rewind button...

USA TODAY BESTSELLING AUTHOR

KAYLA
Perrin

Love, Lies & Videotape

On the verge of realizing her lifelong dream of
becoming an actress, Jasmine St. Clair is suddenly
embroiled in a sex-tape scandal, tarnishing her
good girl image. Desperate to escape the false
accusations, Jasmine heads to the Caribbean and
meets Darien Lamont—a sexy, mysterious American
running from demons of his own.

"A fine storytelling talent."
—*The Toronto Star*

*Available the first week of August
wherever books are sold.*

ARABESQUE®

www.kimanipress.com

KPKP0160807

Essence bestselling author

PATRICIA HALEY

Still Waters

A poignant and memorable story about a once-loving husband who has lost his way…and his spiritual wife who has grown weary from constantly praying for the marriage. Greg and Laurie Wright are perched at the edge of an all-out crisis—and only a miracle can restore what's been lost.

"Patricia Haley has written a unique work of Christian fiction that should not be missed."
—*Rawsistaz Reviewers* on *No Regrets*

*Available the first week of August
wherever books are sold.*

www.kimanipress.com   KPPH0730807